leave the lights on
true crime junkies
book five

Christy Barritt

River Heights

chapter
one

NICOLE WINDSOR PAUSED in the bathroom.

She'd just started running water in the tub, but it took forever for the water to warm.

As she waited, the sound of liquid rushing through the pipes roared so loudly it nearly obstructed any other noises.

Nearly.

A creak sounded from somewhere in the house. Was that . . . door hinges squeaking? A footstep causing the rustic hardwood floor to moan?

She stilled and listened.

The noise teased the periphery of her hearing again.

She *had* heard something.

What was it?

Probably nothing. Maybe the wind even. The breeze had been fairly strong tonight.

Just to be safe, she should check. It would help set her mind at ease.

She threw on her robe and stepped toward the bathroom door, bracing for the cooler air circulating through the drafty old house. She and her husband, Chad, had picked the place out. They'd thought the sixty-year-old home had character, and that had been the main selling feature.

Nicole had quickly discovered that the last thing anyone wanted in Alaska was to live in a drafty house. Chad should have known better. After all, he'd grown up here. But he'd been desperate to make her happy. All he'd wanted was to come back home.

Maybe in a few years, they could move again. Back to the Lower 48 this time if Nicole had her way. Though Alaska was beautiful, she wasn't sure she was cut out to live in America's final frontier.

She stared at the bathroom door without moving for several more seconds. When nothing happened, she chided herself for overreacting.

The sound was probably nothing. But Chad was out of town, and she was always more nervous when home alone.

Speaking of Chad . . . what if he had come back from his business trip early? What if that had been her husband she'd heard? What if he'd returned home to surprise her?

A surge of hope welled in her.

Nicole would love nothing more than to see him. He'd been gone four days, and she missed him terribly.

The two of them had moved to Anchorage, Alaska, six months ago for her husband's job, and Nicole hadn't made any friends in the area yet—which left her feeling restless and lonely.

Tomorrow, she'd told herself. I'll make friends tomorrow.

She said that every day, yet she was still friendless.

She opened the door, stepped into the hallway, and glanced at the steep wooden stairway leading to the dark first floor. "Chad? Is that you?"

No answer.

Maybe he couldn't hear her over the running water.

Gripping her soft pink robe to her chest, she hurried down the stairs.

The dark shadows at the bottom made her skin crawl. She'd turned out all the lights thirty minutes ago when she thought she'd take a bath and go to bed.

When she reached the first floor, she flipped the light switch. But instead of light filling the downstairs, the whole house went black.

The refrigerator stopped humming. The heat stopped rattling.

The only sound was the running water upstairs.

Her throat tightened.

She flipped the switch several more times, but nothing happened.

Had she blown a fuse?

That had to be it, right?

How did she even fix that?

Where was the breaker box? She'd never had to deal with it before.

Hopefully, she didn't have to go outside to find it. She preferred the security of her four walls. Plus, she didn't have a flashlight, and she was only wearing a robe. Her neighbors on the street were closer than she'd like, with only space enough for a driveway between the houses.

That settled it. She wanted to go back home to Illinois. She wanted to buy that nice little house right down the street from her parents in the neighborhood where she'd grown up. She'd always felt so safe there. The neighbors had watched out for each other, and her best friend still lived only a couple of blocks away.

Homesickness hit Nicole with such force she knew she had to do something about it.

When Chad returned home, she would beg him to leave. She didn't care that this new job he'd taken paid more. That it was a good move for his career. Some things were more important than money and climbing the ladder.

She couldn't live like this any longer.

She hated the cold. Hated the isolation.

Hated being here.

She sucked in several deep breaths, trying to ground herself.

The sound of the running water continued in the upstairs bathroom.

No odd sounds came from anywhere else in the house.

This was probably nothing. What if it really was Chad? He always liked surprises. She could see him cutting the lights and then jumping out with flowers.

Was that what was happening now?

"Chad?" Her voice sounded scratchy and thin as his name left her lips.

Still no answer.

Her lungs tightened.

Maybe she'd been hearing things.

She should go back up. Take her bath.

But what were the odds she'd been hearing things *and* the lights had gone out on their own?

Near zero.

She didn't like those odds.

Her panic roared to life.

She pressed herself against the paneled wood wall and scanned the dark area in front of her. Shadows stared back. Shadows that were actually furniture—couches, chairs, and tables.

Yet she felt like a foreigner in her own home. Even the air felt haunted.

In reality, beyond the veil of darkness stretched a coral-colored couch. The sofa was cheerful, adding a nice brightness when the doldrums of winter lingered well into May. Pictures of family smiled at her from various tables and bookshelves. A wildflower arrangement by the fireplace reminded her of spring.

There was nothing to be scared of.

Nicole glanced at the front door.

It was closed and locked.

She couldn't see the back door. But if it was open, she'd feel the breeze.

It had been windy today.

That was probably it. The wind had probably knocked some branches into her house. Maybe one scraped a window.

The wind could even be the reason the electricity had gone out.

A brief—fleeting—moment of comfort filled her.

Then the creak sounded again.

From inside the house.

Her throat tightened.

She wasn't imagining anything.

Someone was inside, weren't they?

She should have grabbed her phone. She needed to call the police.

Everyone in the area had been on edge lately, especially after six people had died recently—had been murdered, to be exact.

The police were probably fielding uncountable calls from people like her who jumped at every sound.

She licked her lips. What should she do?

Go back upstairs and grab her phone?

That was probably the wisest choice right now.

She'd get her phone in the bathroom and then seclude herself there with the door locked until the police showed up.

Another creak moaned in the darkness.

Closer this time.

Behind the stairway.

Just out of sight.

That definitely hadn't been a tree branch being harassed by the wind.

Who was inside her house?

Her throat tightened until she could hardly breathe.

Don't just stand here!

She started to dart up the stairs when someone stepped from the shadows.

A man.

A man not wearing a mask.

The stranger didn't care if she saw his face, Nicole realized.

He didn't plan on letting her walk away, did he?

Her blood turned ice cold.

"Good evening," he murmured, his voice velvety and eerily polite. "I'm sorry to intrude like this. But you must pay. You *all* must pay."

A scream caught in Nicole's throat.

She started to scramble up the stairs.

But the man grabbed her ankle.

She slammed into the wooden risers. Her face hit a stair, and something cracked.

Her tooth, she realized. She'd cracked a tooth.

Blood spilled over her tongue.

"Please," she managed to beg. "Don't . . ."

"Let's just get this over with," the man murmured as he lingered over her. "No need to fight the inevitable. Struggling will only make it worse for you."

He raised an arm over his head.

Something glinted in his hand.

A blade of some sort.

Nicole tried to scream. But it was too late.

The blade plunged into her body.

chapter
two

ANDI SLADE DUCKED around the corner, her lungs so tight she could hardly breathe.

She pressed herself against the brick wall of the high-rise building. If only she could disappear into the night-time shadows here in Anchorage. But that was hoping for too much.

Had she lost those men?

As if to answer, footsteps struck the pavement in the distance.

Her lungs tightened even more.

She couldn't stay here. She had to keep moving.

If she were caught, she'd never find the evidence she needed to put Victor Goodman away. Instead, she would go to prison.

Victor had enough connections to make it happen. That was the way money and power usually worked.

She'd known when she broke into that building

tonight that the move was risky. The key had been not getting caught.

That part of her plan hadn't worked out.

Andi glanced down the deserted street at the downtown area. Where else could she go?

She'd have to figure that out on the fly. Right now, she had to keep moving.

She hurried down the dark, empty street.

The footsteps around the corner became louder, the voices more distinguishable.

"Where did she go?" one of the men asked.

"I don't know," the other one said. "We've got to find her. Keep looking!"

Any time now, Andi's pursuers would round the corner and see her.

More accurately, those *cops* would round the corner and see her.

She swallowed hard.

Yes, the police were after her. How would she explain this? Even State Trooper Logan Gibson wouldn't be able to help her now.

An alleyway bathed in darkness appeared on her left.

The corridor could be a dead end.

Or it could lead to freedom.

Either way, at least she'd be out of sight.

She darted into the alley, sprinting as fast as she could.

But before she even reached the corner of the building, she stopped.

The alley ended . . . just as she feared—at a solid concrete wall.

Andi muttered under her breath as despair clawed at her.

She'd put too much into this investigation. She'd given up everything and still had some fight left inside her. She couldn't let it end like this.

She glanced up at the wall. It had to be at least nine feet high.

There was no way she could scale that. People didn't call her pint-sized for no reason.

She scanned her surroundings, desperate to find a place to hide.

There were no doorways. No windows on the sides of the buildings.

There was nowhere to go . . . nowhere except a dumpster.

More shouts sounded from the street. The cops were getting closer.

Andi pressed her eyes closed and let out an aggravated breath.

Not the dumpster.

But she had no other choice right now.

The cops would find her if she tried to hide behind it.

Which meant . . .

Before Andi could second-guess herself, she darted toward the old metal container, pushed the top open, and scrambled inside.

Careful not to make any noise, she lowered the lid over her.

Darkness—as well as the scent of rot—surrounded her.

Nausea rose in her as she realized the filth she'd just immersed herself in.

Her hand brushed up against something slimy.

She stifled a gag.

Shouts distracted her.

The footsteps were closer.

Those cops had come this way.

They could still find her. All they had to do was open the lid.

She swallowed hard and made another last-minute decision.

Quickly, she shifted a couple of garbage bags—some of them wet and torn—and quietly buried herself beneath them.

Then she remained perfectly still.

The voices and footsteps came closer.

The cops were right beside the dumpster.

Her heart pounded so loudly in her ears it nearly blocked any other noises.

She should have told Duke McAllister what she was doing.

The two of them had driven from Fairbanks to Anchorage together earlier today. Two hours ago, she'd told him good night as she disappeared into her hotel room and he into his.

Before she'd slipped away, she'd briefly contemplated confessing what she planned to do tonight. Then she'd changed her mind. It was better if Duke didn't know.

That way Andi would be the only one in trouble if she was caught.

"Where do you think she went?" one of the officers asked.

"I don't know. Maybe she stashed a car somewhere and took off."

"Did you get a good look at her?"

"Can't say I did. Maybe some cameras picked up her image."

Andi had been aware of each of those cameras. She'd done her research before she came.

She'd kept her face concealed and her signature white-blonde hair pulled into a bun and tucked under a dark baseball cap. Her black yoga pants and oversized black sweatshirt helped her blend in.

Silence passed.

Something oozed down Andi's neck. She forced herself to remain still, to not imagine what the substance might be.

One sound from this dumpster would give her presence away. She couldn't take that risk.

"What do you want to do now?" the first cop asked.

Please, don't say look in the dumpster.

If the cops found her, what could Andi possibly tell them that wouldn't result in her being arrested and put in jail?

She'd simply been out for a late-night stroll and wandered into an office building by accident? Or she was just testing out the security system to look for weaknesses?

No. There was nothing she could say to explain this, Andi realized. There was absolutely nothing she could say to get out of this.

Andi held her breath as she heard the dumpster lid being lifted.

Fifteen excruciating minutes later, Andi climbed from the dumpster and shook stray trash off her.

The police had opened the dumpster, peered inside, and then walked away. No doubt they assumed no one would be motivated enough to burrow in the trash.

They clearly didn't know Andi.

She glanced up and down the alleyway.

It was clear. The police were gone.

Her lungs loosened slightly.

Then she glanced down at herself.

Weird stains marred her clothing and part of a banana peel had stuck to her shoulder. She still wasn't sure what had drizzled down her neck.

It was better if she didn't know.

She'd never felt so disgusting. But at least she was still a free woman.

However, that reality could change in the blink of an eye.

Moving quickly, Andi hurried toward the street.

She peered around the corner, searching for signs of trouble.

Those cops were no longer in sight.

She released her breath. But things could still go sideways if she wasn't careful.

She had to maintain her composure and calmly walk back to the hotel.

The last thing she wanted was to arouse suspicion by acting strangely.

Thankfully, her hotel was only two blocks away.

Also, thankfully, it was eleven at night. Not many people were out at this time.

Finally, she reached the upscale—upscale for Anchorage, at least—hotel where she was staying.

As if she hadn't just been dumpster diving, Andi strode inside, headed to the elevator, and pushed the Up button.

An empty car arrived.

Perfect.

She stepped inside and quickly hit the number for her floor, followed immediately by the Close Door button.

As soon as the doors shut, she let out a long breath and nearly collapsed against the wall.

She was almost home free.

All she had to do was make it to her room without anyone seeing her.

She couldn't wait to take a shower. The warm water would feel glorious—and cleansing.

Afterward, maybe she'd burn her clothes.

Then she'd look at the pictures she'd taken. She needed to see what was on those files she'd taken photos of.

Somewhere in those documents, there had to be evidence she could use against Victor.

The elevator stopped.

But not on her floor.

Anxiety zinged through her blood.

Foul odors emanated from her—odors even she could smell. That wasn't to mention the fact she must look like a total wreck.

She should have taken the stairs.

Whoever stepped inside would clearly know she'd been up to something.

What if it was a cop?

No, what were the chances they were still looking for her, and in this hotel of all places?

You can do this. Just don't make eye contact with whoever gets on the elevator. Play it cool.

Andi took several deep breaths to calm herself.

Most likely, a stranger would step inside. What were

the odds she'd ever run into that person again? Slim to none.

The doors slowly opened, revealing two men on the other side.

Andi sucked in a breath at the sight of them.

You have to be kidding me . . .

"Andi?"

"Duke." She nodded as she stared at him, certain to keep her voice normal and act as if this was just an everyday, ordinary encounter. "How's it going?"

Duke's skin turned paler, and he pressed his lips together as if fighting nausea. "What in the world . . . ?"

"Yes, for real—what in the world are you doing on the fourth floor?" Deflect, deflect, deflect.

"Checking out the gym." Duke's gaze remained narrowed.

Andi's gaze slid to the man beside him. A man who looked an awful lot like Duke with his broad build, tall frame, and square jawline.

The two of them stepped inside the elevator. As they did, the look on Duke's face became even more grotesque. "Andi, no offense, but you smell awful."

"It's a new perfume I'm testing out. What do you think? It's called Eau De Lavatory." She raised her eyebrows, trying to play it off. Humor was usually a great distraction.

Except with Duke. Humor didn't affect his intense focus.

He gave her the side-eye.

The door closed, and Duke pressed the eighth-floor button again.

Then his gaze shifted to the man beside him. "Andi, this is my little brother, Beau."

"Beau as in boyfriend, not BO as in body odor." He winked. "And I'm only younger by eighteen months, but Duke loves to rub that minor age difference in."

Andi's lips curled in a quick grin. Beau was a charmer, wasn't he?

Duke was charming in his own way also. But Beau, by first impression, seemed to be the more lighthearted of the two.

She swallowed hard as she studied the man. Beau was handsome with dark hair and the same GI Joe vibes Duke possessed. But Beau's smile didn't look as weathered by heartache as Duke's.

Andi pushed a lock of hair behind her ear—ignoring something that fell from the strands—and started to extend her arm. Then she noticed something green and slimy on her wrist.

She quickly stuffed her hand back into the pocket of her black sweatshirt and forced a smile. "Nice to meet you."

"I thought you were turning in early for the night?" Duke studied her without apology.

The man was too smart for his own good—and sometimes, he was entirely too tuned-in to how Andi thought.

In the past, she'd mused that the quality was a good thing. But right now, his power of observation felt like a liability.

"I thought *you* were turning in early for the night." Andi glanced at Duke then Beau, trying to turn the tables on this conversation.

"I was. Then I found out my brother was passing through town on his way to Canada," Duke explained. "He's on a layover for work, so we caught up over dinner."

"But now my flight is cancelled," Beau added. "An ash cloud from a volcanic eruption in Russia has shut down flights in Anchorage for the rest of the night."

"It's not every day you hear that," she murmured. "I'm glad the two of you had a chance to catch up then. That's awesome."

Beau nudged his brother. "That's right. We need to get together more often. Ever since you moved to Alaska, you've practically been a stranger—except for those food pictures you love to send."

"That *I* love to send?" Duke raised his eyebrows.

"We know you secretly love them." Beau winked.

"Who doesn't love a food picture?" Duke murmured, a touch of sarcasm to his voice.

Andi had heard him talk on more than one occasion about how food pictures drove him crazy.

"Anyway . . . don't let my brother fool you." Duke shot a pointed look at his brother. "Beau has a pretty busy schedule himself as a motivational speaker."

"Motivational speaker?" Andi cast Beau another glance. That was unexpected.

"I was a POW for six months in Iraq." Beau's voice turned more serious. "Since I got out of the military, I've been asked on a fairly consistent basis to do speaking engagements. That led to a book deal, news commentary requests, and more."

Maybe Beau *had* weathered just as much heartache as Duke—only a different kind. Still, he didn't seem as haunted by trauma as Duke did. Was that because Duke's was unresolved?

Andi gave Duke a look. Why hadn't he ever mentioned what happened to his brother before? The subject seemed like something he would have brought up. They'd had endless hours to chat on their long drives together.

Andi looked back at Beau. "I want to hear more about your story sometime."

"I'd love to share," Beau murmured. "From bomb tech to hot commodity in foreign relations. It's a story Hollywood couldn't have written any better."

The elevator stopped on the eighth floor, and they stepped out. Duke was staying in the room next to her. Several other members of the Arctic Circle Murder Club were staying in the same hallway. Tomorrow morning, the gang would move to a rental house, but the place hadn't been available this evening.

Both men paused outside the door to Andi's room.

"It was nice to meet you, Beau." Then Andi glanced at Duke. "And I guess I'll see you bright and early tomorrow morning."

They were meeting to talk about their next case for *The Round Table*, their true crime podcast.

Their team of six would all be here in Anchorage for the weekend. It had worked out well for Andi because she wanted to do some research in this area anyway—though research might be a loose use of the term.

That "research" had nearly gotten her arrested.

If she kept pushing the limits, she might end up behind bars. As a former attorney, she knew the stakes. Yet the risk seemed worth the payoff.

"So . . ." Duke shifted like he wanted to ask her more questions.

But Andi raised her hands and shot at him with two finger guns, trying to brush off the mess she'd gotten herself into tonight. "Tomorrow."

Right now, she really needed to wash all this sludge off before she threw up.

chapter
three

ANDI COULDN'T STAND the smell on her body a second longer—or the germs. She scrubbed away the grime covering her skin and hair. It took two tries to get all the stink off.

Then she quickly towel-dried her hair and pulled on her pajamas.

Wasting no more time, she grabbed her filthy yoga pants—discarded on the bathroom floor—and felt for her phone.

Her breath caught when she discovered the empty side pocket.

She squeezed more frantically, certain she was wrong.

But she wasn't.

She grabbed her sweatshirt. Felt around.

Nothing.

She stepped from the bathroom. Glanced at the floor.

Nothing.

She opened her hotel room door. Scanned the hallway.

Still nothing.

Her phone was gone.

She returned to the bathroom and pressed her hands into the cool bathroom countertop as her thoughts raced.

If not in her pocket, where could it be?

But she knew.

The device must have fallen out when she was in the dumpster.

No, no, *no!*

She raked a hand through her hair. How could she have been so clumsy?

Everything she needed was on her phone. Even though she set it to automatically back up on the Cloud, she doubted those updates had gone through yet. She had to get to her cell before the city emptied the dumpster.

What was she going to do? Her heart raced as she chided herself.

She paced from the bathroom, her thoughts spinning.

Moving more quickly, she rushed to the window and peered out at the street below.

Two cops stepped toward the front doors of her hotel, their gazes scanning everything around them.

They were still looking for her, weren't they?

Her gut clenched. The lady at the front desk hadn't seen her. The woman had been distracted helping a distraught traveler when Andi crept inside.

She should be safe.

Andi's gaze swerved to the other side of the street, instinctually drawn to something there that beckoned her attention.

A man stood under a streetlight on the sidewalk.

Staring directly up at her in her room.

As if he wanted her to know about his presence.

She sucked in a breath as he smiled at her—a cold, devious smile.

Who was that man? He was too far away for her to make out any features.

But he was dangerous. She knew that for sure.

She stepped back and closed the curtains.

She'd risked everything to get her hands on those files.

Now it seemed like it could be all for nothing . . . especially since that stranger outside was taunting her.

Going back out tonight was too risky.

Tomorrow. Andi would go tomorrow.

She'd dumpster dive and find her phone.

Because she needed those photos and the information they contained.

Duke and Beau stayed up late talking and catching up. The conversation was good for his soul.

Beau had always been his best friend, and too much time had passed since they'd been together. Duke should have remedied that sooner, but he'd been distracted with too many other things as of late.

When he'd finally gone to bed, Duke's thoughts kept him awake.

Thoughts about Andi.

It wasn't unusual that thoughts about her kept him from resting. But tonight, the reasons were different. His curiosity was fully ablaze.

He turned over in bed and punched his pillow beneath him with a little too much force.

Why in the world had Andi smelled as if she'd been rummaging through trash? She'd looked as if she'd been burrowing her way through the city dump.

Just what was she up to? Did it have something to do with Victor Goodman?

Duke would bet everything he owned that answer was yes.

He turned over in bed again, unable to get comfortable.

Victor was trouble, and Andi was determined to bring the man down. But the oil mogul was also rich and powerful with more connections than an international airport. Anything remotely connected to that man put Andi in danger.

That fact left Duke uneasy.

Would she try something else tonight?

He didn't know.

But he'd sleep with one ear open, just in case.

Andi was too stubborn to ask him for help . . . but that didn't mean Duke wouldn't be there to offer assistance if she got herself in a bind.

He let out a sigh and glanced at the time. One-thirty.

Realizing sleep wasn't going to happen, he stood and threw on his clothes. Quietly, he crept from the room and paused in front of Andi's door.

Should he knock? See if they could talk?

He frowned. That seemed like overstepping. Besides, she could be asleep.

Instead, he decided to wander down to the lobby. They sold chocolate milk in a small store area. Maybe that would help him sleep.

But as he got off the elevator on the main floor, he paused.

Two cops talked to the front desk clerk. They asked her about a petite blonde wearing a black hat whom they were searching for as a person of interest.

Duke narrowed his eyes. A petite blonde woman?

It couldn't be Andi . . . right?

One thing was for sure: wherever Andi went, trouble seemed to follow.

chapter
four

THE NEXT MORNING, Duke wandered to the suite where the gang was meeting.

Thoughts from last night continued to haunt his mind. He hadn't heard Andi leave her room—and he'd been listening for any telltale signs. However, he *had* gone downstairs to get that chocolate milk. He supposed there was a chance she'd slipped out then.

He frowned at the thought.

However, based on that conversation he'd heard at the front desk, she probably hadn't shown her face since those police officers sounded like they were looking for Andi.

Duke hoped she hadn't gotten herself into trouble. Maybe today she'd finally open up.

His curiosity continued to grow by the minute.

Andi was definitely up to something, and he hoped the worst-case scenarios in his mind were all overblown.

Duke walked into the room and noted the smell of

cinnamon and vanilla. An arrangement of grab-and-go breakfast pastries sat on a table in the corner, along with a pot of coffee. Perfect.

As he grabbed a cup, he noted that he was the last of the Arctic Circle Murder Club to arrive. They'd all seen each other only a couple of days earlier when they'd taken a visit down to Salmon-by-the-Sea to solve an impromptu case.

This weekend had already been scheduled. Duke couldn't take too much time off work, but there *were* some perks to being his own boss. Thankfully, he had trustworthy employees he could depend on to take the reins when he was gone.

Mariella Boucher organized the group and acted as their spokesperson during the podcast.

Her twin brother, Matthew, oversaw the technical aspects of their show.

Ranger Garrett was a man of mystery—a gruff survivalist who never talked about his past. He wasn't a people person per se, but he had skills that had gotten them out of tight spots before, especially while in the wilderness.

Simmy Samuels worked at the secluded Almost Halfway Trading Post up near the Artic Circle. She wasn't much for investigating, but she had a way with people. Her genuine spirit made others trust her.

As they all greeted each other, Duke's gaze stopped on Andi. She looked much better this morning. Her hair was clean and flipped out near her chin. She wore a black leather coat and tight jeans with a pale blue top.

Duke gave her a look, making it clear he still had more questions about last night.

Instead of acknowledging his silent question, she asked, "Where's your brother? Did he leave?"

Nice conversation change, Duke noted. "Flights were delayed again this morning so he's hanging out in our hotel room while we each do our thing."

"He seems nice."

"He's a good guy." Duke didn't want to acknowledge the truth, but he'd felt a twinge of jealousy last night when Beau and Andi had been flirting.

Maybe flirting was too strong a word. But Beau and Andi had joked with each other and laughed together a little too warmly.

Duke didn't like it. Which was stupid. But if he were honest with himself, that was how he truly felt.

Before they could talk more, Mariella stood at the front of the living room area and clanked her spoon against a water goblet.

Everyone turned toward her. With her long, blonde hair and affinity for wearing pink, Duke had initially thought of her as Malibu Barbie. But there was so much more to her than that.

"I hate to break up this happy reunion, but we did come here for a purpose," she started.

They all found their seats on the various couches and chairs in the living area.

"Okay, so we're here for two reasons," Mariella continued. "One is clearly more pressing. The family of Stuart Downing has asked us to look into his murder."

Duke knew some of the details, but he settled back to hear Mariella's take.

"For the last twelve days, a killer has been haunting Anchorage," Mariella continued, her voice dramatic—perfect for the podcast but a little extra at this moment. "Six people have been murdered, including Stuart. His parents are heartbroken and want answers. Even though the police are working the case, Stuart's parents want to bring us in also."

Duke continued to listen, his mind racing over the facts.

This killer didn't seem to have a pattern—only that at night he cut the power to his victim's property, snuck into their house, and used a knife to kill them.

Each person had been alone.

But the victims had been women and men of different ages, ethnicities, and social standing.

Everyone in the area was now living in fear, wondering if they'd be the next victim. No one felt safe.

"Josiah and Elma Downing want to meet this morning," Mariella continued. "Duke and Andi, I'm hoping the two of you will talk to them."

"Absolutely," Duke answered.

Duke and Andi seemed to be the official boots-on-the-ground members of the team—and Duke was okay with that. He preferred it, in fact. With his background as an investigator with the Army CID, it made the most sense.

"Be glad to," Andi murmured before taking a sip of coffee.

Duke couldn't help but notice how she kept glancing at the door, almost as if she expected someone to barge in.

Again, he remembered those police officers he'd seen at the front desk last night, the ones who'd been asking about her.

What kind of trouble had Andi gotten herself into?

Before Mariella could continue, Matthew held up his phone where a news story played. "Hey, guys. Listen to this."

A story about the Lights Out Killer. That was what the media called him.

Nothing like giving a killer a name to make him infamous. Sometimes, people played right into the hands of these psychopaths.

The air left Duke's lungs as he listened to the report.

Another woman had been found dead this morning in her home in Anchorage.

The seventh victim in twelve days.

This guy had struck again . . .

The Lights Out Killer wasn't slowing down, was he? In fact, his rampage seemed to be accelerating.

How many innocent people would this guy murder before he was caught?

Duke's jaw hardened at the thought.

Andi's mind raced through everything Mariella said as she sat with coffee in hand.

She tried to remain focused on the main reason she'd come here this weekend. But it would require all her energy to do so.

Especially since she kept thinking about that man who'd been watching her from outside the hotel last night.

About the cops who'd chased her.

About her missing phone.

She'd started to leave early this morning to go look for it. But as soon as she'd stepped outside, she'd spotted a cop driving by. Not casually driving by either.

The officer had been scanning the streets as if looking for someone.

Were the cops still searching for her?

Andi didn't know, but she couldn't chance it.

Her best bet was to wait and go back to look tonight.

Which meant she'd have to spend all day today without her phone . . . and without the answers she'd risked everything to obtain.

That seemed to pale in comparison to the fact another

murder had occurred here in Anchorage . . . it was equally as horrific as the previous ones.

And terrifying.

The man couldn't continue his killing spree. She and the rest of the team needed to pour everything into finding some answers about this case.

"Maybe someone should go to the scene of this newest crime," Andi suggested. "Get a feel for the crowd. Listen for any police cross talk."

Mariella nodded and glanced at Ranger and Simmy. "Could you guys do that?"

"No problem." Ranger rubbed his dark beard, his eyes narrowed. He seemed to operate at one speed: intense.

"Great." Mariella nodded again as if relieved. "Matthew and I will stay here and continue to work on the technical aspects of the podcast."

"We need to be careful not to spread ourselves too thin," Simmy murmured.

Andi agreed with Simmy's assessment. However, it was too late for Andi. She already had personal business she wanted to attend to while she was in Anchorage.

She'd moved to Alaska with the sole intention of bringing down Victor. Nothing was going to stop her.

He was the reason she'd lost her license to practice law back in Texas, and she was certain he'd had Stockton, her colleague at the law firm and someone she'd briefly dated, killed.

The man had already tried to have her killed as well.

She was nearly certain he'd hired someone to run her off the road once and on another occasion to harm her in a hit-and-run. Thankfully, he'd been unsuccessful.

Those incidents had only strengthened her resolve.

Mariella's grin faded. "Before we go, I need to mention Steven Calderson."

That was right. Steven Calderson.

The man had reached out to them for help. He'd been arrested and imprisoned fifteen years ago for first-degree murder, but he claimed he never committed the crime. New evidence appeared to prove his innocence, and he needed someone to look into it.

"I'll be happy to look into him more," Andi said.

"I was hoping you could do that this weekend," Mariella said. "But the truth is, he came down with pneumonia. He's being treated, so you won't be able to talk to him right now. We'll have to shelve his case for next time."

"Noted."

If they were going to get anything done, they needed to move.

Stuart's parents wanted to meet them in forty minutes.

Andi hoped for the sake of everyone here in Anchorage that they could find answers.

chapter
five

ANDI WAS glad she and Duke had been paired together.

He always kept an eye on her. The "I am woman, hear me roar" part of Andi wanted to pretend she could do things on her own without any fear. But the truth was, she always felt safer with Duke by her side. Part of her even liked his protectiveness—though she'd never admit it to him.

But as they stepped out of the suite several minutes later, another thought slammed into her mind.

Being alone with Duke would give him many opportunities to ask questions.

Being alone with Duke was actually a terrible idea.

More than anything, Andi wanted to tell him the truth. She wanted him, in all his infinite wisdom and experience, to be her sounding block.

But sharing that information wouldn't be wise. Not

telling him would ultimately protect him. She had to remember that.

However, how did she get out of it now?

An idea hit her.

She paused as she stared up at him in the hallway. "You probably want to spend time with your brother, don't you? I can go talk to the Downings by myself."

The brothers *had* seemed eager to catch up.

Duke shrugged nonchalantly. "Maybe he'll want to come with us if his flight hasn't been rescheduled yet."

She resisted a frown. That hadn't worked.

What other excuse could she use?

As her mind raced through the possibilities, she sensed Duke studying her expression, thoughts clearly brewing in his mind.

"Andi, what happened last night?" he finally asked.

Andi's throat tightened. Swallowing hard, she glanced at her watch. "This is a bad time. We're going to be late."

Duke's gaze lingered on her, and Andi knew he wanted to say more. To press for answers.

Instead, he finally asked, "Later?"

Relief swept through her. "Later."

Andi just wasn't sure how much "later" it would be.

~

Beau met them downstairs ten minutes later. Apparently, flights still weren't leaving the airport, so he was stuck in Anchorage a while longer.

Duke and Andi both had brought their bags with them since they had to be out of the hotel by eleven. Around lunchtime, they could move into their rental, where they'd stay for the rest of the weekend.

Duke had mixed feelings about how today would go. He'd love to spend more time with Beau. He just didn't want that time to be around Andi.

Which was ridiculous.

Because Duke and Andi weren't dating. Andi was free to date whomever she wanted, as was Beau.

Duke's life had been in a holding pattern since Celeste, his fiancée, went missing nearly two and a half years ago. He'd originally thought the same person who'd abducted women from the Dalton Highway had taken Celeste. But that hadn't been the case.

Then he'd stumbled upon a woman who looked just like Celeste. But when he'd tried to confront her, she'd disappeared, almost as if she'd never been there. She'd shown up later with a man who'd held Duke at gunpoint, told him to drop his investigation into Celeste, and then knocked him out. Then she'd shown up at Andi's place and left a note saying, *Stay out of this*.

It was enough to both break Duke's heart and make his head ache.

Andi had insisted Duke needed resolution before he started a new relationship. Though he wanted to argue, he couldn't. She was right.

He'd lived with guilt for a long time, feeling it was his fault Celeste had gone missing. He should have gone on the backpacking trip with her. Or he should have insisted she not go alone. That she wait until there was a better time and they could go together.

But Duke hadn't. And Celeste had disappeared.

For more than two years he'd imagined all the horrible things that might have happened to her.

Now he wasn't even sure what to think.

What if the woman he'd seen back in Fairbanks wasn't Celeste? Maybe she was just a look-alike. He didn't know. But he wasn't going to give up until he found out.

He, Beau, and Andi stepped outside, ready to walk toward Duke's SUV, which was parked in a garage a block away.

As they strolled down the sidewalk, they paused on the corner, waiting to cross. A commotion in the distance caught Duke's eye.

He smiled when he realized what was happening. A moose had wandered downtown, and people were snapping pictures of the animal. Police tried to clear the crowd. Most didn't realize just how dangerous the creatures could be.

He waited for Andi to make a smart comment. She always seemed to have one on the tip of her tongue.

But when he looked at her, he noticed she'd gone pale.

He narrowed his eyes as he studied her.

What was that reaction for? Andi was scared, wasn't she?

But of what?

chapter
six

WHEN ANDI DIDN'T EXPLAIN herself, Duke finally asked, "You have a fear of moose or something?"

Andi snapped her gaze toward his. "What?"

"You're staring at that moose as if you're terrified."

She brushed off his statement with a forced chuckle. "No, I'm not."

"I heard they're all friendly just like Bullwinkle." Beau winked.

Duke wanted to roll his eyes. Instead, he decided not to push anymore. Not now. But he wasn't ready to let this drop. The subject *would* be coming up again later.

"We should probably get going," he said instead.

"Probably," Beau agreed.

Andi's gaze remained on the moose another moment before she turned away.

What an odd reaction. Why in the world was she

staring at the scene like that? The woman hardly ever got spooked. And over a moose?

Whatever it was, her reaction most likely tied in with last night's events.

Duke couldn't wait to hear why Andi had looked and smelled so bad. The woman was a mystery to him—and maybe that was just one more reason she fascinated him.

"So where are we going again?" Beau glanced around casually as they headed toward the garage. People already milled along the streets since tourist season was in full bloom.

The train station wasn't far from here, and no doubt many were headed there.

In between the buildings, Duke caught glimpses of the mountains in the distance, still snowcapped even in the summer. The sight was awe-inspiring, no matter how many times he'd experienced the breathtaking vista.

Duke updated his brother on today's schedule.

Beau nodded slowly. "What you're doing sounds interesting."

"What you do sounds interesting also." Andi tucked her hands into the pockets of her jeans, a subtle caginess to her movements. "Like I said last night, I really would love to hear your story sometime."

"I would love to tell you my story sometime," Beau said. "Or maybe you can even come and hear one of my talks if we're ever in the same area."

Andi flashed a smile at him. "You'll have to let me know if you come back to Alaska."

"I will."

As another cop hurried past them on the sidewalk, headed toward the moose, Andi slowed until she walked behind Duke.

"This isn't the Middle East," he murmured. "You can walk beside me."

But that wasn't what she was doing, was it? She was trying to hide.

From the cops.

"Andi . . ." He gave her a warning glance.

"It's a long story." Exhaustion marred her tone as she remained out of sight behind him.

"You've said that before. If we're going to be partners, there can't be secrets between us that will get us both in trouble."

She frowned.

Then she glanced over her shoulder before picking up her pace. "Okay, I'll tell you. But not until we're in the car."

Good. She'd listened to his argument and seen his side of things.

Duke was more curious than ever, especially since a bad feeling lingered in his gut.

～

Relief washed through Andi as soon as she climbed into the back seat of Duke's SUV.

The cops hadn't seen her.

She'd take that win.

She hadn't seen that man again either—the one who'd been outside the hotel watching her.

That was also a win.

She didn't want to share with Duke what had happened last night. However, at this point, she didn't have much of a choice—especially since the cop who'd walked past had been one of the two who'd chased her.

If the man caught a glimpse of her face . . . he might recognize her.

The good news was that Duke and Andi had a definite time set up to meet Stuart's parents, so they didn't have an endless stretch of minutes for Duke to interrogate her.

Andi could make her explanation short and sweet.

Duke started the SUV and then typed the address to Josiah and Elma's place into his GPS. A few minutes later, they headed out of the parking lot and down the road.

"It says we have a thirteen-minute drive, so you can start anytime." Duke glanced at Andi in the rearview mirror.

She let out a sigh. Stared out the window. Rolled her eyes up to the ceiling.

Finally, she began. "If you must know, I got a lead on . . ." She glanced at Beau. "*That thing* I'm working on. So I decided to do some research myself."

She didn't want to share too much information in front of Beau. The situation was complicated, and she'd only shared the truth with a few people. She didn't want to pull Beau into her drama.

"Did this research involve anything illegal?" Duke asked.

Andi shrugged, hating how Duke had so easily guessed what she'd done. "I'd rather not share too many details. But I was very careful. Somehow, the police were called. I panicked and took off in a run so I wouldn't be caught."

His gaze remained narrowed. "Let me guess: you hid in a dumpster?"

She twisted her lips in disgust at the memory. "What gave it away? The smell?"

"And the tomato seeds stuck to the side of your face."

She frowned. "Those too."

"That wasn't a smart move." Duke rubbed his jaw in exasperation. "The situation could have turned out differently—badly."

"I know." Andi had known Duke would lecture her. She should have done more to prepare her winning defense.

"If you'd been caught . . ."

"I know," Andi repeated as she glanced out the window at the towering mountains in the distance—mountains that reminded her of how small she was, how her life was like a grain of sand, the smallest of rocks. "But I tried playing by the rules, and it didn't work."

"I think she's got moxie." Beau's voice lilted as if he were impressed. "I kind of like it."

A smile tugged at Andi's lips, especially when Duke's scowl deepened.

Before they could talk any more, they arrived at a modest house on the outskirts of Anchorage, the home where Stuart's parents had resided for the past forty years.

Perfect timing.

Because Andi didn't want to discuss this situation anymore.

Now it was time to do what they'd come here to do: talk to Stuart's family and maybe find answers that would help stop a serial killer from terrorizing this city.

chapter
seven

BEAU HAD INSISTED he had phone calls to make, so he waited in the car while Duke and Andi went to talk to Josiah and Elma Downing. It was better that way, Duke mused. For more than one reason.

As soon as Duke stepped outside and had a moment alone with Andi, he turned to her. "You are *so* frustrating."

The words weren't especially nice, but he needed to say them. What Andi had done had been stupid. Risky. There were other ways to do things. *Legal* ways. She should know that better than anyone.

Andi's hands went to her hips as she turned toward him, fire flashing in her gaze. "You are equally as frustrating."

"Why am *I* frustrating?"

"Do I need to mention all your many opinions and the way you always think you're right?"

He stared at her as they paused on the sidewalk. "I usually *am* right. And what's wrong with having opinions?"

She popped out a hip and tilted her head to the side. "I'm perfectly capable of forming my own opinions and making my own decisions!"

"Well, you made a poor one last night!"

Andi stared at him, the flames in her eyes only igniting more.

Duke stared back, his gaze hard and unyielding.

Neither made any moves to back down.

There was so much Duke wanted to say to Andi.

But none of his arguments would do any good. Andi was hardheaded and stubborn, not to mention determined. If that made him opinionated, then so be it. He was opinionated.

Andi was dead set on bringing down Victor Goodman.

Even more so, Duke was powerless to stop her. Even if he could keep an eye on her twenty-four seven—which would be impossible since the woman had a mind of her own and would never let him—she'd *still* find a way to get into trouble.

Andi sucked in a deep breath as if trying to compose herself. Then she glanced at her watch. "We should get inside. We don't want to be late."

Duke clamped his jaw shut and nodded. She was right. It was almost time for them to meet.

But he hadn't felt this frustrated with someone since . . . since he couldn't remember the last time.

He'd already lost Celeste, and if Andi kept acting like this . . .

Duke shoved that thought out of his mind as they headed toward the house.

He and Andi would talk about this more later.

Right now, he needed to move from one crisis to another.

Josiah and Elma were a lovely couple in their early seventies who'd lived in Anchorage their entire lives. Josiah was on the shorter side with a mostly bald head and kind eyes. Elma had faded red hair cut to her chin, green eyes, and a plump figure.

Andi noted that their yard was well-kept. The house average in size and design, though Elma bragged that Stuart—their only child—had paid for them to renovate their kitchen only two years ago. The cabinets, appliances, and finishes looked top-notch.

They'd been seated in the living room with coffee and some gingersnap cookies while surrounded by uncountable pictures of Stuart. The photos were everywhere—on the coffee table, the fireplace mantel, the walls. Stuart with his red-tinged hair, square jaw, and hopeful eyes.

Pictures of a smiling, happy Stuart at various stages of

his life. Yet in each one, he'd had his whole life ahead of him.

Until that had been snatched away.

"Thank you for coming," Josiah started, his coffee untouched. "Our nephew listens to your show and contacted you on our behalf. He wishes he could be here now, but his wife just went into labor."

"We're glad he reached out." Duke leaned forward, arms perched on his knees. "We're so sorry to hear about Stuart."

As soon as Stuart's name had been mentioned, visible sadness swept over the couple.

Andi's heart physically ached with empathy at their grief.

Though Andi and her team were true-crime enthusiasts, there was nothing entertaining about crime—especially not when it was personal. The main reason Andi even got involved with the podcast was to bring justice to criminals who thought they were untouchable.

"We still can't believe it." Josiah rubbed beneath his eyes, the skin there saggy and bloated. "I keep expecting the phone to ring and for Stuart to be on the line."

Andi's throat tightened at the imagery. Loss was so difficult. Life couldn't be taken for granted. She'd learned those lessons the hard way.

"Tell us about your son." Duke's voice rumbled across the room, low with compassion.

"He's a—*was* a—wonderful man." Josiah took a few

seconds to compose himself by absently running his finger along the top of his coffee mug. "He never married. But he loved his job."

"What did he do?" Andi asked.

"He worked in research for a clean-energy company." Elma's gaze filled with pride. "He truly thought he was making a real difference."

Andi took another sip of her drink before asking, "Was his work controversial?"

Josiah shrugged. "I can't say it was. He never mentioned anything. Really, things seemed to be running so smoothly for him."

Duke shifted and rubbed his lips together before speaking. "I hate to ask this because I realize the crime wasn't personal. I'm just trying to get a better picture." He paused. "Did Stuart have any enemies?"

Josiah and Elma exchanged a glance.

Finally, Elma spoke. "Not really. But if I had to pick someone, it would be Melanie Wooden."

"Who's Melanie Wooden?" Andi stored the name away, wondering if this woman could be the lead they were looking for.

"She and Stuart dated for about a year." Josiah continued to run his finger along the rim of his mug, almost as if he needed to do something to hold himself together. "She wanted to get married. Stuart didn't—and he made that clear from the start of their relationship. But eventually, Melanie became angry because he wouldn't fully commit."

"What do you mean by angry?" Duke narrowed his gaze as he listened.

"I mean, Melanie flew off the handle." The corner of Elma's lips pulled down in a frown as she spoke. "She seemed obsessed with Stuart. She kept calling and stopping by. She even came to our house to see if we could change Stuart's mind."

That definitely sounded off-balance.

But just because Melanie was off-balance didn't mean she was a serial killer. However, it couldn't hurt to confirm that the woman didn't have any connections with any other victim.

"What else can you tell us about Melanie?" Andi asked.

"She lives here in Anchorage and works for a car dealership," Josiah said.

"Maybe we should start by talking with her," Duke suggested.

"Maybe. But the police say these crimes are random." Josiah's forehead knotted as if he were second-guessing himself.

"That's understandable," Duke continued. "But it can't hurt to talk to Melanie. Even killers who, on the surface seem to have random victims, usually have a deeper psychological reason they choose who they do. If we can figure that out—"

"Then you can figure out who killed our Stuart . . ." Elma's voice drifted as more tears filled her eyes.

Josiah squeezed his wife's hand before saying, "There's one other thing."

"What's that?" Andi's breath hitched as she wondered what else he had to share.

"When we identified our son's body, we noticed a mark on his chest." Josiah's voice cracked.

"Stab wounds?" Duke clarified.

Josiah shook his head. "No. Well, yes. Maybe. I don't know. The wounds . . . they were in an X-shape on his chest."

"What?" The question left Andi's lips in a breathless rush.

Josiah nodded, rubbing away his tears. "The police didn't say anything. I think they want to keep it hush-hush. But I can't get the image out of my mind. Why would the killer leave an X on his chest?"

"That's a good question," Andi murmured. "We'll keep that detail to ourselves."

"Please, help us." Elma buried her face in her hands as a sob captured her. "Please. I don't think we'll have any peace until this monster is behind bars."

chapter
eight

DUKE AND ANDI walked back to his SUV after talking to the Downings.

Duke wanted answers now more than ever. Not for the sake of the podcast but for the sake of Stuart's parents. Their grief had been palpable . . . and Duke understood it all too well.

He glanced at Andi as they paused near his vehicle. "What do you think?"

Her gaze looked heavy with grief. "I think everyone in this area should be terrified. The X on Stuart's chest? That's just creepy."

"Definitely." Duke rubbed his jaw as he scanned their surroundings—standard operating procedure for Duke.

"But you're right—we need to examine this guy's patterns. Then maybe we can figure out who the killer is. I think we should start by talking to Melanie."

"I agree." Andi nodded. "Maybe this guy staked out

his victims, and she saw something. Or maybe Stuart told her something that seemed unconnected at the time. We should definitely ask."

They reached the SUV, climbed inside, and gave Beau a recap on their conversation.

"I'm glad you're back into the investigation game, Duke." Beau flicked a glance his way and nodded. "It fits you."

Everything had changed after Celeste went missing.

So much had changed.

Sometimes Duke felt as if he'd been scammed.

His life had been turned upside down because of Celeste.

But what if she'd chosen to disappear without telling him? What if she'd left Duke to suffer, knowing how badly this would hurt him but making no effort to explain?

At night when Duke lay in bed, those questions haunted him the most.

"Where to now?" Beau turned toward them as he sat in the front passenger seat.

"Now Andi and I need to head to the rental house," Duke said. "You want to go back to the hotel?"

"I'd rather go with you." Beau shrugged. "I mean, not to invite myself..."

"I don't think anyone would mind," Andi murmured.

"Why not?" Duke said. "But it may not be that exciting. We'll meet with the rest of the team and discuss what we learned.

As they started down the road, Duke wondered if Ranger and Simmy had discovered anything at the latest crime scene. One thing was for sure: life definitely hadn't been boring since this group had stumbled onto one another.

Yes, stumbled.

That was how it felt.

The Arctic Circle Murder Club had come together by chance—a group with little in common except a love for true crime investigations and an admiration for now-deceased podcaster Craig Rogers.

Yet somehow, they worked.

Duke's phone rang, and Gibson's name appeared on the screen on his console.

Logan Gibson was a state trooper up in Fairbanks. The team had interacted with him several times. Plus, Gibson had been the officer who'd handled Celeste's disappearance, so Duke had known the man longer.

"Hey, Gibson. It's Duke. You're on speaker. I'm here with Andi and my brother."

"Hey, guys." Gibson's deep voice filled the SUV. "I take it you all aren't up in Fairbanks right now?"

"How did you know?" Andi's forehead wrinkled in confusion.

"Because I just got an APB from Anchorage."

Duke glanced at Andi in the rearview mirror, but she

shrugged as if clueless about what Gibson was about to say.

"What kind of APB?" Duke was unsure if he truly wanted to know. If Gibson was calling to tell them this, the man had a good reason.

"A woman broke into Senator Glassine's office last night and stole some classified documents . . . and that woman looks an awful lot like you, Andi."

The blood drained from Andi's face. Certainly, she hadn't heard Gibson correctly.

Senator Diane Glassine had represented the great state of Alaska for the past fifteen years. People often compared her to a bull in a China shop. When she believed in something, she held nothing back.

People in the area either loved her or hated her.

Andi leaned toward the front seat and murmured, "Come again?"

"Officers across the state are on the lookout for someone who broke into Senator Glassine's office last night," Gibson repeated. "That woman looks a lot like you, Andi."

Duke cast her a knowing look.

"I did *not* steal classified information." Andi crossed her arms defensively.

"But you're not denying breaking into a senator's

office?" Gibson paused. "On second thought, don't answer that. I don't want to know."

Andi's throat tightened as she realized how serious these charges could be. "Are you for real, Gibson? The state police are looking for me right now?"

"That's right. Because the crime occurred in a senator's office, local police, state police, and the FBI are involved. The picture was sent out statewide just in case 'this woman' is on the move."

Andi started to defend herself but stopped.

Gibson was right. The less he knew, the better. Besides, if Andi confessed anything, her friend might be obligated to arrest her.

"If I may ask . . . how do they know what she looks like?" Andi asked.

"Security video and eyewitness description."

"Thank you for the heads-up," she told him. "I'll also be on the lookout for a woman who looks just like me."

Gibson let out an airy but unconvincing chuckle. Then his tone turned serious. "I don't know what you've gotten yourself caught up in, Andi. But whatever it is, be careful."

"Will do."

Duke ended the call.

Andi wished the McAllister brothers hadn't heard those details. But it was too late now. They'd heard every word.

Duke veered off the road. A couple of turns later, he

stopped in the parking lot of a big box store, threw his SUV into Park, and turned toward her. "You want to tell me what's really going on, Andi? All of it—not just the sanitized version you shared earlier."

She leaned back in her seat.

That would be an affirmative no. But it wasn't that easy.

How much should she say?

Andi ran a hand over her face as she contemplated her next move.

chapter
nine

ANDI'S HEART pounded erratically in her ears as she deliberated how much to say. "I didn't steal classified information. I'm being set up."

Duke's eyebrows flung upward as he turned more fully in his seat to face her. "Come again?"

Andi drew in a deep breath. She really didn't want to go here. But she needed to fess up, especially if the police were on the lookout for her.

She let out another long breath before finally saying, "Everything I told you is true. I was just trying to find information. But I didn't steal anything."

"Could you start at the beginning?" Duke sounded no-nonsense.

"I've been talking to some people, and I found out that Senator Glassine had been meeting with Victor Goodman about this new oil reserve people want to drill."

Prometheus . . .

Andi had come across the word when she followed Victor one night. Then she found out it was associated with the controversial new drilling proposal that was going before the US Senate.

It would need a certain number of votes to pass, and right now it was tight.

Was Victor trying to buy Glassine's vote?

That was what Andi was trying to find out.

"I can't help but think there's more involved than what we see on the surface," Andi said.

"What do you mean?" Duke's eyes narrowed as he listened, waiting for answers.

"I mean, I think Victor is paying off the senator to get her vote and pass this project—all so he can line his pockets. But I need proof."

"You thought she was keeping proof at her office?" Duke gave her an incredulous look.

"Not necessarily, but I thought it would be a good place to check. The proof is in the pudding, right? I'm not going to know anything until I get my hands on some definite numbers."

"If the senator is involved, she's too savvy to keep evidence of any of it."

"I realize that's probably true."

Duke stared in the distance and rubbed his jaw. A moment later, he asked, "How did you break in?"

"Breaking in is a strong word. I simply went into the building to make a flower delivery before it closed. Then I went into the bathroom and hid there until everyone left —that was probably around nine. Then I wandered into the senator's office."

"You wandered into?" Lines formed on Duke's forehead. "It was unlocked?"

Andi frowned, ignoring the loud sound of someone walking past with a shopping cart loaded with a big screen TV. "Not exactly. But it wasn't hard to pick the lock."

Duke shook his head. "Andi . . ."

"What? How else am I going to get this information? It's not like anyone is going to hand it over to me. So anyway, I got into her office and went through her files. I didn't take the files themselves. I took pictures of them. Then I left. Except something went wrong. Before I reached the front door, I heard someone behind me. Then two cops appeared out of nowhere. I panicked and ran."

"Maybe you triggered an alarm." Beau draped his arm across the back of the seat as he stared at her.

She swung her head back and forth. "But I didn't. I was careful. I studied the building before I went inside."

"If you didn't trigger an alarm then how did the cops know you were there?" Beau asked.

Her lips twisted in a frown. "That's what I'm trying to figure out. The only thing I can think of is that . . . someone has been watching me, waiting for me to mess up. Maybe this person even saw me go into the building and realized what I was doing. Then that person called the cops on me."

"You think someone is watching you?" Beau glanced at her in surprise.

"You could say that." She didn't mention the man she'd seen outside the hotel last night.

"Did you get the proof you were looking for, at least?" Duke asked.

"Kind of." She frowned.

"Kind of?" Duke cast her another look.

"I took pictures . . . but I lost my phone. Probably in the dumpster."

"What?" Duke's voice lilted.

"I've got to go back and find it . . . but I have to wait until I can be certain no one is watching. Rookie mistake, I know. I'm still beating myself up. But my cell must have slipped out of my pocket."

Beau grunted before asking, "Why do you think this Victor guy is behind this?"

"Because he is." Her voice left no room for doubt. Victor was the only one who made sense. "He's powerful and affluent, and he's got people in his pockets."

"And if you try to turn him in for whatever he did, no one will listen," Beau continued.

"That's right." Andi's jaw tightened at the reminder. "I've tried, and now I know that without concrete evidence, it's never going to happen."

"Andi . . ." Duke murmured as he ran a hand over his face.

Andi hated hearing that tone to his voice. The disappointment mingled with worry.

He wasn't her keeper. They were friends, but they weren't dating. It wasn't his place to lecture her or to think he could control any part of her life.

Not that he'd tried to do that.

But Andi bristled at the thought of it. She'd been independent for a long time, and she intended to keep it that way. She didn't particularly like people telling her what to do.

"You know I won't rest until I get the answers I want," she finally said, crossing her arms and readjusting where she sat as the sun tried to blind her.

"I do realize that," Duke murmured.

"But I've got to be honest right now. If all the law enforcement agencies in this area are looking for me . . ." She paused and rubbed her arms. "I have no idea how I'm going to get out of this one."

Her words were on point.

She'd be in a heap of trouble if law enforcement truly thought she'd stolen classified documents.

With her legal expertise, Andi knew the reality of this situation. It was a federal crime that could send her to prison.

But she'd been careful to conceal her face from any cameras. She'd done her research first.

So how in the world had cops gotten a description of her? Who was the eyewitness? Had someone set her up?

Andi knew the answer.

Yes, there were people in the world who hated her enough to do that very thing.

She was in big, big trouble.

Duke pulled back onto the road to head to their rental.

They hadn't traveled for more than five minutes when Andi saw Duke's shoulders tighten.

"Duke?" What did he know that she didn't?

He glanced in the rearview mirror. "Someone's following us."

Andi sucked in a breath as she glanced behind her and saw the sedan there.

Any attempts on her life had failed.

But one day, that fact might change.

She prayed today wasn't that day.

Duke glanced in the mirror again at the dark sedan with tinted windows.

He'd noticed the car behind him before he'd pulled into that parking lot. Then it had reappeared again when they left.

That couldn't be a coincidence.

But who would be following them now? They hadn't dug into this new investigation enough to make anyone mad.

Unless this went back to Andi and Victor. That was Duke's best guess.

Beau glanced over his shoulder also. "What are you going to do?"

"Lose them," Duke muttered, his grip tightening on the steering wheel.

The last thing he wanted was to lead this person right to their rental. That wouldn't work.

Instead, he accelerated as he merged onto the interstate.

The car behind them accelerated also.

The other driver wasn't even trying to hide his presence, was he? That wasn't comforting.

"Be careful, Duke." Andi's voice thrummed with tension.

She was a fine one to talk about being careful.

She'd really snuck into a senator's office and taken pictures of classified information? Had she lost her mind? Duke wished he could give her a stern talking to. But this wasn't the time, nor was it his place.

Instead, he wove between traffic as he tried to lose this guy.

But the other driver stayed close.

Despite the persistence, the guy didn't appear aggressive. He wasn't trying to run them off the road or shoot out a tire.

He only followed them.

Was he trying to send a message? Maybe.

If so, it was working.

Just ahead, traffic ground to a halt.

But Duke pressed harder on the accelerator.

"Duke . . ." Andi's voice wavered again.

"Trust me," he told her.

As he charged toward traffic, tension stretched taut in the car. By the looks of it, he was barreling toward a certain death.

But he had a plan.

Beau grabbed the bar above his door and braced himself.

Andi gasped "Have you lost your mind?"

At the last second, Duke jerked the wheel to the right and onto an exit ramp.

Cars behind him slammed on their brakes and veered onto the shoulder to avoid hitting each other.

The cars zigzagging on the lanes effectively blocked that guy from getting any closer.

But how long would they be clear?

They were about to find out.

chapter
ten

DUKE LOOKED in his rearview mirror again.

The car hadn't reappeared.

He'd lost the driver.

His shoulders relaxed slightly. But he knew better than to let down his guard too much.

Besides, he was still turning over in his mind everything Andi had said.

Finally, they pulled to a stop in front of the rental house.

Before they got out of the SUV, Andi turned to them. "Please don't share any of the details I told you with anyone. I need to figure out my plan before I pull anyone else into my mess."

Duke could understand—and respect—that. Besides, the team certainly had enough on their plate right now. But it would be hard to focus on anything else, especially if Andi's arrest was imminent.

Unless they could keep her out of sight.

However, staying out of sight wasn't one of Andi's skills. A spotlight seemed to shine on her wherever she went.

"Promise?" Andi locked gazes with him, waiting for him to respond.

After a moment of hesitation, he nodded. "Promise."

Duke hoped he didn't regret that, however.

After grabbing their luggage from the back, they stepped toward their oversized house for the weekend. The sprawling two-story home was located on a sparkling blue lake with views of the snowcapped mountains in the background.

The lots in the neighborhood were large and, based on the boats and floatplanes Duke had seen tied to various piers, this wasn't just a vacation rental area. Many people were full-time residents—and wealthy ones, at that.

No doubt Alpine Grist had found this place and booked it for them. The accommodations fit his tastes.

They were afforded luxuries like this lodging because of Alpine, an investor who'd come onboard earlier this summer. The man had made millions in the tech world and now had more money than he knew what to do with. He'd chosen to pour some of those funds into their podcast in hopes they'd solve crimes.

The group also brought in their own money through podcast sponsorships. But for now, it wasn't enough to do what they needed. Duke knew Andi needed the money.

Her accounts had been wiped clean about a month ago, and none of that money had been recovered yet. He'd been trying to help her out by giving her a few jobs with his company. But he knew money still had to be tight for her.

As far as Duke was concerned, the sooner they could get rid of Alpine, the better. There was something about the man he didn't trust. Maybe Alpine's actions were altruistic, but Duke had trouble believing that was true.

In the meantime, Alpine could be the hero for financing their operations.

They stepped inside a moment later.

"Everyone, this is my brother, Beau." Duke nodded at his sibling, who stood beside him near the door. "I hope you don't mind that I brought him with me. His flight was canceled again."

"And I'm fascinated by what you do and anxious to see you guys in action," Beau added with the ease of an aristocratic politician pining for votes.

"It's great to have you here," Mariella said before the rest of the gang chimed in with similar sentiments.

They all chatted for several minutes. Then Mariella directed them to some food that had been delivered—a sandwich tray, some cut-up fruit, and individual bags of chips. Everyone grabbed something before settling at the table—the round table.

Since that was the name of their podcast, Mariella always tried to arrange for them to have an actual round table to gather around. It made sense for them to sit in a circle, where no one took the head of the table. They were all equals, just like the Knights of the Round Table. Andi had jokingly said once that they should call their podcast "Plights of the Round Table."

Duke noted that Andi didn't sit next to him as usual. Instead, she sat beside Simmy. Based on the way she kept shifting in her chair, she was definitely on edge.

As she should be.

"Who wants to start?" Mariella began from her seat in front of the blinged-out murder board.

Everything is better with sparkles. That was Mariella's mantra. But she *had* tamed down her pink obsession ever so slightly since they first started meeting.

Right now, photos of each of the victims hung on the board, along with descriptions including their name, age, location, and job. Post-it notes displayed the date they died, and a map of Anchorage had been placed on the other side with pins to show each victim's location.

"We'll start." Ranger raised a finger. "Simmy and I went to the scene of the most recent murder. The police were still there collecting evidence, and a crowd was gathered outside, as you can imagine."

"Did you find out anything?" Duke asked.

"Nicole Windsor was only twenty-five, and she was a 'housewife,' for lack of a better term," Ranger said. "Her husband was the breadwinner, and she didn't work."

"Her husband?" Andi's lips twitched with a frown.

"His name is Chad, and he was out of town on business." Simmy's voice turned wistful. "He actually returned to the house while we were there. Seeing him . . . well, it was gut-wrenching, to say the least."

"I can imagine." Mariella frowned as if picturing his heartache. "Anything else?"

"We talked to some of Nicole's neighbors," Ranger said. "Apparently, they didn't know her very well. Said she was quiet and kept to herself. The neighbor who found Nicole said she was probably about to take a bath. The water had been left running and flooded the house. He noticed the water coming from beneath the front door, and that's when he knew something was wrong."

"We also overheard two officers talking together." Simmy gingerly pulled a pretzel from the snack-sized bag in her hand. "They mentioned that Nicole went grocery shopping yesterday. She also took a walk and talked to her parents on the phone. The day was so normal until . . ."

Duke's jaw tightened. "Until the Lights Out Killer chose her."

Ranger's gaze darkened. "Exactly."

When Ranger and Simmy finished their update, Duke and Andi shared about their conversation with the Downings.

Afterward, Matthew distributed paper packets—neatly printed and stapled—to everyone. "I printed information about all the victims to see if we could find a connection. I also included photos."

"Hold up . . ." Beau shifted and glanced over Duke's shoulder at the papers. "You guys think you can find a connection the police missed?"

Duke shrugged. "We have before. Law enforcement is looking at this case through a different lens than we are. The cops know things we don't, which could work to their advantage. But the fact is we're looking at this objectively from all angles and different perspectives. Sometimes that allows us to pick up on clues other people don't."

Beau nodded slowly, his ankle crossed over his knee as he leaned back casually in his chair. "I like that."

Duke flipped through the list of victims.

- Mark Williams. Convenience store owner. Divorced. Fifty-two.
- Sherri Blanchard. Housekeeper. Single. Thirty-eight.
- Jevonne Whitaker. DJ. Married. Twenty-nine.
- Stuart Downing. Clean-energy researcher. Single. Forty-four.
- Wyatt Jenkins. Unemployed. Divorced. Forty-nine.
- Tex Lanyard. Retired. Widowed. Sixty-four.

- Nicole Windsor. Homemaker. Married. Twenty-five.

"It seems random to me." Simmy frowned as if bothered by that idea.

"It does, but this guy is choosing his victims for some reason." Andi stared at the papers as if she couldn't look away. "Serial killers almost always pick their victims— whether strangers or not—based on some kind of similar characteristic. Other killers have chosen prostitutes or single women or brunettes. We just have to figure out what links these people."

Everyone here in Anchorage had the right to be nervous about this.

This guy was scary.

Until authorities could figure out his pattern and motive, everyone should be on edge.

Including all of them, Duke realized.

Before they could talk any more, noises sounded outside the house.

Loud, frantic shouts.

Everyone sprang up and darted outside.

Duke paused for only a minute as he comprehended what was happening.

The neighbor's house was on fire . . . and a child leaned out the second-floor window, screaming in terror.

chapter
eleven

DUKE SAW three people huddled outside the house looking up at a window. Probably a father, mother, and preteen daughter. They all stared up at the window as they tried to coax a girl, around eight years old, to jump into their arms.

Smoke billowed out behind her, and the entire downstairs was ablaze.

It was only a matter of time before the upstairs would be as well.

That girl was on borrowed time.

Duke darted toward the house.

"Come on, Sophia!" The mom held her arms outstretched as she stared up at the girl. Desperation strained her voice, and her eyes looked wide with fear. "You can do it!"

"We won't let you get hurt, honey." The dad also had

his arms out. Beneath his calm voice quivered a deep-set fear that any parents would feel in a situation like this.

Tears poured down the girl's face as she shook her head, blonde pigtails slapping her cheeks. Terror captured her gaze. "I can't! I can't do it! Please! Please, help me, Daddy! Please!"

Duke's gut twisted into tight knots when he heard her words.

He could run inside to grab her. But going into that house would be a death sentence. Neither he nor the girl would get out alive.

He glanced back at the rental house.

When he'd pulled into the driveway earlier, he'd seen some tools propped against a shed in the back.

"Come with me!" He grabbed Beau.

He and his brother took off toward the shed. As soon as they reached it, Duke spotted a ladder.

His brother grabbed one end and Duke the other. Then they darted back toward the burning house, toward the girl's window.

"Watch out!" Duke told her family, who stood too close.

They took a few steps back, just enough to let him work.

He leaned the ladder against the house. The yard was on an angle as the ground tapered toward the lake. He'd need to be careful to keep his balance.

"Hold it for me," Duke yelled to Beau.

His brother nodded and grasped the sides.

Duke hadn't even climbed the first rung, yet he already felt the heat of the flames billowing from the house. Though he was outside, smoke already began to infiltrate his lungs.

He lifted a quick prayer for not only the girl's safety but his and Beau's also.

"Be careful, Duke!" Worry stained Andi's voice as she yelled to him from below.

Halfway up, an explosion rocked the air.

The ladder quivered.

Then it began to teeter.

Andi gasped as the windows shattered, sending a rush of hot air out from the house.

The fire must have reached a gas line inside.

The dad grabbed his wife and daughter and pulled them toward the lake. Then his eyes went back to Sophia, and tears began to stream down his face.

Sophia screamed.

A gut-wrenching sob escaped from the mom.

Life itself seemed to hold its breath.

Then Beau caught the ladder and righted it.

It hadn't fallen.

Duke hadn't hit the ground.

Andi let out a breath of relief.

If Beau hadn't been there . . . Duke would have been blown back and seriously hurt.

Thank goodness, that hadn't happened.

But they weren't out of danger yet.

Duke reached the top of the ladder and leaned toward the girl. He said something indecipherable, and the girl's eyes widened. She stepped away from the window.

The trauma of the situation had taken away her logic.

Please, let the girl go with him. Before it's too late.

If that wall collapsed, the ladder would topple into the house and Duke would go with it.

There were so many deadly ways this could end.

Andi held her breath as she waited to see how everything would play out.

Finally, the girl reached for Duke.

He scooped her into his arms.

Holding her in front of him, he quickly descended the ladder.

Just as he reached the ground, the wall collapsed.

The ladder toppled into the fire.

Only a few seconds difference . . .

Andi's throat tightened. She didn't want to think about it.

The little girl . . . she was safe. So was Duke.

Thank You, Jesus.

The dad sprinted toward them and swooped the girl from Duke's arms. He held the girl to him, his eyes closed.

Despite the touching moment, Duke put his hand on the dad's back and led them away from the house.

Just in time.

Another explosion rocked the air.

No one was injured. Thank God, they'd all moved far enough away.

Andi wanted to rush to Duke. To tell him how glad she was he was okay. To gush that he'd been brave and selfless—just as he always was.

As much as the man drove her crazy, he was a good person. Maybe too good. Too loyal.

But Andi didn't dare do any of those things. Instead, she remained where she was. All those ideas seemed too intimate, like she'd be overstepping.

But she was so glad he hadn't been hurt. So glad he'd been brave enough to take that chance and rescue that little girl.

As sirens sounded in the distance, Andi knew she couldn't stay outside much longer.

The police would be here soon.

If the cops saw Andi's face . . . they might arrest her.

chapter
twelve

DUKE STOOD with Beau and watched as the fire consumed the rest of the house.

Ranger, Mariella, and Matthew had grabbed a water hose. They doused out any fires in the grass that might spread to neighboring homes. Simmy stood beside the mom, an arm around her shoulders as she spoke to her in gentle tones.

He'd seen Andi scurry back inside the rental house several minutes ago.

He knew exactly what she was doing: hiding.

He wanted to catch up with her. But he couldn't leave. Not yet.

As Duke stood there, the girl's father approached him. The man still held Sophia in his arms as tears cut rivers in the soot on his face.

"I can't thank you enough," the man started.

"Of course. I'm glad I saw that ladder earlier."

"You and me both." The man, probably in his late thirties, with a ruddy complexion and reddish hair, extended his hand. "Dabney Eldridge."

Duke took the man's hand into his own. "Duke McAllister. Nice to meet you, despite the circumstances. This is my brother, Beau."

"Duke and Beau . . . if there's ever anything I can do to repay you, you let me know." His voice sounded throaty with appreciation.

Duke couldn't imagine what that might be. "There's no need for that, but thank you. Do you know what happened? How the fire started?"

"No, one minute my family and I were downstairs getting lunch together. The next moment, I smelled smoke. By the time I got to the stairs, it was too late. Fire covered the steps, and I couldn't get to Sophia. She'd just gone upstairs to grab a toy ten minutes earlier." Dabney held his daughter closer and seemed to swallow back a sob. "I thought we were going to lose her."

Flames cracked behind them, followed by another crash.

Sophia let out a cry and buried herself in her father's chest.

Duke turned, putting himself in front of the father and daughter. He watched as more of the house collapsed.

The good news—if there was good news—was that the family appeared to have a guest house closer to the lake at the back of the property. It looked big enough that the four of them could stay there if they chose.

Firetrucks and ambulances roared onto the scene. Firefighters emerged, grabbed their hoses, and quickly went to work dousing the flames. Paramedics checked out the family.

That had been a close one. Too close.

Duke was thankful he'd been nearby—not because he liked to be the hero. But because he liked to help.

He glanced back at the rental where he was staying this weekend.

Now . . . would Andi also let him help?

Andi settled at the dining room table, hating that she couldn't be outside with the rest of the team.

A few minutes after she came inside, Mariella followed. Based on the look in her eyes, she was worried about Andi. Andi knew why—she was acting out of character.

It was only a matter of time before everyone realized something was going on. Andi couldn't put off sharing the truth much longer. But she wished she could.

Mariella paused near the table. "You okay?"

Mariella didn't know the police were looking for a woman who looked like Andi.

"I'm fine," Andi said. "I just thought I'd get to work studying this new case."

Mariella sat across from her at the table. "Makes sense, I guess."

Andi quickly glanced out the window and saw firefighters extinguishing the flames. The smell of smoke had crept into the house. Or maybe it was on her clothes and hair?

She wasn't sure.

But the aroma of soot wouldn't leave her.

Andi glanced back at Mariella, knowing a change of subject was in order before Mariella pried anymore. "How's Jason doing?"

Mariella's eyes brightened at the mention of her new boyfriend. "I went straight from Salmon-by-the-Sea to come here. I hated to leave. But I did, of course. Jason is doing . . . so far, so good."

Jason Somersby had been accused of killing his girlfriend five years ago, but there had been no evidence to arrest or convict him. Still, speculation in the small town had rendered him an outcast.

Thankfully, the real killer had been caught and Jason's name had been cleared. Andi knew it would be a process for Jason to readjust to life in his small town, however.

Jason and Mariella had hit it off, and Andi was happy for her friend. Mariella had changed—for the better—in the few months since Andi had known her. She'd let down some of the superficial masks she'd often worn.

The former influencer still liked taking her selfies and posting on social media. But more depth of character had been emerging, and Andi liked seeing this new side of Mariella.

"How about Alpine?" Andi watched Mariella's face closely, remembering her earlier reaction to the man's name. "How is he?"

Something fleeting passed through Mariella's gaze before she finally shrugged. "Fine, I guess. I mean, he set up this house and everything for us, so that's cool, right?"

Andi closed her laptop and leaned back, giving Mariella her full attention. "Are you having second thoughts about that contract we signed with him?"

"Second thoughts?" Mariella let out a feeble laugh. "Don't be silly."

Andi didn't buy her reaction for a minute. "It's okay if you are. It would be normal."

Andi had tried to persuade everyone in their group not to sign that contract, but Mariella had been convinced it was the right choice. As a compromise, Andi had changed the legal wording and taken out a few worrisome phrases.

Still, she couldn't help but think Alpine had ulterior motives for being involved with them. He wasn't a simple man. No, Andi could see the gears turning in his mind, could see that there was more to him than he let on.

Through her years as an attorney, she'd become attuned to reading people.

And she didn't like Alpine. Plus, he had a strange connection with Victor. Alpine claimed the two were enemies, but Andi was still cautious.

"Everything with Alpine is fine." But Mariella's words sounded short and clipped. "How about you? How are things with you and Duke?"

Andi noticed the subject change. Mariella had taken a page out of Andi's book.

"Duke and I are friends," Andi reminded her. "We've been over this."

Mariella twirled a lock of hair around her index finger. "I mean, I know you're friends. But everyone can see the chemistry between you two."

"Just because there's chemistry or feelings doesn't mean you have to act on them." Andi told herself that often. Until Duke had some more resolution with Celeste, he wasn't relationship material.

For that reason, Andi constantly reminded herself to keep her distance.

The last thing she needed right now was a broken heart.

Besides, staying single helped Andi concentrate on figuring out this whole Victor situation.

As if speaking of the devil, the door burst open, and Duke stood there.

Andi held her breath, waiting to see what he had to say—because he clearly had something to say.

"Beau's flight is on, so I'm going to take him to the airport," he announced.

"Sounds good," Mariella called.

He nodded toward Andi, his gaze lingering on her another moment. Then he closed the door. A minute later, an engine roared to life outside.

Then silence stretched.

"There's nothing between you two?" Mariella studied her face with open curiosity.

Andi shrugged, determined to brush off this conversation. "No, nothing."

But the words left a bad taste in her mouth and caused regret to instantly fill her.

chapter
thirteen

"THERE'S nothing between me and Andi," Duke told his brother as they drove to the airport.

"There's nothing between you?" Beau echoed, his eyebrows raised. "Are you sure, man? Because that's not what it looks like to me."

Andi's image filled Duke's mind—her spunky intelligence and admirable bravery. Her winsome grin and confident gaze. Her petite figure and white-blonde hair.

There was nothing not to like about her.

And that was part of the problem.

Duke cleared his throat. "Andi and I . . . we both have different goals. Besides, the Celeste situation has taken a toll on me, to say the least."

"She's been gone for more than two years." Beau's voice dipped with compassion "How long are you going to hang on?"

Duke hadn't told his brother about the latest developments.

Everyone had assumed Celeste was one of the Missing Women of Dalton Highway. But she wasn't. Her disappearance still remained a mystery.

His grip tightened on the steering wheel. "I'm not sure, but Andi and I are just friends."

"Just friends, huh?" Beau cast a glance at his brother.

"That's right. Andi is great. Really great. But I just don't know that I'm ready to move on." The words were true.

Duke had been tempted. Very tempted. But Andi had reminded him that his heart still had some healing to do. Sometimes Duke thought finding answers was the only way he would get that restoration he needed.

But the fact remained . . . what if Duke never found those answers?

"So if you're not interested in her, does that mean I could ask her out?"

Beau's question jerked Duke away from his thoughts.

His gaze swerved toward his brother, and he quickly reminded himself to keep his cool. "Do you *want* to ask her out?"

Duke's throat tightened at the question. He hadn't expected this turn in the conversation.

He'd seen Beau and Andi flirting, but he'd assumed nothing would come of it. But . . . what if he'd been wrong?

"I wouldn't have asked if I didn't." Beau sounded confident—just like always.

He had a way with women and had never been afraid to go after what he wanted. Duke was more the type to put a lot of thought into what he wanted before pursuing it. He operated with more caution when it came to his heart.

"But you don't even live around here." Duke felt the need to point out the obvious.

Beau shrugged. "I travel a lot with my job and have some flexibility. But I'd never step into my brother's territory if you like her."

Duke's thoughts collided as he contemplated how to respond. If he said no, that would make it clear that Duke wanted Andi for himself. Was there anything wrong with that?

No, absolutely not.

But it still somehow felt like a betrayal to Celeste. At the surface level, the reasoning didn't make sense. But maybe he held a smidgen of hope that the woman he'd seen wasn't Celeste. That maybe the real Celeste was still out there. Maybe her hope of being reunited with him one day was what kept her going.

And maybe Duke was just a hopeless romantic—though he'd never admit it.

Finally, he cleared his throat. "Of course, you can ask her out."

Maybe that would be good for Duke. Maybe it would help him to stop thinking about Andi.

Yet he knew his thought process wasn't really accurate.

His only hope was that his brother would catch that flight and forget about Andi.

Just as that thought went through his head, Beau's phone buzzed with a text message.

Beau glanced at the screen. "Good news. Kind of. My flight is canceled again so it looks like I'm stuck here longer. The two of us can hang out more, after all."

The two of them and . . . Andi.

Duke forced a smile "Sounds perfect."

He had to get his head on straight . . . and figure out how to finally get some resolution to the Celeste situation before his whole life passed by, leaving him holding the bag.

Then Duke's phone beeped. He was at a traffic light, so he glanced at the screen.

His heart rate kicked up a beat.

Someone had sent him a picture of his sister, Suzie. She was out shopping, totally clueless that someone was watching her.

Then another photo came through, this one of Suzie outside her house.

Someone was stalking her. And this person wanted Duke to know exactly what they were doing.

His throat tightened.

Duke had to let his sister know . . . especially if she

could be in danger.

After Mariella went to her room to work on some social media, Andi studied the paperwork Matthew had given them.

She couldn't go anywhere until the police next door left. The rest of the gang was still outside watching the fire being extinguished, and Duke and Beau had left for the airport. So she might as well get some work done.

She made columns where she listed information about the victims and tried to find something they all had in common.

To do so, she scoured not only news articles, but she looked at each person's social media.

They already knew all the victims were different ages, races, genders, with various socioeconomic positions.

This killer didn't seem to be a respecter of any of those.

Something else had to link them.

As she continued to study the list, her thoughts drifted to last night's misadventure.

Should she simply go to the police and explain what she'd done?

Andi frowned. No, that was too risky.

There was only a small chance the cops would believe her and let her go. Most likely, she'd end up behind bars. If

Victor had his way, she'd spend the rest of her life there. The man outside her hotel? The car that had followed them?

It was most likely people sent by Victor.

Andi glanced at the time again. The minutes seemed to crawl by.

She'd go crazy if she had to stay in this house all weekend.

Then again, the police had certainly identified her by now. That meant when she got back to Fairbanks, they could be waiting for her at her apartment.

She frowned at the thought.

She had to figure out what to do.

As if on cue, Mariella gathered everyone.

Good. Maybe there was an update.

When Andi joined the gang in the living room, she saw Duke and Beau were back. It appeared Beau's flight hadn't worked out again.

"Guess what?" Mariella started, once they were all settled. "The police are holding a press conference later today about the Lights Out Killer. I think we should go hear what they have to say. Any volunteers?"

Andi would love nothing more than to be there.

But she couldn't go.

Not with her image being available to the cops.

But maybe there was an update or a new clue the club could work on . . . because she needed something to keep her thoughts occupied.

chapter
fourteen

I HAD A LIST. I called it a manifesto because I liked the ominous sound of it.

In order to get my point across, I would keep killing.

The secret was finding my victims alone.

Having other people in the house made it too complicated.

But maybe now that I was getting the hang of it, I could branch out.

I had a message to send, and if I didn't work quickly on bringing these people down, then my declaration would never be heard.

I smiled at a woman as she passed me on the sidewalk. I stood there, waiting for the press conference to start. I wanted to watch people's faces.

No one would ever suspect me.

After all, I'd just won employee of the month two months ago. Everyone in the office loved me. The news had even written me up in an article that espoused the great things I'd done for the community.

They had no idea who I really was.

And I couldn't let them know.

Because I knew how they'd react.

I needed to do something more extreme. Which was what I was doing now.

I remembered last night.

Remembered the feeling I'd experienced as I'd watched the life drain from that woman's eyes.

When I'd taken my first life, I'd been nervous. But I'd had to send a message.

Now, I found myself liking the act more and more.

In fact, I was looking forward to tonight.

Yes, tonight. I touched my chest, the area where my scar was located. It reminded me . . . well, it reminded me of everything I needed not to forget.

My fingers ran along part of the X shape there.

Xs were so important. They represented the unknown.

And life was full of unknowns.

It had been an important—and painful—lesson for me to learn.

My blood lust was strong, and I needed to feed it again soon. I needed to stop people who thought they were unstoppable.

No one would ever believe I was the one responsible.

That was the beauty of this whole setup.

I smiled again as someone passed me. The breeze—cool and refreshing—swept over me and seemed to promise everything would be okay.

The crowd around me, with their murmuring and restlessness, seemed anxious for the press conference to start.

As was I.

I had three choices for tonight's victim.

In fact, one of them might be here today at the press conference. I would watch for her.

Still, I would need to drive by each of their houses. See who was home. Who was alone. Watch for their lights to go out.

Then I'd make my move.

Soon, more fear would spread and consume people's lives.

Fear meant power.

I needed to use that power to make my mark.

Warmth spread through my chest as a grin tugged at my lips.

I couldn't wait for people to know the truth.

For the evil to be exposed.

I even had a grand finale planned.

The opportunity had practically been handed to me.

But my time was running out. I wouldn't be able to cross off everyone before the big event.

For now, I'd wait and watch. Nothing would bring me more pleasure than seeing my future victim here.

chapter
fifteen

DUKE HAD VOLUNTEERED to go to the press conference—and Beau would go with him.

But his thoughts remained on that photo. He'd shown Beau, and they'd called Suzie.

She'd had no idea.

They asked her to go stay with a friend for a few days, just to be on the safe side.

The good news was that Suzie, who happened to be a schoolteacher, was also well-versed in self-defense and had a concealed carry permit. She was out of school for the summer, which would work to her advantage right now.

Still, Duke didn't like the thought that someone had pulled Suzie into this.

Who would have done that? An enemy from a past case from the Army CID? Or was this photo somehow connected with Celeste's disappearance? Or could it be connected with one of the cases he was working on now for the podcast?

He had no idea.

He and Beau found a parking space near City Hall and made it to the press conference just as it started. The mayor, police chief, and lead detective stood on a small stage in front of the municipal building. Reporters with microphones had gathered around, as well as a crowd of spectators.

The sheer number of people interested in this press conference served as a testimony to how scared people in the area were.

Duke hoped he might get some new insight on this killer.

He scanned the crowd again and saw several cops on the perimeter of the area.

He recognized one from last night. The cop had been looking for Andi.

Duke's gaze zeroed in on the man's name tag.

Eisenhauer.

Duke stored away the man's name and face, just in case.

Mayor Tomlin, a man in his sixties with stark white hair and a stocky build, tapped the microphone before getting the press conference started. He said a few words before introducing the police chief, a man named Ricky Hines. The guy was in his mid-forties with thick light-brown hair and red cheeks.

"We want to assure the public that we're using every resource at our disposal to find the person responsible for these murders," Chief Hines said. "We've asked both the FBI and the state police to assist us in this investigation."

He then introduced Ron Rasmussen, the lead detective on the case. He took over the microphone. "We're asking anyone who knows anything to come forward, for the sake of our community. In the meantime, keep your doors locked, don't stay alone, and . . . keep the lights on."

The ominous sound to his words sent a shiver down Duke's back.

He thought about people who lived on their own, not by choice but because of life—the elderly, single moms whose kids were at their dad's for the weekend, widowers with an empty nest.

Duke worried about those people the most.

As soon as Hines asked for questions, everyone began to talk at once.

The chief quickly controlled the crowd and called on a reporter.

"Helena Gray with KTKR," a brunette said. "Has this person left any clues behind to identify him or her? Has the FBI done a profile so we can know who to be on the lookout for?"

A fleeting emotion passed through the chief's gaze. He knew something, didn't he? Most likely he was thinking about the X that had been left on Stuart's chest. That mark had probably been left on all the victims.

"We believe the perpetrator is a white male," Hines said. "Someone who may be in their late twenties or early thirties. We believe he's never been on the police radar before he started killing, that he's someone who's kept a low profile."

"That's it?" Helena continued. "No footprints or trace evidence?"

"That's correct. This killer has been careful. Minimal evidence has been left." Hines's voice sounded coldly professional.

"Would you say it's accurate that no one is safe?" the reporter continued. "That everyone in this area is in danger?"

Based on the murmurs rushing through the crowd, other people here shared that same sentiment.

Fear.

Without a victim profile, everyone felt at risk.

Maybe that was this killer's plan. Duke glanced at the crowd around him and their worried expressions. If the killer wanted to strike fear into the heart of everyone in town, it was working.

Andi was still reviewing her notes on the victims of the Lights Out Killer when she heard a car pull up outside. She walked to the window to see who was here. She knew a few members of the team were outside, still helping with the fire.

Had Duke and Beau returned from the press conference? It seemed too soon.

The breath left her lungs when she saw a police car in the driveway.

She shrank from the window as a tremble overtook her.

"Andi?" Mariella looked up from the couch where she sat with her legs pulled beneath her, a notebook on her lap, and a pen with a puffy pink poof on the end in her hand.

"The cops are here." Andi glanced around, looking for a way to escape.

Mariella put her notebook and pen down and stood. "Wait . . . they're *here*? At this house?"

Andi nodded. "That's what it looks like."

Mariella stared at Andi, not bothering to hide her scrutiny. "Why do you look scared?"

"It's a long story."

Mariella eyed her another moment before asking, "Since you clearly don't have time to explain, what do you want me to do?"

That was an excellent question.

Andi darted toward a bedroom. "I don't want them to see me."

A knock sounded at the door, and Andi knew her time was running out.

She couldn't let Mariella get into trouble for her.

She didn't have it in her.

"If the police ask for me, I'll come out," Andi told her. "But I'm not ready to give up yet . . . not on my own accord, at least."

chapter
sixteen

ANDI REMAINED IN THE DARK, careful not to move—just in case.

Could the police have tracked her to the rental house? If so, how? They couldn't be tracking her phone since Andi didn't have it on her.

She listened as Mariella opened the door.

"Good afternoon, Officer." Mariella sounded as perky as ever.

"Sorry to bother you, ma'am. I'm Officer Townsend. I'm hoping you can help me."

Andi's heart continued to thump against her chest. Was he looking for her? Or was this visit because of something else?

"Help you with what?" Mariella asked.

This was it. The moment Andi found out if she'd been caught or if she was still a free woman.

"As I'm sure you know, there was a fire next door," the cop said.

Was this about the fire? Andi still didn't let her guard down.

"Yes, I know." Mariella's tone dipped lower at the serious turn of the conversation. "It was horrible. But I'm glad everyone is safe."

"We believe the fire may have been set on purpose, and I'm wondering if you saw anything suspicious over at the house. Anyone strange lingering outside or any cars driving by a little too slowly?"

"Set on purpose?" Mariella gasped. "While the family was inside?"

"We're still trying to figure out the details."

"That's horrible."

"Yes, it is," the officer said. "So . . . did you see anything?"

"Unfortunately, I only got here a couple of hours before it happened, and I was busy with something else and not paying attention." Mariella paused, and Andi pictured her shrugging. "I'm sorry I can't be more help."

"I understand. We're talking to everyone to find out what might have happened."

Why would someone purposefully set the house on fire with people inside—and in the middle of the day, at that?

There was clearly more to this story.

"As you may know, your neighbor is the attorney

general for the state," Officer Townsend continued. "He's been targeted before."

The attorney general? Andi had thought the man's name seemed familiar.

She stored that information away for later.

Why did she have a feeling Alpine had picked this rental on purpose? Was she reading too much into this?

Maybe.

Maybe Alpine wasn't that calculated.

But maybe he was.

Duke and Beau drove down the street toward the rental.

Just as they pulled into the driveway, Duke saw a cop car pulling away. The sun's glare on the windshield made it impossible to see if anyone was inside the vehicle with the officer or not.

What if Andi had just been arrested?

"That could be bad," Beau muttered, his gaze on the patrol vehicle also.

"Yes, it could be." Duke's hands tightened on the steering wheel.

Adrenaline raced through him.

Quickly, he pulled into the driveway, threw the SUV in Park, and rushed inside.

To his relief, he spotted Andi sitting at the table.

She was still here and not in the back of that police car.

The breath left Duke's lungs in a whoosh.

Before he could ask more questions, the rest of the gang flooded inside.

He'd seen Simmy distributing water and snacks for the family next door. While she did that, Ranger observed everything from a distance, almost like a bodyguard. Matthew recorded something with his phone.

Everyone grabbed drinks and snacks before settling in the living room.

Everyone except Duke. He stayed near the door, not ready to relax.

"Everything okay?" Andi stared at him, concern in her gaze as if he was the one in trouble.

"I thought . . ." He nodded toward the door where the police car had disappeared.

"The cops are investigating the house fire next door," Andi explained. "They believe it may have been arson."

Duke's thoughts shifted from worry about Andi. "Arson? Why arson?"

"Because the man living there is the Alaska attorney general."

Duke's eyebrows shot up. "I thought his name sounded familiar, but I didn't put it together."

"Neither did I."

"I wonder if he lives there or if he's just vacationing," Ranger said before taking a long swig of water.

"I did some research, and I believe that's where he lives," Andi said. "He travels to Juneau for government business, but Anchorage is his home base."

"What kind of case is he involved with that makes someone want to kill him?" Simmy asked. "I mean, is that what happened? Was this arson like the police think? Or was the fire truly an accident?"

Those were excellent questions, Duke mused. Excellent questions.

He shifted, knowing he needed to change the subject.

He told them about the pictures of Suzie, and a murmur traveled through the room.

They all had the same questions he did—but no answers.

Someone was making this personal, and he needed to figure out who.

chapter
seventeen

A LULL FELL in the conversation, and Andi's thoughts raced.

Finally, she stood. "I just can't stay inside for the rest of my time here in Anchorage."

Duke stared at her from across the room, and it was clear he wanted to say more. But not here with an audience.

"Why would you have to stay inside?" Ranger shifted in his seat as if trying to get a better look at her expression.

"It may or may not be because the police are looking for me." Andi pressed her lips together as soon as the admission left her mouth.

She hadn't wanted to say it. But she had to. She had to let them know something was going on.

"Wait . . . the police are looking for you?" Mariella gasped. "Are we harboring a fugitive? Is that why you acted weird when that officer came to the door earlier?"

"It's nothing like that," Andi assured everyone. "I mean, there's not a warrant out for my arrest or anything."

"Did you kill somebody?" Simmy asked.

Andi's mouth dropped open. Had Simmy really just asked that?

"Of course, I didn't kill anybody!" Andi's voice lilted with frustration. "I just got myself in a bit of a predicament, and I'm going to figure things out."

"You don't want to share any more details?" Ranger stared at her, his eyes cool and assessing.

"It's better if you all don't know. That way, if anybody asks you questions, you won't have any answers. I didn't even want to tell you this much, but I felt like I should." Andi's chest ached as tension pulled at her.

"Andi . . ." Simmy's voice turned soft with compassion. "How can we help you?"

"I'm not sure you can help. I just wanted to make you aware of the situation. It's like I said, I can't hide away until all of this passes. I need to be out there doing something. We don't have much time."

"What are you suggesting?" Duke crossed his arms and stared at her, something close to a challenge in his gaze as he remained standing.

"I think I should talk to this Melanie," Andi said. "She dated Stuart, and Stuart's parents didn't have the best impression of her. It seems as if we should check her out, at least."

Mariella stared at her this time. Everyone in the room was staring at her, for that matter.

"Are you sure it's wise for you to go out?" Mariella asked.

Andi nodded, careful not to show any doubt. "I can be careful."

Mariella stared at her, quiet with thought. Finally, she said, "I still have those extensions you wore back in Salmon-by-the-Sea. I haven't unpacked since I left, and if you wanted to use them again . . ."

Andi considered the idea a moment. "It's not a bad idea."

Mariella rose. "I'll go grab them, just in case."

Andi stole a glimpse at Duke.

Was it her imagination or did he look irritated? She tried to brush the thought off.

It didn't matter what he thought. That was what Andi told herself.

But she knew the truth was that it did matter to her, even if she didn't want to admit it.

Twenty minutes later, Duke headed down the road with Andi and Beau.

Andi had added those extensions to her hair, making her short, pale hair suddenly look long and luscious. She'd shoved on a black baseball cap, some sunglasses, and wore baggy khakis with a shapeless white top—an outfit that wouldn't get any notice.

Duke had an extra burner phone in his glove compartment, and he'd given it to her when they got into his SUV. It was only wise that she have some way to contact people if things turned ugly.

If Duke had his way, Andi would be locked up in that rental house for the rest of the weekend. But he couldn't force her into a corner.

"I know what you're thinking," Andi murmured from the back seat.

"What's that?" His curiosity blazed to life as he wondered what she would say.

"You're thinking I deserve this. Am I right?"

Disappointment quickly replaced his curiosity. Did she really assume he would think that? "Wrong. I don't think you deserve this."

"That's what your expression says."

"Don't let his expression fool you," Beau added. "Duke has always been a man of mystery when it comes to what's really going through his head."

"I just don't want to see you getting in trouble or to get hurt," Duke finally said, stealing a glance at her in the rearview mirror.

Andi eyed him a moment as if uncertain if she believed him. Finally, she nodded and leaned back, slightly more relaxed.

"I guess we should focus on Melanie now," she

murmured instead.

"Probably a good idea," Duke added. "Have you been able to find out anything about her?"

Andi glanced at the notebook in her hands. "As a matter of fact, I have. She's thirty-two years old. She's been married and divorced twice. And she currently works at an off-road vehicle dealership."

"An off-road vehicle dealership?" Beau muttered. "Does anybody else see the irony in that or is it just me?"

"You mean the irony that she was dating a man who dedicated his life to clean energy?" Andi questioned. "Meanwhile, she works at a car dealership specializing in gas-guzzling off-road vehicles?"

They continued down the road. The dealership just happened to be located right on the outskirts of downtown Anchorage, within walking distance of many of the high-rises.

Duke wasn't sure what that meant for Andi since a higher concentration of police would be in this area.

"Okay, what's our approach going to be?" Duke turned to face Beau and Andi. "Are we going to be direct and ask questions? Or do we come up with a cover story?"

"I think we play it by ear." Andi stared at the dealership office in the distance. "It's nice to get a feel for people before making those kinds of decisions."

That sounded just like Andi. Duke was more the type that liked to go in with a plan.

Before they could talk about it anymore, Andi opened

the door. She adjusted her hat and straightened her clothes before slamming the door and waiting for Duke and Beau to follow suit.

Duke prayed this went well, but he wasn't holding his breath.

chapter
eighteen

BEFORE ANDI MADE it halfway across the parking lot, a fortysomething salesman wearing a Hawaiian shirt stopped her. "I'm Sam. Are you guys shopping for a new off-road vehicle?"

She glanced back at Duke, quickly formulating a ruse. "We sure are. Nothing better than going off-roading here in Alaska. Have any good sales for us?"

"We always have good sales. Are you looking for just you? Or do you have a family?" His gaze scanned them as if he tried to figure out the dynamic.

On a whim, Andi looped her arm through Duke's. "Just me and my boyfriend. His brother might come along too sometimes." She nodded at Beau.

Sam chuckled as if he felt better knowing more details. "I know just the vehicle for you. I have a sense about these things."

He led them to a bright yellow Jeep Wrangler and

began talking details. However, Andi tuned him out. Instead, she scanned everything around her, looking for any sign of Melanie.

It was Friday at four p.m. Most likely, if the woman was working, she wouldn't get off until five or six. Which meant she should be here.

Andi murmured something about needing to use the restroom before excusing herself.

No one questioned her.

She quickened her steps as she hurried toward the building housing the dealership's office. The one-story building was small and outdated, with cedar siding and plain-looking letters across the top proclaiming, "Bergenske Auto."

As she walked, she glanced around.

No cops.

Part of her still feared that one of them might pop out of nowhere and arrest her.

But so far, the coast was clear.

She stepped into the showroom and glanced around, looking for Melanie. The polka music playing overhead distracted her—but only for a few seconds.

Andi's gaze stopped on a woman with curly dark hair sitting behind the reception desk.

Melanie. Andi had looked up her picture earlier.

But Andi was three seconds too late.

The woman didn't seem to notice Andi's entrance.

Instead, the woman glanced at her phone before rising to her feet.

As Andi followed the woman's gaze, she spotted a man standing in the doorway leading to a hallway to her left. Something about him looked dark and mean.

Melanie glanced around one more time before heading toward the man.

Something was going on here. Andi felt certain of it.

She needed to figure out what—especially if it tied in with these recent murders here in Anchorage.

Making a split-second decision, Andi started toward the hallway where Melanie had disappeared.

She glanced around to see if anyone was watching. The only person she saw was a janitor mopping the floor in the corner. The older gentleman didn't even look up at her, though.

She glanced out the window one more time. Duke and Beau were still talking to the salesman. Duke's gaze fluttered toward the building as if he were concerned about her.

He always seemed concerned about her.

Andi wasn't sure if it was touching or annoying. It probably depended on the day.

She slipped down the hallway, which led to several offices.

But Melanie was nowhere in sight.

Where had she gone with that man?

Andi slowly crept down the hallway, listening near doorways.

Masculine voices sounded on the other side of the walls. But no one she imagined to be Melanie.

Finally, she reached a door at the end of the hallway, one with an exit sign above it.

Andi hesitated a moment, her hand on the bar to unlatch it.

She wasn't sure what was going to be on the other side. If she just simply pushed the door wide open, she'd be too obvious.

Instead, she barely cracked it.

As she peered out, she spotted Melanie and a man talking behind the dealership.

A man who had a distinct Russian accent.

Based on his tone, he wasn't happy.

And Melanie was practically cowering in his presence.

Fire ignited inside Andi, and she wanted to step in.

Before she could, Melanie pulled herself together and began barking back at the man.

Maybe the woman wasn't a shrinking violet after all.

Andi tried to tune her ear to the conversation. But . . . they'd switched from speaking English to Russian.

She couldn't understand a word they were saying, only that the conversation was heated.

She frowned. Maybe if she pulled out her phone, she could find a translation app. But did she have time?

Quickly, she grabbed the burner Duke had let her borrow and found a translation app. But it was taking forever to load.

"Come on . . ." she muttered as she stared at the screen.

Just then, a shadow fell over her.

She glanced up and saw a man step out from one of the offices—and he stared right at her.

A man with a dark expression and hulky build.

And he didn't look happy as he muttered in a Russian accent, "What do you think you're doing?"

chapter
nineteen

WHAT WAS TAKING Andi so long in there? Duke wondered. Had she found Melanie?

Or had she gotten herself in trouble?

If this Melanie woman was wrapped up in something dirty, what were the odds that Andi found herself in the middle of it?

"Excuse me for a minute." Duke interrupted the salesman's soliloquy on the glories of the Jeep Wrangler. "My girlfriend is taking a while inside, and I need to make sure she's okay. She hasn't been feeling well lately."

Sam's forehead knotted at that revelation, and he nodded. "Of course. I can finish telling your brother more of these details."

Beau sent him a withering look. They were both tired of listening to this guy as he went on and on in an effort to make this sale. The man would be sorely disappointed when they left.

Duke would worry about that later. Right now, he hurried into the building.

When he stepped inside, the janitor was the only one in sight. The man didn't even glance Duke's way. Instead, he limped toward a closet, almost as if he'd hurt his knee.

Two hallways stretched on either side of the room and another door in the back probably led to the garage.

With no signs of Andi, Duke decided to go left.

He pushed through the door and spotted Andi.

Along with a very large, intimidating looking man who stood directly in front of her.

Andi swallowed hard as she stared up at the man. "I was looking for a bathroom."

The man's gaze darkened. "It's on the other side of the building."

A Russian accent tinged his words, although the brogue wasn't strong. Still, it was there.

Was it significant? She wasn't sure.

"Perfect." She wanted to skirt around him, but he blocked the hallway. Andi took in a deep breath before looking back up at him. "No one was at the reception desk, so I didn't know who to ask."

Someone cleared his throat behind the big man. "Everything okay here?"

Andi peered over the man's shoulder and spotted . . . Duke.

A wave of relief washed over her. He always showed up just in the nick of time.

The man glanced back at the door Andi had been peering out of. He still didn't believe her, did he?

"What's on your phone?" he grumbled.

"What do you mean?" She glanced at the device in her hands. "Nothing."

"Were you taking pictures?"

"No, I wasn't."

He held out his hand. "Let me see it."

Duke stepped closer. "She doesn't have to do anything."

The man bristled. "This is my business, and I want to see that phone."

This guy was definitely on edge about something.

Andi slipped her phone into her pocket. There were no pictures on it. But out of principle, she wouldn't let this guy bully her.

"I said give it to me." The man jutted his hand closer.

Andi ducked under his arm and stepped toward Duke. "I'll be going now. And if you want a good review online, I'd back off. Reviews can make or break a business. Am I right?"

The man grunted.

Before he could come after them anymore, Andi took Duke's arm and led him away.

But when she heard a footstep behind her, she knew that man was following them.

chapter
twenty

DUKE BRISTLED when he heard the footsteps.

Then it went silent.

The man had stopped following them.

Relief swept over him.

But they still needed to get out of here.

"What was that about?" Duke whispered as they stepped outside.

"I followed Melanie," Andi whispered back. "She was meeting with some Russian guy behind the building. I was trying to download a translation app when that guy found me."

"What do you think was happening?" Duke asked.

"I couldn't understand a word they were saying, but the conversation was heated. However, I'm still having trouble wrapping my mind around the idea that Melanie could be involved. A bad girlfriend? Definitely. But I don't see her being a killer."

"You're probably right. Most serial killers aren't women. But maybe she knows something or maybe she saw something. Especially if she was stalking the guy."

Duke glanced back at the building as he and Andi strode across the parking lot. The man hadn't come outside—thankfully.

"It's going to be hard to talk to her while she's at work," Andi said. "She's definitely hiding something, but maybe not about the murder."

"So we're right back to where we started?" Duke clarified.

"That's how it appears . . ."

They joined Beau again. The salesman still talked to him, this time about the fallacy of bad gas mileage, and Beau looked bored to tears.

"We've had a bit of an emergency." Duke grasped Andi's elbow. "I'm really sorry, but we've got to go."

"You sure about that?" The guy looked up at them, desperation fluttering through his gaze. "I don't know how long this Jeep is going to be here."

"If it's meant to be, it's meant to be," Duke called. "Thanks for all your help!"

Then he steered Andi toward the sidewalk, Beau beside them.

"Everything okay?" Beau stole a glance their way.

"Now it is." Andi tucked her hands into her pockets, having the ability to appear casual even in the tensest of situations. "But I'm not sure how much coming here really accomplished."

They took several more steps down the sidewalk toward Duke's SUV when Andi froze.

Cops.

They seemed to be everywhere lately. That one cop—Eisenhauer—was one of the two walking toward them now. The man could easily recognize Andi.

He glanced at Andi and saw the panic in her gaze.

They needed to think quickly.

"Hug me," Andi murmured.

Duke slowed his steps, unsure if he'd heard Andi correctly. "What?"

"I don't have time to spell this out for you."

"I've got you," Beau said.

The next moment, his brother wrapped his arms around Andi.

Her arms circled his neck as she buried her head in his chest.

Duke resisted a scowl.

He knew that it was just a ruse. If he'd been three seconds quicker comprehending what Andi was hinting at, then she might be in his arms right now instead of Beau's.

He held his breath as the cops continued by.

Would one of them recognize Andi?

She did look like a completely different person with those extensions in her hair.

But it was risky for her to even be out here. Certainly she knew that.

Duke watched as the cops glanced their way. When they saw Andi and Beau embracing, they quickly averted their gaze.

Just what Andi wanted.

Moments later, Beau and Andi pulled away from each other, and Andi glanced up at Beau. "Thank you."

Beau grinned. "Anytime."

They'd maintained that embrace for several seconds longer than necessary. In Duke's opinion, at least.

Not that it was any of his business.

"We should get going before we run into anyone else," Duke muttered.

"Smart thinking." Beau rolled his shoulders back as he glanced up and down the street.

They reached Duke's SUV.

As they did, Duke checked the time. Six p.m. He knew Andi needed to get her phone sometime tonight. But only once it was dark.

The unfortunate thing about Anchorage in June was that the sun didn't set until close to midnight.

But there was no need to go all the way back to the rental house only to return to the downtown area to retrieve her phone.

"What do you guys say we grab some fast food, and we can wait for it to get a little darker outside before we hunt for Andi's cell phone?" he offered.

It would be good to have some downtime to talk everything through as well.

"That sounds great." Gratitude filled Andi's gaze.

As Duke looked up, a familiar face in the distance caught his eye.

It was that reporter . . . the one he'd seen at the press conference. Helena, if he remembered correctly.

And she was striding toward them as if she were on a mission.

chapter
twenty-one

ANDI WATCHED AS DUKE FROZE.

Then she saw a brunette with dark, thick hair and shapely legs.

Who in the world was that?

Based on the way the woman's eyes were set on them and the steadiness of her gait, she was looking to talk to them.

Duke stepped forward, his gaze on her. "Helena, right?"

The woman paused, a glint of satisfaction in her gaze. "I am. I saw you at the press conference."

"You made quite the impression as well."

Andi crossed her arms. "Can someone fill me in?"

"I'm Helena Gray, a reporter with KTKR. Who are you guys?" The woman's gaze scanned the three of them.

Andi and Duke glanced at each other, a silent conversation passing between them. Finally, Andi nodded and let Duke take the lead.

"We're true crime podcasters who are looking into the Lights Out Killer."

"True crime podcasters, huh?" She raised an eyebrow. "Which one? Maybe I've heard it before."

"*The Round Table*," Andi said.

Familiarity crossed her gaze. "I saw that interview you guys did on *Dateline NBC*. It was impressive. Your team has done really good work."

"Thank you," Duke said. "And this is my brother, Beau."

Beau extended his hand. "Nice to meet you."

Helena didn't hesitate to return the handshake. "Same."

Helena glanced at the car dealership in the distance. "So I guess that I'm running into you here because you were talking to Melanie Wooden?"

"I guess you're on your way to do so also?" Duke crossed his arms.

"I am. Her name came up in my research, and I thought it couldn't hurt to get her take on this situation since she knew Stuart. I'm not expecting much. Did you guys find out anything?"

"Not really." Duke shrugged.

She paused. "Let me guess—you don't want to tell me because you want to break the news first?"

"It's not that," Andi said. "But we didn't even get a

chance to talk to her. We saw her meeting with a Russian, and that was as far as we got."

Helena's eyebrows rose higher. "A Russian? We have a lot of Russians in this area. That's not too unusual."

"Maybe not," Andi said. "But they were having a pretty heated discussion."

"You know anything about this car dealership?" Beau stepped into their circle.

"I did my homework before I came, and I know it's owned by Alex Bergenske," Helena said. "He grew up in a small Russian Orthodox community on the Kenai Peninsula, but he left to come to Anchorage."

"While you were snooping, did you run a background check on him?" Duke asked. "Does he have a police record?"

Helena raised a shoulder in a guilty-as-charged look. "He does not have a police record per se, but he *is* affiliated with people who've done some prison time. However, I have trouble connecting him with the murders in the area. A murder spree doesn't seem like something this Alex guy, or any of the other Russians he affiliates with, would do—especially not considering the victims."

"I agree," Andi said.

As they talked, Andi glanced down the street to make sure those cops hadn't come back.

That was when she spotted the black sedan with the tinted windows parked a couple of blocks away.

The same vehicle that had followed them yesterday.

It was following them again today.

She sucked in a breath.

That meant that they were all in danger right now.

"Duke . . ." Andi grabbed his arm.

He glanced at her, her voice pulling him from his thoughts. "Yes?"

She nodded at something in the distance. He followed her gaze and saw the sedan.

The person who'd followed them yesterday was back again.

His hands fisted.

Part of him was tempted to storm over to the car and find out who was inside. But that could be a good way to get shot. He had to play it smart here.

"Is there something I should know about?" A knot formed on Helena's forehead.

He turned toward Helena. "It's not safe out here. Come with us."

Duke didn't leave room for her to say no. Instead, he ushered everyone into his SUV. He didn't release his breath until they were all inside with the doors locked and the engine cranked. Even then, he still didn't relax.

"Does someone care to explain?" Tension emanated from Helena's voice.

"Someone's watching us," Andi quickly clarified.

"Someone dangerous. We couldn't all just stand out there. We could be knocked off like bottles on a fencepost."

"So what do we do now?" Fear crackled through Helena's voice, yet her gaze remained steady.

"We've got to lose this guy." Duke put his SUV into Drive. "I'd drop you off at your car, but I'm afraid you might be targeted now too."

Helena shivered and rubbed the side of her arms. "Do you even know who it is?"

"No, we don't." As he pulled away, he glanced in the rearview mirror.

The lights on the other car came on also.

"They're coming after us." Helena's voice cracked.

Duke had to figure out a safe way out of the situation. A high-speed chase through downtown would only garner police attention—which was the last thing Andi needed.

But he'd rather her be arrested than dead, and he had no idea what this other driver was planning.

He pulled onto the street as the light on the corner turned yellow. He jammed on the accelerator, despite the gasps of the two women in the back seat.

"Are you crazy?" Helena sounded breathless. "You're going to get us killed."

"No, he's not," Andi interjected. "He's former law enforcement. He knows what he's doing."

Duke took a sharp left, immediately followed by a right on the next street.

He'd need to do some fancy driving to get away from this guy.

He glanced at his review mirror again.

Nothing.

But he didn't dare think he'd already lost his tail.

It wouldn't be that easy.

Duke prepared himself for whatever would happen next.

chapter
twenty-two

ANDI CRANED her neck to see what was happening.

She fully expected to see that car again. She'd seen the headlights come on. Had seen the driver pull out behind them.

But there was no one behind them now.

Not yet.

Her heart pounded against her chest as she anticipated what might come next.

For all she knew, this guy could appear again out of nowhere and slam into them.

Two innocent people—Duke and Beau—had already been pulled into this, and now Helena.

The person following them wasn't affiliated with the podcast.

He was affiliated with Victor.

Andi was the target. She was certain of it.

She wouldn't forgive herself if something happened to these people because of her.

Duke continued to weave through the streets.

She nibbled on her lip as she waited for whatever would happen next.

The car didn't reappear.

"I think we've lost them," Duke announced.

"Are you guys sure you weren't imagining something?" Helena offered a thin laugh. "Looking for an excuse to get me alone so you could pick my brain?"

"Is there something to pick your brain about?" Andi stole a glance at her, curious about her words.

Helena shrugged. "I want to find answers about this as much as you do."

"So you can get your news story?" Andi immediately regretted the sharp tone to her voice.

"No, because my neighbor was one of the victims."

Guilt flooded Andi. "I'm sorry."

Helena's jaw hardened. "It's okay. You didn't know."

"Who was your neighbor?"

"Tex Lanyard." She pressed her lips together. "He was a good man."

As Duke eased off the accelerator, his shoulders also softened. "I think we're okay now."

"That was easier than I thought," Beau said.

"Agreed," Duke said. "Listen, what do you guys say we grab something to eat, and then talk? I think we could all benefit from that."

"I'm game," Helena said.

Andi glanced behind her again. "Do you really think we've lost this guy?"

"I don't know where he went or what his game is." Duke glanced in the rearview mirror again. "But I don't see him. I don't necessarily trust that the coast is clear, but I can't keep driving around like this for the rest of the day."

"We can get some food," Andi said. "But I suggest we eat in the car."

It seemed like the safest thing to do.

Going into any restaurant near Anchorage would be risky. Maybe too risky.

Besides, they could discuss things privately in the SUV, and Andi desperately wanted to hear what Helena had learned.

The group decided on pizza at The Moose Caboose, one of Helena's favorite places in Anchorage. Duke picked the food up from inside and brought it to his SUV.

Eating in his vehicle wasn't ideal. He could be a bit of a neat freak at times. But desperate times called for desperate measures, and that was exactly what this was. A desperate time.

Sitting in the parking lot of the restaurant, he let everyone grab their own piece of pepperoni and reindeer sausage pizza. Then he perched the pizza box on his dash-board and handed out bottles of soda and water he'd also bought. He'd grabbed plenty of napkins to hand out as well.

As they ate, he didn't take his eyes off everything around them. At any minute, he expected someone to surprise him. For danger to show up.

However, it hadn't taken much to lose the guy. In fact, Duke wondered if the guy simply stopped following them.

Unless he was playing some kind of game or had some kind of alternate plan.

Duke didn't like those options.

When Duke saw Helena was nearly finished with her first piece, he asked, "Is there anything that you can tell us that would help us figure out who's behind this?"

Helena wiped her mouth with a napkin and twisted the top off her drink. "This has to be a fair exchange."

"You mean the fact I bought you pizza isn't enough?" He raised the slice in his hands.

She let out a dry chuckle. "Almost but not quite."

"I'm going to be honest." Andi frowned as she plucked a piece of pepperoni from her pizza. "We haven't learned a lot. So I'm not sure how much of a fair exchange of information this would be."

Helena nodded slowly. "I can appreciate your honesty. I think everyone is finding it difficult to chase down the bad guy on this one."

She went quiet a moment as if in thought. Then she let out a long breath.

"Here's something that might help us find this guy," Helena said. "The weapon this guy is using . . . it's not your typical knife."

"What is it then?" Duke asked.

"It's an ulu."

"What's an ulu?" Beau asked.

"An ulu is an all-purpose knife developed by the Inuit people," Duke explained. "It's got a short handle and the blade itself is rounded, like a half-moon. They're very handy."

"Do a lot of people around here have those?" Beau sounded fascinated by this new discovery.

"They're not uncommon," Helena said. "But I think it's safe to say that the police don't often see them used in crimes."

"Thank you for sharing that," Duke said. "We really appreciate it. The killer is using that to leave Xs on the chest of his victims."

Helena's expression remained unchanged.

She already knew that, didn't she?

"Thanks," she finally said. "It's chilling really, isn't it?"

Andi turned toward her. "Just curious—how did you find out that information concerning the ulu? The police haven't released that information."

Helena smirked. "I have an inside source. That's all I can say."

"Very well then." Andi shrugged, certainly under-standing the importance of confidentiality.

This information was something else they could use.

But was it enough?

chapter
twenty-three

I GLANCED in the mirror and straightened my collar.

Tonight, I had a date.

Kate was her name, and I'd met her on a dating site. She was pretty and perky with blonde hair that came just below her ears and a wide grin. Twenty-eight years old. Slim. A nurse.

She was just my type.

I was thirty, but I'd never been married. Really, I had no desire to be married. I'd seen what marriage could be like, and I didn't want anything to do with it.

But if I didn't date, people might notice and ask too many questions. So on occasion, I went out. It seemed to appease the people around me.

Maybe one day I'd find someone I was compatible with. But I doubted it.

I could never truly trust someone.

Because everyone had secrets. They had their ghosts in the closet.

I had more than my fair share. And they'd literally been created in the closet.

My throat tightened, and I looked away from the mirror.

The closet had been a place of nightmares for me.

It had been pitch-black in the space, with not even a sliver of light peeking from under the doorway.

There was no carpet on the floor. Only concrete.

And it was cold. So cold.

The door had been locked, and I'd been left there for hours.

No one had come looking, even as blood drizzled from my skin.

Not long ago, I'd had the opportunity to see the closet again. A new door had been hung. The marks I'd left as I tried to claw my way out were gone—along with the memories of what had happened.

Except not for me.

I'd never forget, even if everyone else had moved on.

I'd promised myself I'd never feel that way again.

And I haven't. I won't.

I refused to feel powerless.

I shifted my thoughts from the bad memories and glanced down at my jeans and polo shirt. I hoped Kate would like what she saw. Most women did. I tried to use my trustworthy appearance to my advantage.

My handsome face didn't hurt either.

I glanced at my watch. It was time to go.

I would pick her up and take her to Barry's, one of my favorite restaurants here in downtown Anchorage. Their salmon linguine was off the charts.

I preferred to take my dates out for ice cream to start. It wasn't too much of a commitment that way. But I'd been craving that linguine for a while, so I figured, why not? With any luck, while we were there, the people around us would talk about the Lights Out Killer.

I smiled at the thought.

Nothing made me feel the surge of delight more. I wanted people in this town to live in fear.

They hadn't realized yet that there was a connection between my victims. There was a purpose behind what I was doing.

They had no idea.

Because they were all so stupid.

I would have to keep on killing until they got the message.

In fact, tonight, after my date with Kate, I had another date with the darkness.

I knew exactly who I'd be visiting. I'd studied all three of the potentials today until I narrowed it to one. Of course, it depended on whether or not the chosen one was alone. Maybe she wouldn't be.

But I knew that the reporter wasn't married. Most nights, she was alone.

I hoped that would be the case tonight as well.

Because even she was connected.

People might think I chose her just so she would stop investigating. Stop reporting. After all, she seemed to take her stories very seriously.

But that wasn't why I'd chosen her.

I'd have to wait and see if the police could figure that one out.

In the meantime, I would keep doing my thing. Maybe I'd even take Kate with me to the Grand Finale. I could only imagine the look on her face when she learned what I'd planned.

It would be fantastic.

I grabbed my wallet and keys and slid them into my pockets. Then I stepped outside to go pick up Kate.

But I'd be counting down the minutes until this date was over. Until I was able to fulfill my true mission.

I was stopping the evil.

I was just the only one intelligent enough to see it.

chapter
twenty-four

THEY DROPPED Helena back off at her car and thanked her for the information.

Then Duke found a parking space on the street near the dumpster.

Andi braced herself for another night of dumpster diving.

She wasn't looking forward to doing this again.

But she had no choice.

She climbed out with Duke and Beau and started toward the alley. When they reached it, she turned toward the men. "Well, here goes nothing. Will you stand guard for me?"

Duke gave her a look. "I'll help you. Beau, can you stay on the corner and keep watch?"

Andi's eyes widened. "You don't have to help me."

"I know. But I will."

She swallowed the lump in her throat. "Thank you. I really appreciate this."

"Of course. You owe me one—and mine might involve the sewer. You never know." He offered a playful grin.

While Beau stood lookout, Duke and Andi hurried down the alley. Thankfully, no one else was down this way, nor had Andi seen anyone on the streets. They'd need to be quick about this if they didn't want to draw any attention to themselves.

Duke was a good ten inches taller than Andi, which would be a big help. He'd be able to reach into the dumpster, whereas Andi, being petite, would have to jump inside.

As they reached the big metal box, Duke opened the lid. The stench of rot rose around them and turned Andi's stomach. Memories of her time inside the metal box flooded her.

How did she get herself in this predicament?

She peered inside and felt a rush of relief.

"It hasn't been emptied." Andi tapped her heart. "I was a little nervous."

"Not only has it not been emptied—it's full. And some of that looks fresh."

She turned her nose up. "Yes, it does."

She dreaded trying to find her phone. But she had to get it back.

Duke grabbed the first several bags and put them on

the other side of the dumpster, out of sight of anyone who might casually glance down the alley toward them.

While he did that, Andi searched through any bags that were torn or ripped.

She found a lot of stuff—a lot of really gross stuff—but no phone.

This was going to take longer than she anticipated and possibly be even grosser.

Duke kept pulling bags out, but there was no phone so far.

He paused for a moment and let out a sigh as he stared at the still half-full dumpster.

"Maybe I can call it," he said. "And if we hear it—"

"I turned the volume off in case someone walked in on me at the same time I got a phone call."

"Of course, you did." He frowned.

They might have to empty this entire dumpster before they found that phone.

The possibility wasn't one she looked forward to.

Before they could dig any deeper, Beau signaled to them.

Someone was coming.

Quickly, she and Duke moved the bags out of sight and ducked behind the dumpster.

Then they waited.

∾

Andi held her breath. Would someone come this way? Had they been followed?

The voices became louder.

And louder.

They were right at the entrance to the alley. It sounded like three people, and they sounded joyous.

Not like assassins—or cops.

But she didn't dare relax.

A few minutes later, the voices faded. The people had passed.

The coast was clear.

She released the tension from her lungs. "It was nothing."

"Thankfully," Duke said. "But we need to keep going. Next time we might not be so lucky."

He was right. They had no time to waste.

Bag after bag, Andi tried not to lose hope.

If her phone had fallen out while she was hiding in there, she should be able to find it.

But . . . what if her phone hadn't fallen out in the dumpster? What if it had fallen out somewhere else? In the senator's office?

Panic fluttered inside her.

If that was the case then Andi was pretty much a sitting duck.

She had to keep those thoughts at bay. There was no need to think in worst-case scenarios. Not yet. It would only throw her off her game.

She glanced at Duke as he reached into the dumpster again. He really was taking one for the team.

No, not the team.

He was doing this for her.

And she greatly appreciated it.

She kept telling herself that the man drove her crazy. And he did in some ways because the two of them were opposites.

But in another way, she let him drive her crazy as a way of putting up walls and not getting too close. Not getting hurt.

"We've got three more bags, and then we're going to be at the bottom," Duke murmured.

That same hopelessness tried to rear its head again, but she pushed the emotion down.

Duke turned his phone light on and shone it around.

"I think I've got something," he murmured.

Andi's breath caught. Was it her phone? She could only hope.

But before she could find out, police sirens sounded in the distance.

No, not in the distance.

They were close.

Too close.

chapter
twenty-five

DUKE WORKED FASTER, just in case.

But the sirens were coming closer.

He prayed this wouldn't be anything.

But he couldn't take any chances.

As the sirens grew louder, he pulled Andi behind the dumpster again so they could wait this out.

He sucked in a breath when the sirens stopped—right at the end of the alley.

Then he heard voices.

Were those officers talking to Beau?

His heart pounded in his ears as he and Andi exchanged a glance.

Had someone reported them?

If so, there was a good chance Duke would be arrested right along with Andi. He was now an accessory to a crime.

"I'm going to peek," Andi whispered.

"I'm not sure that's a good idea . . ."

"I have to know what's going on."

Duke knew there was no stopping her. She'd be careful. She usually was.

She rose up and peered over the dumpster. "They're definitely talking to Beau."

"Are they pointing this way?"

"No, I don't think so. I don't know what they're talking about."

She watched a few more seconds before ducking back down beside him. "I think they're leaving."

"Really?"

"Really." Andi nodded.

Duke peered around the dumpster and saw the police car was indeed gone. Beau motioned for them to keep working—but they were going to need to move faster.

He was going to have to go all in for this last part of the search.

Taking in his last deep breath of fresh air, Duke hopped in the dumpster. He started searching the area where he'd thought he'd seen something. He tossed aside a few more bags before he spotted the object at the bottom of the dumpster. He grabbed it and held it up.

A phone.

"Is this yours?"

Andi's eyes brightened. "That's it! It was there at the bottom?"

"Of *course*, it was at the very bottom," he muttered.

Her shoulders slumped with relief. "I could hug you right now."

"You might not want to do that. I think I just stepped in a dirty diaper." He glanced at his shoe and frowned.

She scrunched her nose. "Sorry about that."

He hopped out and landed with a thud on the asphalt. "You can thank me by helping me load these bags back in the dumpster. Then we can get out of here."

Working quickly, they put all of the trash back where they found it. Then they glanced at each other. As their gazes caught, Duke saw the thankfulness in Andi's eyes.

A moment of tension passed between them.

Finally, Andi cleared her throat and raised her hand. "High five."

A high five would have to do. But, if he were honest, Duke would admit he craved Andi's touch. How long would she wait for him to resolve the Celeste situation?

The question weighed on him heavily.

Duke slapped his hand against hers before heading back to Beau.

Andi's phone was safely in her pocket now. He knew she was anxious to see what was on it.

He had to admit, he was also anxious to know what she might have found out.

But right now, he was even more anxious to take a shower.

～

Andi couldn't wait to see what was on her phone. To study the images that she had taken. But first they dropped Beau off at the hotel.

Then she wanted to get back to the house, somewhere private. Out here, she was too distracted with worry that the cops might find her.

Thankfully, it only took about fifteen minutes to reach the rental house.

As soon as she and Duke walked inside, everyone stopped what they were doing and stared at them.

They must be a sight to see.

She caught a glimpse of herself in the mirror by the front door and saw that her extensions were now crooked. Dirt smudged her cheek. Then there was the smell . . . she had no doubt it was atrocious.

Duke didn't look much better than she did.

"What in the world happened to you two?" Mariella paused near the murder board and craned her neck toward them.

"Were you in an accident?" Simmy asked.

"Did you lose a bet?" Ranger paused with a bottle of water in hand.

Andi and Duke exchanged a look. Andi was tempted to say "long story" again. It was her normal schtick.

But she felt like she owed the team more than that.

"I lost my phone and had to retrieve it," she admitted. "It was a dirty job, to say the least. Duke helped."

"Did you lose your phone at the dump?" Ranger's

eyes remained narrow with doubt.

"Something like that." Andi shrugged. "Again, the less details you know, the better."

Duke cleared his throat and glanced around. "What have you guys been doing?"

"We've been talking to the neighbors and family members of some of the victims," Ranger said. "Most people are still in shock, in grief."

"So you didn't find out anything?" Duke asked.

A grin tugged at Ranger's lips. "Now, I didn't say that."

"So what did you learn?" Andi was eager to hear more.

"A neighbor of the fifth victim couldn't sleep," Ranger said. "She went to her window and glanced outside. When she did, she thought she saw a shadow near her neighbor's house."

"And?" Duke said.

"She was already jumping at shadows, like most people here in Anchorage after they learned what was going on, so she didn't dare go outside," Simmy said. "But she did notice something about the shadow."

Simmy glanced at Ranger, as if passing the torch.

"The man had a distinct gait," Ranger finished.

"What do you mean?" Andi wanted to make sure she understood.

"She said the man's walk was a little different, and he looked like he had long arms," Simmy said. "You know, kind of tall and gangly."

The janitor . . . he'd had an unusual gait and walked like he'd hurt his knee. But that wasn't entirely unique. Still, Duke stored that tidbit in the back of his mind, just in case.

Duke twisted his head. "That's something, but it's not much."

"Not much is better than nothing," Ranger said.

No one could argue with that.

"Did she tell the police?" Duke asked.

"She called the police, but it was too late. The man was gone. Her neighbor was already dead." Simmy rubbed her throat as her voice cracked

"We learned that the killer used an ulu to leave that X mark on his victims," Andi shared.

"Wait . . . how did you find that out?" Mariella squinted in confusion.

"We have a source," Duke said. "A reporter who's a fan of the podcast."

"That was nice of her to share." An edge of caution stained Mariella's voice.

"She just wants this guy to be stopped." Andi glanced at her watch. "Sorry to cut this conversation short, but it's been a long day, and I need to get cleaned up. Then I'm going to turn in early for the night."

Before anyone could argue, she hurried down the hall to her bedroom.

Andi couldn't wait any longer to look at those photos.

chapter
twenty-six

DUKE HOPPED IN THE SHOWER, scrubbed the smell off, and quickly changed into fresh clothes.

Then he glanced up and down the hallway.

The rest of the group was talking among themselves in the living room. But he had no desire to join them.

All he could think about was what Andi had discovered.

Maybe she wouldn't welcome his questions or interference.

But maybe she would.

He quietly walked across the hall and tapped on her door, trying not to draw any attention to his actions.

The door opened, and a freshly showered Andi stared at him.

She didn't say anything. Instead, she nodded toward her room, and Duke slipped inside.

Andi softly shut the door behind them. She hurried to

the bed and sat down. She'd printed several pages and pulled a few onto her lap to study them.

Duke hesitantly sat on the other side of the bed but remained close enough to peer at the papers she'd printed.

Yes, that she printed. Mariella had brought a printer with her.

"Well?" He waited for her to share.

"This is a start." Andi still stared at the papers as if sorting through all the information.

"So there's something there that will help you?" he clarified.

"I think so." She paused and glanced up at him. "This all just skims the surface. It's not enough information for me to bring anyone down. But it gives me a better idea of what's going on."

"And what is it that's going on exactly?"

"I'll show you." Andi scooted closer and held up one of the pages.

Andi heard the excitement rising in her voice as she pointed to the paper. "Victor has been trying to get this new drilling project approved by the government. But a lot of people have been against it, as you know. Huge social media campaigns have been started to prevent it, and members of Congress have had a lot of pressure not to let this go through, especially by people concerned with the environment."

"Which is where Senator Glassine comes in," Duke murmured.

"Exactly. She's one of the deciding votes as to whether or not this will pass."

Duke nodded slowly. "So you think Victor was paying her off?"

"From what I've read about Glassine, she's not the type who can be paid off."

"So what exactly are we looking at here?" Duke leaned back against the headboard, appearing deep in thought.

Andi pointed to one paper. "You can see numerous proposals were sent to her by people affiliated with Victor. They were putting a lot of pressure on her to get this done."

"Doesn't surprise me. That's probably normal with politics."

"I also found this Environmental Impact Statement. It's probably public record, but I haven't seen it before. It spells out the dire consequences of more drilling in that area."

"I know that's a hot topic, and it can get heated on both sides."

"Yes, it can," Andi agreed. "But people will be willing to take that to extremes. I mean, this new oil reserve they're proposing is the size of Indiana. I don't think most people realize that."

"I didn't."

She flipped through some more papers. "And this one shows that Victor has made large campaign contributions to her—probably as a way of trying to win her favor."

"That's illegal, but I know that happens also."

"This is the one that most interests me." Andi pulled out another sheet of paper. "It's a letter from Victor. It's worded as if it's a friendly commendation. But I think there's more to it than that."

"May I?" Duke reached for it.

Andi handed it to him and watched as he read through it.

"You're right," Duke said. "The wording is strange."

She leaned closer. "Right? Look at this. *I know how much your family, your job, and the great state of Alaska mean to you.* I almost feel like that's a veiled threat."

"In other words, do what I want or there will be consequences?"

"Exactly!" Andi turned back to her papers. "I still have more to go through."

"How about if I help you?"

"I'd love that."

They worked for several minutes in silence before taking a break.

"These papers may be your first real piece of evidence as to what Victor is up to." Excitement laced Duke's voice.

Andi nodded slowly, leaning back to give her neck a break "He was buttering up the people down in Texas too, some of those oil tycoons, so they could pitch in and be part of this project. I have no doubt that's why he had a base down there and why he's been traveling up here to Alaska as much as he has recently."

"What it doesn't prove, however, is that Victor has done anything illegal."

She nibbled on her bottom lip. "No, he's very careful, and he's very good at covering his tracks."

A moment of silence passed.

"What are you going to do about the police, Andi?" Duke shifted to look at her, a dead serious tone to his voice.

She shrugged at his question before answering, "I . . . I don't know, to be honest."

"This isn't going to go away."

His statement made that familiar heaviness press on her chest. "I know. But I just need more time. If I'm behind bars . . ."

"Then you can't keep researching."

She nodded somberly. "Exactly."

"Let's keep searching for more."

Warmth filled her. His support meant everything. Made her realize she wasn't alone.

There was no one else she'd rather have to help her but Duke.

Andi tried to clear her thoughts and keep reading.

Duke was out of reach right now.

But maybe putting Victor behind bars wasn't.

chapter
twenty-seven

ANDI'S EYES fluttered open as light filled the room.

She stretched. Based on the ache pulsing through her neck, she must have fallen asleep in a bad position.

The last thing she remembered was studying those papers. She'd leaned back and closed her eyes just for a second . . .

She'd clearly been more exhausted than she thought.

She sat up straighter in bed and rubbed her eyes, trying to get the cobwebs out of them.

As she did, her gaze drifted beside her on the bed.

She sucked in a breath.

Duke.

Duke had fallen asleep while looking at these papers also.

Panic swept through her.

When the rest of the team realized Duke spent the

night in her room . . . they were going to draw some inaccurate conclusions. Conclusions she didn't want to face.

How could they have let this happen? They'd both been so caught up in studying the documents . . .

She swallowed hard before reaching for Duke and nudging his shoulder.

"Duke," she whispered. "You've got to wake up."

Maybe everyone else in the house was still asleep. With any luck, Duke could creep out of her room, and no one would ever be the wiser.

Duke blinked a few times before his eyes fully opened. Then he shot up in bed. "Andi?"

He sounded just as confused as she felt.

"We must have stayed up too late working on this because we both fell asleep." She raked a hand through her hair.

"I guess so. I didn't mean to . . ." He rubbed a hand over his face and shook his head.

"Neither did I. I don't really care that you fell asleep in my room. The only thing I care about is how everyone else on the team might perceive this."

"Ditto for me." He stood and stretched before his gaze fell on the alarm clock on the table. "It's only six a.m. Maybe everyone is still asleep."

"That's what I'm hoping." Andi stood and took his arm, ushering him to the door. "Open it quietly."

"I will." A touch of impatience filled his voice.

If the team knew he'd slept in here . . . it would just make everything awkward.

That was the last thing they needed.

Duke wasn't sure how he'd let this happen.

He didn't even remember closing his eyes. The last thing he remembered was reading about the environmental effects of oil on animals in the Arctic.

Then he'd felt Andi waking him up.

He gripped the doorknob and slowly turned it.

It didn't so much as let out a creak.

Slowly, he opened it. His room was just down the hallway. With any luck, someone might think he was headed to the bathroom. After all, they each had their own accommodations.

But just as he stepped into the hallway, his gaze latched onto someone else's.

Mariella's. She stood there with coffee in her hand, a pink robe, and an eye mask that she wore like a headband.

"Wait . . ." Her voice lilted with surprise. "Duke?" Then her gaze shifted over his shoulder. "Andi?"

"It's not what it looks like," Andi and Duke both said at the same time.

Mariella shrugged a little too quickly. "I didn't say anything."

"We know how this looks." Duke's voice sounded

calm as he explained. "I accidentally fell asleep in Andi's room. That's it."

Someone else stuck their head out of their room and glanced at them. Ranger.

"You accidentally fell asleep in Andi's room?" Ranger's voice came out entirely too loud. The whole house had probably heard him.

And apparently, they did. Because slowly doors began to open until the whole team had joined them in the hallway.

"What's going on?"

"Did something happen?"

"Are you two . . . ?"

"It's about time."

Suddenly, Duke felt as if he and Andi were on trial over a relationship between them that didn't exist.

Andi stepped forward and sliced her hand through the air to silence everyone's questions. "Look, y'all. Duke and I were reviewing some papers until late in the night, and we both accidentally fell asleep. That's all."

But as Duke glanced around the group, he saw the skepticism in their eyes.

Thankfully, instead of pressing them more on the issue, Mariella asked, "What kind of papers?"

Duke was nearly certain Andi would rather talk about their lack of a relationship than about those papers. But he left the ball in her court.

"I'd rather not say," she started, a weariness to her voice.

"Does this have to do with whatever secret it is that you don't want to tell us about?" Ranger asked.

After a moment of hesitation, Andi nodded. "It does. It involves Victor. I don't want it to intrude on any of our time together this weekend, which is why I thought I'd work on it at night."

"I wish we could help you with it." Simmy stepped out and tugged at the oversized cardigan she wore.

"I know. I wish you could too, but it's just not a good idea." Andi glanced around the group. "And why are you all awake? It's not even seven."

"Voices carry here in this house." Ranger shrugged. "I heard someone talking and thought something was wrong."

"Me too," Simmy said.

"Me three," Matthew added.

Mariella shrugged. "I guess if we're all up then we should get ready, have some breakfast, and dive into this case again."

"That's a good idea." Matthew held up his phone. "Because this guy struck again last night. There are now eight victims in thirteen days. You guys, he's not slowing down."

Duke's throat tightened at the words. Matthew was right. This guy was on a rampage.

What was it going to take to stop him?

chapter
twenty-eight

EVERYONE GOT ready and met back in the living room in just under twenty minutes.

Andi had taken time to brush her teeth, comb her hair, and put on some fresh clothes. She'd worry about the rest later.

Right now, she wanted to hear about this newest victim.

There weren't enough clues to figure out who this guy was. But even the most skilled killers messed up sometimes.

Ted Bundy bit someone and left teeth marks that helped identify him.

Jeffrey Dahmer had a victim escape.

John Wayne Gacy's last victim told his mother where he was going.

She grabbed a cup of coffee and a banana nut muffin

from the counter. Then she took her place in the living room, careful not to sit beside Duke.

It wasn't an absolutely terrible thought for people to assume the two of them were a couple. But Andi and Duke weren't together, and she was working really hard to keep it that way.

Because if she let down her guard . . . Andi might find herself in Duke's arms. That wasn't the way she wanted to start a relationship.

He needed resolution with Celeste first. In all honesty, Andi probably needed resolution with Victor too.

"So who is this victim?" Andi asked once they were all there.

"They haven't announced his or her name yet," Matthew said.

"I'm sure the cops are probably trying to notify the next of kin," Duke added.

"Did they give any clues?" Andi asked. "Location or . . . anything?"

"Nothing," Matthew confirmed. "Just a warning that this killer isn't going to stop until he's caught."

The cops weren't wrong.

And that thought was terrifying.

Duke's gut clenched at the thought of what had happened last night.

The team didn't have any time to waste. But finding clues didn't follow a timeline or include a checklist. Since none of them were official investigators, everything was a little harder. Police today relied on trace evidence and DNA and fingerprints.

All things their group wasn't privy to.

The things they *were* privy to were witnesses, firsthand accounts, and articles.

This case . . . it felt harder than some of the other ones. But Duke wasn't sure why.

Maybe because of how fast the victims were piling up. It put more pressure on everyone to find answers as quickly as possible.

When he thought about what they needed to do next to find more leads, Duke didn't have a lot of great ideas, other than talking to the friends and loved ones of the victims. But since none of these people were there when the victims had been murdered, that didn't really help much.

Just then, his phone rang. He was about to dismiss the call when he looked at the screen and saw it was his brother.

He excused himself from the group and put his phone to his ear. "Hey, what's going on? Was your flight rescheduled?"

"That's not why I'm calling." An unexpected tension stretched through Beau's voice.

Duke instinctually knew that there was more to this.

Something had happened. "What's up?"

"Last night after you dropped me off . . ." Beau started. "I noticed someone following me."

"What?" Duke's voice rose.

He glanced over his shoulder and saw the rest of the group staring at him. He turned away, trying to gain privacy, even though he knew there wasn't any in the house.

He could go to his room, but the walls were too thin to block out the sounds of his voice.

"What happened?" Duke asked his brother.

"I saw these guys follow me into the hotel, so I veered away from the elevator and took the stairs. Stepped out on the third floor. A maid had just left a room as I walked down the hallway. I caught the door and slipped inside."

"And?"

"I peered out the peephole and saw one of the guys walking by. He was talking on the phone to someone, and he had a Russian accent. He also had a gun in his hand, and he was clearly looking for me."

Duke's heart pounded harder. "Did he find you?"

"Thankfully, no. I don't know what you or Andi—or whoever this is about—has gotten themselves into. But I'm telling you, this guy had blood in his eyes. If he had caught me . . . I don't want to think about what he would have done to me."

chapter
twenty-nine

ANDI LISTENED as Duke updated the group.

Who would have followed Beau? What sense did all this make?

"Is he okay?" Andi rushed.

"He's fine. Thankfully, he's a pretty sharp guy."

"I'm sorry he was pulled into this."

Duke rubbed his jaw, the way he always did when he was deep in thought. "Me too."

"Is he still leaving today?" Andi asked.

"Some flights are opening up today, but Beau said he might stay a couple more days," Duke said. "He already missed his speaking engagement, and he doesn't have anything else scheduled for several days. He thought he might hang out."

"He might be safer if he didn't stay." Andi hated to say the words, but they were the truth.

"You think he's in danger because we're looking into

this Lights Out Killer guy?" Mariella tucked her legs
beneath her on the couch.

Andi shook her head. "At this point, that's not what I
think. I think this has to do with me, unfortunately."

"Andi, whatever you've gotten yourself into, is it really
worth all this danger?" Simmy's sweet voice cut through
the tension in the room.

"What's that quote? All that's necessary for evil to
triumph is for good people to do nothing?" Andi asked. "I
can't just let Victor get away with what he's doing. I have
to fight."

"Even at the expense of your own life?" Duke's question hung in the air.

"Why not? I'm single. I don't have a family. I don't
have anything to lose. If anyone is capable of fighting this,
it's me."

Duke's gaze locked on hers. "You do have people that
care about you. People in this room. We don't want to see
anything happen to you."

Her cheeks flushed at the sincerity in his voice. "I
appreciate that. I care about all of you too. You've become
like my family here in Alaska, something I never thought
I'd say when we first met. But I meant what I said. If
anyone is capable and in the position to do this, it's me.
Nothing's going to change my mind."

She forced herself not to look at Duke as she said the
words. She sensed he might have an injured look in his
eyes, and she couldn't bear to see that.

Instead, she cleared her throat and glanced at the rest of the group. "Now, enough about me. What's on our agenda for today?"

Duke took a seat as they talked about their plans for today. He tried to keep his mind focused on the task at hand. But instead, he kept going back to that conversation they'd just had with Andi.

She was being foolhardy. He understood her drive to find answers and find justice. But she needed to protect herself in the process.

Because there truly were people who cared about her.

Like him.

He'd promised himself he wouldn't start a new relationship until he had resolution with Celeste. But how long would that take? He'd been doing research on his own time for the past two years. *More* than two years.

But ever since Duke had thought he'd seen Celeste . . . he had upped his efforts.

Yet there was still nothing. It was like his fiancée was a ghost.

Maybe that was exactly what Celeste wanted.

As the team doled out tasks for the day, Simmy raised a hand in the air. "I know this probably doesn't have anything to do with our investigation. But it just seems like something I should mention to you guys, just in case."

Everyone turned to her.

"Like I said, it probably doesn't relate to anything, but yesterday I went over to check on the Eldridge family. They're staying in the guest house behind their property. I heard them talking to the fire chief, and he said something about a matchbook being used to start the fire."

"What kind of matchbook?" Duke asked.

"That's what's weird. I'm pretty sure he said it was from the Breaking Dawn Casino in Nevada."

Simmy was right. Duke didn't know what this might have to do with their investigation. It did, however, sound like there could be a whole different crime that had taken place right next door.

He was about to brush the idea aside when he caught a glimpse of Andi's face.

She'd gone totally pale.

What was going through her mind right now? Why in the world would that update personally affect her?

Clearly, Duke had missed something significant.

chapter
thirty

ANDI'S THOUGHTS REELED. She had to have misunderstood what Simmy said.

But she knew she hadn't.

"Andi . . . ?" a deep voice said.

She looked up, sensing someone staring at her. She was right—and it wasn't just Duke. Everyone studied her.

Had Andi been that obvious?

"Did that trigger something for you?" Duke narrowed his eyes as if trying to figure her out.

She licked her lips, not wanting to dive into the subject. But there was no need to hide the truth either. She was already hiding enough things from everybody in an effort to protect them. But protecting them was feeling more and more impossible.

"When I was twelve, my best friend died in a house fire."

"I'm so sorry to hear that, Andi." Familiar compassion encompassed Simmy's voice.

"I found out later, when I was older, that her death was considered suspicious. Someone used a matchbook to start the fire."

"What kind of matchbook?"

"One from the Breaking Dawn Casino."

Silence stretched through the room a moment.

"That has to be a coincidence," Duke murmured. "You don't think somebody purposely killed your friend then all these years later came here to kill some strangers next door?"

Andi shook her head. "No, that's not what I think. But I think if someone dug into my background and found out about that fire . . . they might have set this one next door just to send a message to me."

As the words left her lips, Andi realized that they were some of the most vulnerable, honest, and raw sentiments she'd shared in a long time.

Duke and Andi had been assigned to work together today. The pairing seemed to be an ongoing thing at this point.

Which was fine because they made a good team.

They planned to question Melanie. Ranger and Simmy were going to track down friends, family, and neighbors of the other victims, while Mariella and Matthew worked on the podcast itself.

Duke couldn't stop thinking about what Andi had told him about the fire.

She'd never mentioned her friend who'd died in a fire before. He could see where it wasn't something she would want to bring up. And it had happened so long ago . . .

Still, the similarities were eerie.

He didn't believe it was a coincidence either.

What if Victor had set that fire—or had one of his men do it—to send a message? But why target the neighbor's house instead of the house the murder club had rented?

It didn't make sense.

So many questions swirled through his head.

He didn't mention any of them. He sensed Andi didn't want to talk about the subject any more right now.

She was quiet for most of the ride to Melanie's house. Talking to the woman seemed even more important now that he knew the person following Beau also had a Russian accent. Coincidence? Maybe.

But it was worth checking out.

When they pulled up, he spotted a Jeep in the driveway. Maybe this meant the woman was home.

Duke could only hope.

He turned toward Andi before they got out of the SUV.

"You ready for this?" he asked softly.

"More than ready. I want some answers."

"Then let's go." He climbed out, and his gaze swept the street.

No signs of that car that had been following them.

He'd still keep his guard up.

He and Andi walked together toward the front door of a small house located only five minutes from the downtown area. The place was painted a purplish gray, and the outside was plain without any shrubs or flowers or embellishments.

Just as they took the first step onto the porch, the front door opened.

Melanie stood there.

But as soon as she saw them, her eyes widened with surprise.

Clearly, she hadn't been expecting to see them there.

"Melanie, we need to ask—"

She slammed the door in their faces before Duke could finish his sentence.

Then footsteps pounded inside the house as if she were fleeing.

chapter
thirty-one

"I'VE GOT THIS," Andi muttered before taking off in a run toward the back of the house.

Just as expected, Duke was on her heels.

As she scaled the short picket fence into the backyard, she saw Melanie darting down the back stairs.

"Wait!" Andi called. "We don't want to hurt you. We just want to talk. Please."

Melanie kept running, all the way to the back fence. But when the woman reached it and tried to jump it, a picket snagged her shirt.

She froze as if realizing she wasn't going to get away and resigning herself to whatever was to come. She raised her hands, nearly pulling her tiny green skirt up above her hips in the process.

She had a pretty face, that was for sure. The guys at the dealership probably liked that fact.

"Please." Andi paused in front of her, sucking in a deep gulp of air.

Melanie turned and looked at her. Then she glanced behind Andi.

Duke stood there, not looking winded at all.

Melanie's shoulders slumped. "Who are you with?"

"We're not with anybody," Andi said. "Stuart's parents hired us to look into his death."

Melanie seemed to consider her words a moment. "What are you? Private investigators or something?"

"Or something." Andi shrugged. "We're true crime podcasters."

"It's a long story," Duke added. "We just want to help."

Melanie crossed her arms. "I didn't kill him."

"We're not saying you did," Andi said. "We don't think you even fit the MO for a killer. We just want to ask you some questions."

Melanie's eyes narrowed with caution. "Like what?"

"Like did Stuart ever tell you he felt as if he were being watched, or did you notice anything that disturbed him the last time you talked?" Duke asked.

Tears glimmered in her eyes. "That's been all I can think about. But I haven't been able to pinpoint anything. As far as I know, this killer is just random. There's not really a pattern to what he's doing, right?"

"Maybe," Duke said. "But sometimes, subconsciously, these people have a pattern they're following, and we're just trying to figure out if there is a link between the victims."

Melanie shrugged. "I'm sorry, but I can't help you. I mean, we broke up a while ago."

"When was the last time you saw him?" Duke asked.

Her cheeks reddened. "I saw him . . . the night he died."

Andi's lips parted. "The same night Stuart died?"

Melanie's shoulders stiffened as if she second-guessed admitting that. "I may have been a little obsessed with him."

"So you were stalking him?" Duke clarified.

"That seems like such a harsh word." Melanie frowned. "I was just looking for an opening where I could talk to him again, tell him that he should give me another chance."

"Did that opening ever pop up?"

She shook her head. "No, he didn't want to talk to me. He wasn't interested."

"So while you were watching him and *waiting for the right opportunity*," Andi chose her words wisely, "did you see anything suspicious?"

She swallowed hard. "Maybe. I don't know. But there is something I can't stop thinking about."

"What's that?" Andi tried to keep the eagerness out of her voice.

"The day before Stuart was murdered, as I was watching his house, I saw another car parked just up the street. There was a man just sitting inside, but I couldn't see his features. It was too dark."

Duke jerked to life beside her. "What did the car look like? Did you get a license plate?"

Melanie shook her head, clearly getting frustrated. "No, I didn't. I wish I had. But I didn't know then what I know now."

"Do you remember anything about the car?" Andi asked, holding her breath as she waited for Melanie's response.

The woman let out a long sigh. "The only thing I remember is that it was a dark color. Blue, I think. But it was dark. It was a sedan. Four doors. Not too junky but not fancy either."

"That's a great start," Duke said.

"He did have some kind of bumper sticker. It was red, white, and blue. Maybe with some stars on it or something."

That sounded vaguely familiar, like he'd seen one like it recently.

Then he remembered where.

Dabney had a similar bumper sticker on his car. His black sedan.

Coincidence?

Hard to say.

He stored that fact in the back of his mind also.

"Did the man ever get out of the car?" Duke asked.

"No. He didn't. I thought it was kind of weird, but I tried to brush it off. After all, I was doing the same thing, right?"

The woman had a point.

"Did you tell the police this?" Duke asked her.

Melanie nibbled her bottom lip. "I didn't. I didn't want to draw attention to myself. I . . . I was arrested on stalking charges before. I knew how it would look and . . ."

"You should tell them," Andi told her. "More people are going to die unless this guy is stopped. Maybe that clue will mean something to the police."

Uncertainty flared in her gaze. "I . . . I'll think about it. But I'm making no promises."

If Melanie didn't tell the police, maybe Andi could leave an anonymous tip.

At least, this was *something* to go on.

And maybe they were slowly creeping closer to finding some real answers.

chapter
thirty-two

BEFORE THEY WALKED AWAY, Duke had one more question for Melanie. "We went to the dealership yesterday to talk to you. We didn't have a chance to because some Russian guy pulled you aside. The conversation looked heated. Do you mind if I ask what that was about?"

Duke watched Melanie's expression carefully. But she didn't show any signs of concern. In fact, she thought briefly about his question before letting out a laugh.

"You mean Dominic?" she asked. "We work together at the dealership."

Andi narrowed her eyes. "Was he giving you a hard time?"

"He wants me to go out on a date with his brother, which I think is weird."

"Why is that?" Andi asked.

"Because Stuart got me a job at that dealership. Dominic was his friend."

"So why is he pushing you to date his brother?" Duke asked.

"Apparently, Dominic and his girlfriend need a double date for an upcoming wedding they're going to. The problem is that I find his brother repulsive. Dominic was ready to pay me to go with his brother." She let out an airy and nasally laugh. "Crazy, huh?"

"You speak Russian?" Andi asked.

Melanie responded in a different language before laughing again. "I do. My mom was Russian and made sure I learned."

So maybe there wasn't really anything going on with the Russians after all. But it had been worth asking and finding out more information.

"Why did you run when we came to your door?" Andi asked.

Tension stretched across Melanie's face. "Ever since Stuart died . . . I've been afraid the killer saw me. I mean, I was staring at the car, and a moment later, the driver pulled away. Maybe he was the killer. Maybe he saw me. Maybe he'll find me and silence me, all so I don't share his secret."

"It's understandable that you'd be cautious," Andi murmured.

"Thanks for speaking with us, Melanie," Duke said as

he stored that information away. "If you think of anything else, please call us."

He handed her a card Mariella had made up for the team. Originally, the card had been pink with a sparkly silver font. Everyone had told her she had to make it look more professional, and she'd agreed.

So now they had neat, precise business cards with their podcast name and contact info.

He and Andi strode back to his SUV to talk about what Melanie had shared and to develop their next plan of action.

Andi waited until she was seated in the SUV with Duke before speaking.

"So what do you think?" she started.

He placed the key in the ignition but didn't start the engine.

"I've never thought Melanie was the killer," Duke said. "I don't think she's involved with the Russian mafia either."

Andi leaned back and crossed her arms. "What do you think about that car she saw?"

"It definitely seems like something worth looking into. Maybe it wasn't the killer."

"But maybe it was." Andi dabbed the air with her finger as if she were Tinkerbell with a wand.

"It's not much to go on, however," Duke said. "Without a license plate or a more distinct description, it will be like looking for a needle in a haystack."

"But it does seem to show, if it was the killer in that car, that maybe he does stake out his victims' homes before attacking them."

"He would almost have to," Duke said. "Otherwise, how would he know that they're alone?"

"Good question." Andi shifted slightly. "Do you think he knows them? You know . . . personally?"

"It's hard to be sure, but I doubt it. You've studied the list, right? You didn't see any similarities between the victims?"

She shook her head. "No, none. But I agree he's choosing them for a reason. But for the life of me I can't figure out what that would be."

"Maybe if we keep digging we'll find more answers."

"The only thing is . . . I'm uncertain about where to even keep on digging," Andi said. "Where else do we look at this point?"

Duke let out a deep breath. "I do agree that every lead seems to be going cold. But we can keep talking to neighbors. Keep looking for patterns and links. Maybe we can examine the map again and see if the locations are key."

Just as he said the words, sirens sounded in the distance. Not one. But several.

She exchanged a concerned look with Duke.

It almost sounded as if the sirens were coming this

way. Had someone spotted Andi and reported her to the police? Were the cops coming this way to arrest her now?

"Get down in your seat, just in case," Duke said.

Andi slid down low.

But anxiety thrummed through her as she considered what might happen next.

chapter
thirty-three

CONCERN PULSATED THROUGH DUKE.

Were the police coming for Andi? He had a hard time believing that was the case. There were too many police cars. And while breaking into a senator's office and potentially stealing information was a crime, it wasn't a crime that needed this kind of response.

Besides, as far as they knew, Andi hadn't stolen anything. Everything was right where it had been when people in the office had left for the night. Andi had merely taken pictures of some files.

He glanced in his sideview mirror, anxious to see what would happen next.

The police cars zoomed their way.

He held his breath with apprehension.

Then he glanced at Andi and saw the fear on her face.

Fear wasn't something Duke associated with Andi.

No, she was tough. Headstrong. Perhaps even foolish at times. Not usually scared.

The sirens came closer and closer.

The cars weren't slowing down.

The first police car whizzed past.

Duke's lungs loosened slightly. But it was too soon to fully relax.

Sure enough, another car sped past. Then another. Then another.

They were all headed somewhere on the outskirts of Anchorage.

Whatever had happened, it was clearly serious.

Finally, all the cars had zoomed past.

Duke glanced at Andi. "You can sit up now. The coast is clear."

She pulled herself up and glanced around as if double-checking his statement.

"I wonder what that was about?" she murmured as she smoothed her shirt.

His jaw hardened. "I have no idea. But at least it wasn't about you."

Just then his phone buzzed, and he glanced at the screen.

Matthew had sent a message. Duke quickly scanned it before reading it out loud.

"The police released information on the newest victim," Duke said. "His name was Albert Clubber. He was fifty-eight years old and had lived in Anchorage for twenty years. He was divorced, and his kids were grown and out of the house."

"What does he do now? Or what *did* he do?" Andi corrected herself.

"He worked for Child Protective Services. Nothing too controversial."

"No, that doesn't really help us, does it?" Andi murmured.

If this killer stuck to his pattern, there would be another murder. Not tonight, but Sunday night.

That meant that there was an unknowing victim out there right now, someone who had no clue they were living on borrowed time.

Maybe one day this guy would get sloppy and leave a clue behind.

But even if that was the case, there was a good chance the police wouldn't share any of the information with them. The other issue was that they'd be returning to Fairbanks on Monday.

Andi felt her jaw harden.

This might just be the one case they couldn't solve.

Andi and Duke started back toward the rental for now. But Andi's thoughts raced over everything.

Before they left downtown Anchorage, Duke pulled

into a parking lot at a coffeehouse. Said he needed some more caffeine.

Andi told him she'd wait in the car while he picked up the drinks.

Before he climbed out of the SUV, his phone rang again.

Andi assumed it was one of the murder club members calling with another update.

But when she saw Duke's expression tighten, she knew that wasn't the case.

"It's Gibson," he said.

Gibson? What now?

Duke answered.

But before he could explain he'd put it on speaker, Gibson spoke. "Duke . . . is Andi with you?"

Andi's chest tightened at the tone of his voice.

Duke glanced at her before opening his door and stepping away.

He was putting distance between them, probably so his response could contain a measure of the truth.

"No, she's not," Duke said. "What's going on?"

"Things just went up another notch, Duke. The police are looking for her."

"But the police have already been looking for her, right?"

"This time it's even more serious," Gibson said. "Senator Glassine was shot in her home last night. She's in ICU right now as the medical team fights to save her life."

The air left Andi's lungs.

Someone had shot the senator? Andi had trouble wrapping her head around it . . . and wrapping her head around the thought she was wanted by the police for the crime.

"I'm not sure what that has to do with Andi." Duke threw another glance her way. "She didn't do it."

Andi heard the tension in his voice. Duke knew how serious this was. Both of them did.

"If you see her, you need to call me," Gibson continued. "You don't want to get yourself mixed up in this. Do you understand?"

Duke's gaze lingered on Andi as he murmured, "I understand."

He ended the call and slid his phone back in his pocket. Instead of getting that coffee, he climbed into his SUV and slammed the door.

"Forget the coffee," he said. "We need to get you out of here."

chapter
thirty-four

DUKE'S THOUGHTS KEPT SPINNING.

Someone had shot the senator? Why in the world would the police think Andi was responsible? She didn't have a violent history or anything against the senator even.

Nothing made sense.

He started down the road before Andi could say anything. A moment later, he felt her hand on his arm.

"You shouldn't be seen with me." Andi's voice sounded throaty. "I'm going to get you in trouble too."

"You're my friend. I'm not just going to push you out on the street and let you fend for yourself."

"I appreciate that, but you need to think of what this might mean for your own future."

Duke continued down the road, knowing he wouldn't change his mind.

"I know you didn't shoot the senator. In fact, I've

been with you literally all night—though by accident—and all this morning. I can vouch that you're not guilty."

"I appreciate that. But the fact still remains that I *did* break into her office." She stared out the window, a disturbing mellowness to her voice.

"It sounds like someone is trying to set you up." Duke gripped the wheel tighter.

Andi pressed her lips together, a grim expression on her face. "I think you're right. If I'm behind bars then I can't go after Victor anymore."

"You really think he'd take things this far?" He stole another glance at her, determined to see her expression and figure out how she really felt.

"I know he would." Her voice left no room for doubt. "Nothing is going to stop him from getting what he wants. And what he wants is this oil deal that will make him millions of dollars."

Duke couldn't argue with her statement. She was right. Victor was single-minded. Greedy. Power hungry.

The list could go on—and none of the qualities were positive.

"So where do we go from here?" Andi pulled her gaze from the window and glanced at him.

That was an excellent question.

"Back to the rental until we can figure things out," Duke said. "We can lie low."

"You don't think the police are going to find me there?"

"It was booked in Alpine's name. Right now, that could work to our advantage."

"I suppose that it could . . . but I hate the fact that I could pull everyone into the middle of this."

"No podcaster left behind," Duke quipped.

Andi gave him a look.

"All for one and one for all?" he offered.

She still didn't seem impressed.

How could he convince Andi that they could help her? That secluding herself would be a mistake?

The task seemed impossible.

But Duke wasn't going to back down.

Instead of going to the rental, Duke decided to take Andi to the hotel where Beau was staying.

Even if the rental was in Alpine's name, the hotel was a safer bet. And that way Beau could keep an eye on her.

He wouldn't tell his brother what was going on. Beau needed to be clueless.

It would be Andi's decision about whether or not to tell the rest of the team. He understood why she didn't want to do that and put them at risk.

But they all knew something was going on.

Duke would like to stay with her to help navigate this, but Andi was fully capable of doing that herself. In fact, the best thing he could do right now was to put distance between them—just in case Gibson decided to track his phone.

He looked up and saw Beau waiting for Andi near the front doors.

Before Andi could slam the door of the SUV, Duke called her name. She paused and looked back at him, uncertainty in her gaze.

Another emotion that he rarely saw on Andi.

"It's going to be okay," he assured her.

Andi still looked unconvinced. "Thank you for your help."

"Are you going to tell the others what's going on?"

She nibbled on her bottom lip a moment before shaking her head. "I still don't think it's a good idea."

Duke nodded slowly. "Just stay out of sight. We'll figure out something. I know you don't like sitting back and not doing anything. But that's the best thing you can do right now. Maybe examine that victim list again and look into this new guy who passed, Albert Clubber. See if maybe there's a connection you can put together."

"And what are you going to do?"

"I'm going to see if Helena will meet with me." He'd already made up his mind. He wasn't going to give up.

"Why would you do that?"

"Because maybe she knows something that we don't."

She stared at him for another moment before nodding. "Okay then. You do that. I'll stay here and see what I can figure out."

But as Duke watched her walk into the hotel, something strange twisted his heart.

He was truly worried about her. He had to figure out why the police thought she might be involved in the senator getting shot.

Maybe Helena knew something that would help.

However, that information would most likely come with a cost.

But no price was too large if it meant protecting Andi.

chapter
thirty-five

ANDI AND BEAU didn't speak until they were in the new room Beau had secured at the hotel. He hadn't been able to stay in his old one—not after that man had tracked him down last night.

Once inside, she collapsed into a chair by the corner.

Beau went to the window, peered outside, and then closed the curtain. When he finished, he sat on the edge of the bed facing her.

"Something must have gone south," he murmured.

"You could say that." Andi nibbled on her lip as she contemplated how much to say. "The police . . . they think I shot Senator Glassine."

"What?" His voice came out sharp. "How could they think that?"

"I'm not totally sure." She ran a hand over her face. "I shouldn't have told you that. Now you can't plead ignorance."

Andi knew better. She'd been an attorney. But she was so tired of playing this game where she kept everything to herself. Secrets were so exhausting.

Still, regret pounded inside her chest.

"What are you going to do?" Beau studied her face.

"I have no idea. Right now, I'm just trying to figure this out. Duke is meeting with Helena to see if she has any more information."

"Smart thinking." He paused, still observing her. "Are you doing okay?"

"Not really. I think . . . I think I'm being set up."

"But you have an alibi, right?"

Andi nodded. "I do. But even if I get out of this one . . . Victor is going to keep coming after me."

"He might. Maybe you're a bit like Esther."

She raised an eyebrow. "From the Bible?"

"That's right. She was created 'for such a time as this.' Maybe you were too."

"So you think I should trust this process?"

"I think where God guides, He provides."

She stared at Beau a moment as she contemplated his words. "I like that. I stopped believing in God for a while, but that's starting to change. I've realized I can't blame all the bad stuff on Him."

"It's tempting."

"Yes, it is."

"God. Church. The Bible . . . they all changed Duke. He was in a bad, bad place. I'm so thankful his friend reached out to him and invited him to that Bible study. That invitation turned Duke's life around."

Andi studied Beau's face. "I'm glad that friend reached out too. Duke and I have been unofficial partners lately."

Beau smiled. "I can tell."

As shouts sounded outside, all Andi's pleasant feelings disappeared.

What was happening now?

Duke headed to a café in Anchorage to meet with Helena.

He pulled up to Wildflowers—the choice had been Helena's—and stepped inside. Based on the signs in front of him, the place focused on vegan foods, which was interesting considering Helena had eaten pepperoni and reindeer sausage just yesterday. But he wasn't going to call her out.

The scent of freshly baked bread filled the air, along with the sound of blenders emulsifying fruit for smoothies.

He spotted Helena already sitting at a corner table. Her upright posture made her appear more than ready for whatever this conversation might hold.

He took a seat at her table, eager to jump right into business. "Thanks for meeting me."

"Of course."

"What do you know about Senator Glassine's shooting?"

Helena's eyebrows flickered. "I figured you'd want to know something about the Lights Out Killer, not the senator."

"I assume you're working both stories."

She lifted a shoulder. "They're both on my radar. But I'm still not sure why *you're* interested in the senator."

Duke's jaw twitched. "Let's just say I have personal reasons."

She nodded briefly. "Very well. Tit for tat, right?"

"That was the agreement."

She let out a long breath before starting. "I know the police have a person of interest on their radar as far as the senator's shooting. Apparently, the shooter was caught on video going to the senator's house, and it's someone who's harassed the senator before."

That couldn't be Andi . . . right? Or was there more Andi hadn't told him?

"Go on," Duke encouraged. "Did they release a name or image?"

"Not yet, but I understand they're about to. It's crazy out there. Everyone is searching for this woman."

"A woman? They believe a woman did this? Usually crimes like this are done by men."

"This time it's a petite woman with white-blonde hair, who weighs approximately one hundred twenty pounds."

She stared at him, an inquisitive look in her gaze. "Sound like anyone you know?"

Duke swallowed hard. Helena knew it was Andi, didn't she? "I know my friend was with me last night and couldn't have done this."

Helena continued to stare at him. "Maybe she has a twin."

"She doesn't."

"I don't know what's going on." Helena did that half shrug again. "But your friend could be in some serious trouble. And that's too bad because I kind of liked her."

He didn't like the way Helena sounded so sure that Andi was guilty. But he swallowed the things he wanted to say. Instead, he asked, "Do you know anything else?"

"I don't. That's all I've been told." Helena crossed her arms and leaned toward him. "Now it's your turn. What do you know that might help me out?"

Duke sucked in a long breath before starting. He'd already thought this through, and he'd decided how much information he was willing to give up. He knew coming empty-handed wasn't an option.

"I was able to talk to Melanie this morning," he started. "She believes she may have seen the killer outside Stuart's house before he died."

Helena's lips parted with surprise. "What?"

Duke nodded. "Apparently, Melanie was basically stalking Stuart after their breakup. While she was doing so, she noticed a car near his house."

"Did she get a license plate? Description of the person inside?" Excitement rose in her voice.

"Unfortunately, she didn't. But she thought it was a blue four-door sedan that was in fairly good condition. There was also some kind of red, white, and blue bumper sticker on the back."

"That's it?"

Duke shrugged. "I know it's not much, but it's something. Melanie said that happened the day before Stuart died. So if this guy truly is the killer then he's staking out his victims ahead of time. It's not as if he's wandering the street at night just trying to guess who might be home and who might be alone."

Helena leaned back and frowned, her gaze shifting toward the window. "Yeah, this guy is too smart for that."

"Yes, he is. That's what makes him even scarier."

chapter
thirty-six

ANDI SAT at the desk in the hotel room studying the victims' info again.

The commotion outside?

It had just been another moose. The animals were out in full force this week.

Thank goodness, it wasn't anything more. She'd had visions of SWAT teams surrounding the hotel, coming for her, or even a gang of Russian gunmen rushing the place.

The thoughts were almost laughable.

Yet they weren't.

Beau was busy doing something, which was fine because Andi had things she needed to do as well.

There had to be a link between these victims. She just had to figure out what.

After studying the list for a good thirty minutes, nothing new stood out to her. Finally, she rubbed her eyes and leaned back in the chair, ready for a break.

"Nothing?" Beau looked up from where he'd perched himself on the brown couch.

She turned in her seat and shook her head. "No, unfortunately."

"You guys are really good at doing what you do. I've been listening to the podcast, and it's impressive." He laced his hands behind his head as he leaned back, looking like the picture of casual.

"It has been kind of amazing the way everything has come together. I still can't believe it sometimes." The shift in conversation seemed almost inappropriate considering the circumstances—yet Andi knew it would be good for her mental health to shift gears a moment.

"It almost seems like you guys were meant to do this."

A smile tugged at her lips. "Sometimes it does feel like that."

Beau continued to study Andi, and she knew he had something on his mind. She waited for him to say whatever it was.

"I think Duke really likes you," he finally said.

Her eyebrows flung up. She hadn't expected him to say that. "Really?"

"Really. I've been worried about him for a while. Ever since everything happened with Celeste, it's been tough, to say the least. He's not the same person he used to be."

"After going through what he did, that's understandable."

"It is. But there has to come a time when you move

on, right?" Beau shrugged, but not as a means of brushing off the seriousness of the situation. The action was full of plenty of thought.

"I don't think your brother will move on until he has answers," Andi admitted, unsure if she should even say anything. Yet it was good to talk to someone who had insight on Duke. "I hate seeing that haunted look in his eyes. I hate how much this has hurt him."

"I get that." Beau slowly nodded, another topic brewing in his gaze. "You know, when I first met you, I wanted to ask you out."

Andi tilted her head. Something else she hadn't expected him to say. "Is that right?"

"Duke said I could, but I knew he wasn't okay with it. I could see it in his eyes."

"The two of us have talked about some things," Andi admitted. "But who knows if he'll ever have answers about Celeste?"

"That's true. The thing about Duke is that he's a loyal kind of guy. He dated this girl in college who had all kinds of problems. Everyone in the family kept telling him to break up with her. But he wouldn't do it. He was too loyal."

Now Beau had her full attention. "So what happened?"

"Eventually, she cheated on Duke, and that was enough for him to finally call things off. But it had to get that serious before it happened. It's not because Duke is insecure or lacks confidence. He just believes that commitments should be kept."

"That's admirable." For some reason, the words made Andi's throat tighten. Probably because she had seen for herself how much Duke would sacrifice for others. It was a commendable quality, but one that had the power to cripple him.

"It is. But right now, that quality is working against him." Beau frowned as if worried about his brother.

"We'll keep looking into Celeste," Andi told him. "Eventually, we'll find some answers. I hope."

"So do I."

Andi leaned back and rubbed her arms as another thought hit her. "If Duke is as loyal as you say he is . . . maybe I should distance myself from him now."

"Why is that?" A knot formed on Beau's brow.

"Because there's a good chance I'm going to end up in prison . . . and if that's the case, he deserves happiness with someone who lives as a free woman, not a jailbird."

The words burned as they left Andi's throat. But they were true.

Gut-wrenchingly true.

Duke thanked Helena and left the café.

But as soon as he stepped onto the sidewalk, he noticed two men across the street.

They tried to look casual—one like he was checking something on his phone, the other like he'd paused from a jog.

They were cops.

Duke was sure of it.

They'd followed him, hoping Duke would lead them to Andi.

He couldn't let that happen.

Remaining casual, he started down the street. He wasn't sure where he was going—but definitely not to the hotel where Beau and Andi were staying.

First, he'd confirm these guys were following him.

He strolled several blocks until he reached Cook Inlet. He paused near a bench and stared out over the water, acting as if he were simply getting some fresh air and enjoying the view.

He slid on his sunglasses before peering on either side of him.

The man on the phone. He was there. A decent distance away, where most people probably wouldn't notice him.

This time he had his phone to his ear as he paced.

A few minutes later, the jogger paced by on the sidewalk behind Duke.

Duke was *definitely* being tailed.

He needed to look into things, but he couldn't afford to have these two following him.

That meant he would need to lose them.

As he glanced in the distance, he saw his answer.

The trolley.

Moving quickly, he rushed toward the nearest stop and mingled with the crowd. He paid his fare and then took his place at the back.

He peered out the window and saw the man who'd been on his phone staring at him.

The jogger had stopped as well.

But they were too late.

Duke had gotten away for now.

But his freedom wouldn't last long.

chapter
thirty-seven

ANDI SAT crisscross on the couch and continued to study the victims. Beau had let her use his computer.

She'd decided to dive deeper into each person's social media.

After several minutes, she hit paydirt.

Maybe . . .

First, she needed to double-check a few things.

Quickly, she visited the social media sites of several victims again, just to make sure she wasn't reading too much into things. She didn't think she was.

She may have found a link!

"Did you find something?" Beau turned toward her from the other end of the couch, clearly sensing her excitement.

"I think. It might be minor. But it's something." She stared at the screen.

He moved closer. "What is it?"

She leaned back, her heart pounding. "I know this seems like a long shot but . . . each of the victims has gone to a hockey game in the past year. There are various pictures of them at the games or mentions by friends they attended the games with."

Beau's eyebrows shot together. "Hockey? You think this guy's targeting them because of hockey?"

"I know it sounds ridiculous. Believe me, I do. But really, these people have nothing else in common. I've looked at their education, at their backgrounds, at restaurants they frequent. I've even looked at books they've read and vacations they've taken—all from social media, of course. But there's nothing else. Nothing I can find. Only hockey."

He tilted his head, still appearing skeptical. "Seems like a lame reason to murder someone, but there *are* people who are really into sports."

"But why murder over it?" Andi nibbled on her bottom lip in thought.

Beau shook his head. "I have no idea."

"Wait . . ." She typed something else onto the computer. "Xs are used in hockey, right? It's a penalty thing. When an official crosses his arms over his chest it means interference. Maybe that explains the Xs carved into the victims."

"Sounds plausible to me. It's definitely worth looking into." Beau shrugged.

"Could you call Duke? Ask him to check into it? I already turned my phone off and took the battery out. I can't risk anyone tracing it." Andi tried to hide the worry from her voice, but it was no use. It was still there, and it was still obvious. "I should have brought that burner phone with me, but I didn't think about it. I already gave it back to Duke."

"Sure, no problem," Beau said. "Besides, it's like you said. It's not like there's anything else to go on right now."

Andi slowly nodded. "You're right. At least, this is something. It's better than the possibility that we've hit a total and complete dead end."

"Yes, it is."

As Duke reached his SUV—after successfully losing the men tailing him—he got a call from Beau.

Andi had found a connection.

The fact didn't surprise Duke. She was one determined woman.

The lead made his blood race.

Though he'd prefer to look into who'd shot the senator, Andi had insisted he look into this lead instead.

He pulled to a stop in front of the Subarctic Sports Complex, which housed an ice hockey rink where players of the Anchorage Golddiggers practiced. The place had closed down for years but had recently reopened. Based on the signs outside, it appeared their official grand reopening was coming up soon.

This wasn't hockey season, but from what Duke understood, most professional hockey players practiced year-round. This was the preferred practice facility for the Gold-diggers, and it looked big enough to host games as well.

Duke hoped this wouldn't be another dead end.

He parked and grabbed a leather crossbody bag he'd thrown some information in that Matthew had put together for him.

Then Duke strode inside. Instantly, the chilled air hit him along with the sounds of whistles and blades scraping against the ice.

The place was larger than he'd thought it would be. A rink sat in the middle, surrounded on two sides by rows of stadium-style seats. A concession stand stood on one edge, a skate rental on the other, and some unmarked doors appeared to be offices.

He rolled his shoulders back and tried to look like he knew what he was doing as he nodded at the woman behind the desk. Then he casually strolled toward the rink.

No one batted an eye.

From where Duke stood, he saw at least six players practicing as well as a coach on the sidelines.

Duke stood behind the Plexiglas and watched. These guys were intense, as was their coach as he yelled out corrections in not-so-nice terms.

Duke had looked up the man's name before coming inside. Thomas Pence.

Duke had played hockey some while growing up in Wyoming, so he knew the rigors of the game.

What kind of connection could this killer have to hockey? Had one of the players built up some rage and decided to take it out on innocent civilians?

Part of him thought the idea seemed far-fetched, but another part of him thought it could be a legitimate motive, especially if someone was off-kilter in some way.

As the players began a new drill, Duke saw his opening.

He approached Coach Pence, praying the man would receive him well. Duke didn't know much about the guy, but his yelling and frantic motions made him seem like a hothead.

The man glanced at him. "You here to try out?"

"Not exactly."

"Then I don't have time to talk." He turned away from Duke.

Not a great start.

"It's about the Lights Out Killer," Duke stated.

That got his attention, and he glanced back at Duke again. "What does that have to do with me? And who are you?"

"Duke McAllister, former Army CID, and I work with the true crime podcast *The Round Table*."

Pence stared at Duke another moment as if contemplating whether or not he believed him.

Finally, he asked, "What do you want to know?"

"I have confirmation that all the victims have been to a Golddiggers' game."

"What?" Pence barked out the word with what sounded like genuine surprise.

Duke pulled out his phone. "We have social media proof that they were all at games during the past year."

"So you think someone here has something to do with this?" Defensiveness now edged his voice. Then he let out a rough, skeptical chuckle clearly meant to dismiss Duke's theory. "Do you have any idea how many tickets are sold to our games each year? Thousands."

"I'm not saying that someone here is responsible," Duke said. "I'm just trying to find some answers, to figure out if this is truly a lead or not."

Pence's gaze went to the guys practicing on the ice. "Be vocal and stop stick tapping!"

Then he turned back to scrutinize Duke without apology for several moments.

Finally, Pence nodded. "What can I do?"

"Do you recognize any of these people?" Duke showed him some photos on his phone.

Pence flipped through the pictures, his expression stony.

After he went through the pictures once, he looked at

them again and stopped on the photo of one man. "Him. I remember him."

Duke's pulse raced as he waited to hear what Pence had to say.

chapter
thirty-eight

LAST NIGHT'S date had gone surprisingly well.

So when Kate asked if I'd like to do a late lunch or early dinner today, I'd agreed. I didn't have to work until later, so I figured why not?

At least, she was easy on the eyes.

I'd offered to make her one of my famous lasagnas, and she'd agreed to come to my place.

It was already in the oven, and the smell of cheese and ground beef and oregano made my stomach grumble.

This should work out well because I had to be at work in three hours.

That would give us a definite time when she needed to leave.

Right on cue, the doorbell rang, and Kate stood there. I could see her on the other side of the glass wearing a pale-yellow sundress.

She had such a sweet smile. She'd brought some fresh bread with her, and she held it up when she spotted me.

I greeted her with a friendly smile and ushered her inside, giving her a quick kiss on the cheek.

She blushed.

I showed her where she should sit while I finished up lunch, but she insisted on helping.

I figured, why not let her? I was still in a good mood from last night.

It had been amazing. And I wasn't referring to the time I'd spent with her.

I was referring to the time afterward.

That man hadn't known what was coming. When I'd surprised him, he'd put up a good fight. That made my experience even more exciting.

People here in Anchorage were starting to be more on guard. It was better if I could slip into the house at night while they slept and surprise them.

But sometimes things didn't work out that way.

This guy had probably been listening to the news. He'd slept with a baseball bat beside him.

If he'd had a gun . . . well, it would be a totally different story right now.

But before he could swing his bat, I'd plunged my knife into him.

The move had been effective.

A smile tried to tug at my lips.

Then I'd left my calling card.

I could hardly wait for the next time . . .

But for now, I cast those thoughts aside to focus on lunch.

Kate was skirting around me in my small kitchen with a glass of red wine. She'd peeked on the lasagna, though I'd told her she shouldn't open the door. It would take longer to cook.

As she scurried away from the oven, her shoe caught on the rug.

She tumbled forward, her wine glass tilting.

The merlot sloshed.

Then liquid hit my shirt.

I stared down at the red stain.

Anger whipped through me.

She should have been more careful! Now my shirt was ruined—and I'd just bought this one.

I took several deep breaths, trying to get my temper under control. People who weren't careful drove me insane. So clumsy and inconsiderate!

"I'm so sorry," Kate murmured, reaching for my shirt. "If you take this off, I can wash it and get the stain out."

"That won't be necessary—"

Without listening to me, she tugged at my clothing, untucking it. She yanked my shirttails from my pants as if prepared to take my button-up off me herself in her frenzy to make things right.

The next thing I knew, my chest was exposed.

As was the scar of the X.

My heart pounded in my ears as everything seemed to happen in slow motion.

She wasn't supposed to see that.

No one was.

I quickly shoved my shirt down and pushed her back —a little too hard. She hit the counter behind her, her eyes wide with a spark of fear and surprise.

I tried to soften my voice. "Sorry about that. But that's not necessary. I can take care of this myself."

She stared at me, clearly shaken. "Your scar . . ."

"It's a long story." My jaw hardened as I said the words.

She had messed everything up.

I should have never agreed to eat with her again today. This lunch date had been a mistake.

No one knew about the X pattern I'd been leaving on people's chests. No one other than law enforcement and paramedics. They were keeping it quiet, probably as a way of testing false leads.

But eventually, that detail might be leaked.

Then Kate would think of me . . . and it would be nearly impossible to explain. She'd be suspicious.

She'd turn me in to the authorities.

I fisted my hands tighter.

I studied her. Saw a few splotches of wine on her dress. Saw the fear lacing her eyes.

She could see the devil simmering down inside me, couldn't she?

I would need to take care of her.

This wasn't the way I'd planned things.

Not at all.

"I . . . I've made a mess of things." She scooted to the side, trying to slip around the counter away from me.

I blocked her. "Yes, you have."

I had a choice to make.

I could end this now, knowing someone could have seen her come in here.

Or I could finish this later and make it look like she was a victim of the Lights Out Killer.

That was an appealing thought. But what if, in the meantime, she blabbed to a friend about what an awful date this had been? What if she ruined everything for me?

I couldn't let that happen.

As more fear welled in her eyes, I knew I had to make a decision, and I had to make it quickly.

However, my plans to take her to the Grand Finale were in serious jeopardy.

chapter
thirty-nine

PENCE POINTED to the photo of Mark Williams, the first victim.

"What do you remember about Mark?" Duke asked.

Pence blew out a long breath. "Forgive me if I don't have all the details right, but I believe that man was the one heckling Raz Burton."

Duke knew enough to know that Raz Burton was a reckless hockey player.

He glanced at the rink now to see if he could identify the man.

"Raz isn't here," Pence said as if reading Duke's thoughts. "But he's a fan favorite when it comes to heckling. And he doesn't handle it well."

Duke turned back to Pence. "What happened?"

"Not much, really. Except things got a little heated. This guy was saying some pretty crude things about Raz, and Raz couldn't take it, so he skated over to the sideboard

and got up in his face. This guy got right back in Raz's
face. We had to call security because we were afraid a fist
fight might break out. It's one thing if a fight breaks out
on the ice, but it's a whole other story if it's between a
hockey player and a supposed fan."

"Do things like this happen often?"

"More than I'd like, especially when it comes to Raz."
Pence paused and stared at Duke a moment. "Certainly
you don't think he's guilty of being a serial killer, do you?"

"I'm just asking questions. Is there any way that I
could talk to him?"

"He's not here today, so I couldn't tell you. He's not
due back to the rink until next week."

That was one connection, Duke mused. But how
about these other people?

"Do you know of any other situations similar to the
one with Raz and Mark? Maybe an argument that
happened after the game?"

"That wouldn't be a question for me," Pence said. "I
would know about some of the incidents if they happened
during the game, but not afterward."

"Do you know who I could ask?"

"You'd probably want to talk to Richard Blackmore.
He splits his time between this place and the arena. He
manages both facilities for the time being. I think he's at
lunch now."

Duke thanked Pence for his help.

This was something to go on.

Duke remembered that Wyatt Jenkins' neighbor had said the killer had a strange gait. That might fit that of a hockey player with all of their injuries.

It was definitely something worth looking into more.

Andi paced the hotel room. She couldn't stop herself.

Beau looked powerless to do anything except watch her.

She knew Duke was on his way. He'd called Beau to let him know and then informed them that he was ditching his phone. He couldn't risk being traced. That meant they had no way of getting in touch with him in the meantime.

She could practically hear the minutes ticking in her head.

Finally, a knock sounded at the door.

Beau motioned for her to stay back, and she scooted out of sight. Tension threaded through her muscles.

Was it the police? The bad guys?

Instead, Duke's voice sounded from the other side of the door.

Her shoulders softened. Duke. Good. He was back.

Maybe he had an update for them.

He rushed into the room, a new urgency to his steps. He headed toward the window and peered outside before stalking back toward them.

He was definitely on edge, probably checking to make sure he hadn't been followed.

He stopped when he saw Andi. "You okay? You look pale."

She nodded. "I'm as well as can be expected."

"You might be onto something with this hockey stuff," he started. "Good job figuring out that link."

Her cheeks warmed. "What did you find out?"

"There's this one player—" Before Duke could finish, Beau's phone rang. His brother handed the device to Duke, who glanced at the screen and frowned.

"Who is it?" Andi peered at the screen.

"Mariella. Let me take this."

Based on his tone, he wasn't expecting good news.

And why was Mariella calling on Beau's phone?

chapter
forty

DUKE PUT the phone to his ear. He had a feeling he knew what this conversation was going to be about, and he dreaded it.

He'd stashed his own phone in a locker near the train station. Later, he'd go back to retrieve it.

But the last thing he wanted was to be traced.

"Duke?" Mariella rushed. "Have you seen Andi? I've tried to call her, but her phone goes straight to voicemail. Your phone does too. So I called Beau's number hoping he could help me reach you."

"Is everything okay?" Duke tried to avoid the subject.

"The police just showed up at the rental house. They're looking for Andi, saying some stuff about that senator who was shot. What's going on?"

Duke stole a glance at Andi, who stood pensively waiting for an update.

"Things have gone upside down, to say the least."

Duke placed his other hand on his hip and rolled his shoulders back as he prepared himself for the rest of this investigation.

It was going to require everything he had, and he couldn't afford to let down his guard, not even for a moment.

"Is Andi okay?" Concern laced Mariella's voice.

Duke glanced at Andi again, and his cheek twitched. "She's fine. For now. What did you tell the police?"

"That she wasn't here and that I didn't know where she was. That was the truth."

"Good. From here on out, we're going to try to keep it that way."

"Duke . . ." Mariella murmured. "I'm worried about her."

"I'll explain more when I can."

"Please keep us updated. We're all worried."

"I will." Duke ended the call and gave the phone back to Beau.

Then he turned to Andi. "The police went to the rental house looking for you. Also, Gibson called again, before I ditched my phone."

Andi's face went still. "And?"

"He's in Anchorage. Local police called him in to help look for you since he has a personal connection to you."

"I see. And . . ." She swallowed hard.

"He wanted to confirm again that I didn't know where you were."

Her face sagged with worry. "I hate the fact you're having to lie to him, especially on my account."

"I need to keep you safe."

Andi nibbled on her lip before turning back to him. "No, what I need to do is to turn myself in."

"Andi . . . that sounds like a terrible idea."

She stepped closer, almost as if desperate to reassure him of her decision. "I can't keep acting like a fugitive. It's only going to make me look guilty. I just need to explain myself."

"But you really did break into the office of a US senator. There will be consequences for that." His jaw hardened in disapproval.

"I know. Believe me, I know. But I can't keep living like this. And I can't keep adding this stress to all of you."

Duke stared at her a moment, his thoughts racing. "So what do you want to do?"

"I want to call Gibson. If anyone brings me in, I want it to be him."

Duke hesitated another moment before nodding stiffly. "Okay then. That's what we'll do."

Twenty minutes later, a knock sounded on the hotel door.

Duke answered, but this time Andi didn't bother to hide. She stood near the entry, watching to see who was on the other side. She knew what was coming.

Gibson stood there in his state police uniform, two officers at his side.

Gone was his normally friendly demeanor. Instead, his chiseled face looked stony and his gaze hard.

His eyes flickered from Duke to Andi and then to Beau.

"I don't even want to know how long this happy arrangement has been going on, especially since I asked you outright if you knew where she was," he muttered.

"I'm sorry," Duke said. "I don't like to lie, but we had to figure a few things out first."

Gibson stepped toward Andi and took her arm. "I don't know what you've gotten yourself involved in, Andi, but it doesn't look good."

"I can vouch for her," Duke said. "We were together all evening, all night, and all morning."

Gibson sent him a look.

"Not like that," Duke explained. "But we've been together. There's no way Andi is responsible for this."

"She's not under arrest yet. Right now, we just want to ask her some questions." His gaze flickered back over to Andi. "Because even if she's not directly responsible for pulling the trigger, some people think she's still involved in some way."

She heard the undertones of accusation in his voice, and her defenses rose. Maybe calling him had been a bad idea.

"Who are you getting your information from?" Andi asked. "Victor Goodman or one of his cronies?"

"Victor Goodman? Why do you think he has anything to do with this?" Gibson's eyes widened with surprise.

Andi clamped her mouth shut, not saying anything else. "I should wait to say anything more. And I need to call a lawyer."

She knew exactly who she would call, but she'd have to swallow her pride to do so.

She wasn't sure what tomorrow was going to look like.

But this wasn't going to be the end of her. She promised herself that.

chapter
forty-one

DUKE HATED the helpless feeling that gripped him. More than anything, he wanted to protect Andi. Not because she'd asked. But because he cared about her— truly and deeply cared.

If Celeste wasn't in the picture, he would pursue Andi with abandon.

But right now, his hands were tied.

Part of him wanted to go to the police station. But Duke knew he wouldn't be able to sit with Andi. In fact, the best thing he could do was keep trying to find answers.

Though the team had come to Anchorage to discuss the Lights Out Killer—and though Duke still wanted that case resolved—right now, Andi was more important.

"What do you want to do?" Beau turned to him as they stood in the hotel room in stunned silence.

"Right now, I need to break the news about Andi to the rest of the team. I don't want to do it over the phone.

They deserve to hear this in person." He ran a hand over his jaw.

"Then?"

Duke blew out a breath. "Then we need to figure out what's really going on."

Beau nodded slowly. "I'm going with you."

"I'd expect nothing less."

Several minutes later, they were outside. Thankfully, there wasn't any fanfare to Andi being taken in. No reporters or parade of officers.

Maybe this could all go away quietly.

But as Duke glanced across the street, he spotted Helena on the sidewalk. Had she followed him?

His throat clenched at the thought.

He hoped he didn't regret trusting her.

She hurried across the street to meet him, anticipation in her voice. "That was your friend I just saw being led out of the hotel, wasn't it?"

Duke didn't say anything.

"Do the cops think she shot the senator?" Helena continued.

"I'm not at liberty to say anything." Duke continued walking.

"The media is going to be all over this." Helena's words came out fast as she kept pace with him. "You could give me the real scoop before all the other reporters fill in the details for themselves. You owe me that, at least."

"I don't owe you anything." Irritation pinched at him. "Like I said, I'm not at liberty to say anything."

She grabbed his arm and stopped him on the sidewalk.

Begrudgingly, he didn't move for a moment. He only glowered at Helena.

"It's going to look bad for your friend," she told him. "Especially when they figure out she lost her law license to some illegal practices not long ago."

So Helena had done her research. Duke shouldn't be surprised.

"There's more to that story." He didn't need to explain any more than that right now.

She stepped closer. "Why don't you tell me what that is?"

Beau seemed to sense Duke's rising frustration and stepped in. "This is a bad time. You should back off."

Helena's eyes flickered with surprise at his assertive tone, and she held up her hands. "I'm not trying to be aggressive. I know it doesn't seem like it now, but I'm just trying to help."

"You can help us by staying out of this." Duke continued walking again and charged past her toward his SUV.

He didn't want to waste any more time in this conversation.

∾

Andi was usually the one defending other people, not the one in the hot seat in the interrogation room.

Even though she hadn't officially been arrested, that was entirely what this felt like.

She'd asked for representation. It was only smart.

Then Andi had tracked down an old schoolmate of hers named Emilia Daughtry, who'd moved to Anchorage. She wouldn't call the two of them friends—not by any stretch of the imagination. In fact, for a while, they'd been sworn enemies.

But Emilia was smart and assertive. That was what Andi needed now.

Andi sat alone in the cold, dim interrogation room. She wished she had a jacket with her. Or water. Or a "get out of jail free" pass.

But when she'd refused to speak, a man named Detective Rasmussen had left her in here, almost as if she'd been forgotten. This was the same guy she'd seen working the Lights Out Killer case. Certainly he couldn't handle two high profile cases at once.

The man seemed gruff anyway with his shaved head, stocky build, and a face that had never dared a smile.

Andi figured it was only a matter of time before the feds took this over anyway.

For a moment, she felt claustrophobic.

Finally, Emilia arrived. She looked as glamorous as ever with her sleek blonde hair, expensive beige suit, and impeccable makeup.

Andi couldn't read her expression, but it seemed like a mix of pity and feeling like Andi must be stupid to get herself into this mess.

No doubt Emilia had heard Andi lost her law license. She'd probably delighted in Andi's humiliation.

Though Emilia shouldn't know any of the details, people jumped to conclusions when they heard things like that. She'd already experienced that multiple times. It had been one more reason she'd been glad to leave Texas.

"Long time no see." Emilia gently perched herself beside Andi, carefully crossing her legs and revealing her nude-colored heels. She was the picture of professional. "Not exactly the reunion I envisioned."

"Me neither if it makes you feel any better."

The smug expression quickly disappeared from her eyes. "What kind of trouble have you gotten yourself into this time?"

This time . . . the words dripped with derision.

In law school, Andi had discovered one of her professors was sleeping with a student and giving her passing grades because of it. The student just happened to be a friend of Emilia's. In true Andi fashion, she hadn't been able to let the issue go. She'd pushed and prodded until finally the professor was fired.

She regretted nothing.

Drawing in a deep breath, Andi did a quick run-through with Emilia on the basics of the past few days.

With each new fact, Emilia clicked her tongue as if she didn't approve of most of what she heard.

When Andi finished, Emilia said, "I don't think you should own up to any of this. It's too risky."

"I'm most worried about the shooting charge."

"As you should be. We need to find out what kind of evidence the police have that makes you look guilty." Emilia observed Andi coolly for another moment. "Something about this whole situation smells stinky. I don't think you're totally innocent, but I think there's more going on here than meets the eye."

"I'm being set up. Someone has been watching me, waiting for the right opportunity to pin something on me."

"And you walked right into it . . ." Emilia gave her a pointed look.

Andi frowned but nodded. "I did."

"You know the drill here." Emilia stood. "The cops are going to question you hard. Not let you get sleep. Try to wear you down until you confess. You need to stay strong."

Andi nodded. But the truth was, she already felt exhausted.

But she couldn't let that affect the fight she had left inside her.

She hadn't come this far to fail.

She wasn't going to start now.

chapter
forty-two

DUKE ARRIVED BACK at the rental house and took a
moment to compose himself before filling the group in on
what had happened. They'd gathered in the living room,
pensive expressions on each of their faces.

Their reactions were as he expected. Surprise.
Outrage. Concern.

"We can't just let Andi go to jail," Mariella said.

"Andi willingly turned herself in," Duke reminded
her. "At least, Gibson was with her. Even though he likes
to follow the law to the letter, I do believe he'll be fair.
Right now, there's really nothing we can do except to let
this play out—and maybe figure out who really did shoot
the senator."

"But what about the Lights Out Killer?" Matthew
pushed his glasses up higher on his nose as he waited for
Duke's response.

"I'm looking into the hockey angle." Duke glanced at

his watch. "I have a meeting with the manager in about thirty minutes. Maybe he'll have some answers."

"In the meantime, we can swing by the scene of the crime," Mariella said. "We'll go to Glassine's house and see if we can find out anything by talking to people in the crowd."

"Or by eavesdropping," Simmy added.

Mariella shrugged unapologetically. "Or by eaves-dropping."

"Good." Duke nodded. "You never know what you might find out."

"It sounds like a plan " Mariella rose as if ready to get busy now. "I just don't want to see anything happen to Andi."

"I know she'll appreciate that," Duke said. "But I also know Andi will want us to continue looking into this serial killer that's on the loose."

It didn't even feel right to investigate without Andi at his side. The two of them had become quite the partners in all the recent investigations.

But he had no choice. Right now, he needed to find answers.

Just as Andi expected, the feds had taken over. They'd questioned Andi, but she practiced her right to remain silent. It was the safest thing to do right now in this situation. Emilia agreed.

Andi didn't like being the one in the hot seat.

Not only that, but the charges she faced were serious. She'd broken into a senator's office. That could land her in prison.

The only comfort Andi found was in the fact she had an alibi for the time the senator had been shot. That had to count for something.

The problem was that she'd seen miscarriages of justice. They happened.

She prayed that wasn't the case now.

The agent interrogating her finally shook his head as if aggravated that he was getting nowhere.

He stood abruptly, his chair screeching across the floor. Then he stomped from the interrogation room.

Even if the police didn't press charges, they could hold her for twenty-four hours. She had no doubt they planned on doing just that. With the bad press the police had already received after so many deaths at the hands of the Lights Out Killer, they didn't need this shooting to stain their reputation as well.

They were anxious to put someone behind bars and appear competent.

A moment later, Gibson stepped inside. But he wasn't the same familiar old Gibson she'd known before. Right now, his gaze was stormy.

"My lawyer is gone," Andi reminded him. Emilia had taken a bathroom break.

"I wanted a moment to speak to you alone. The feds okayed it since I'm sure you're wondering."

The feds were hoping she'd open up to Gibson since they had a personal connection.

She crossed her arms. "I can't promise I'll talk."

"Then maybe you can just listen." He held an electronic tablet in his hand as he sat across from her. "I don't know what you've gotten yourself involved with."

"I think you know me well enough to know I'd never shoot somebody, especially a senator."

His cheek twitched. "That's not what the evidence says."

"I'm not sure what kind of evidence you're looking at, but I've never even had a face-to-face conversation with the senator."

His gaze remained unconvinced.

"What do you know that I don't know?" A trickle of fear shimmied down her spine.

He gave her a cold stare before punching something on his tablet.

Then he turned the screen toward her.

She sucked in a breath when she saw her image on the screen.

The footage was dark and grainy, but it clearly looked like Andi walking down a sidewalk at night.

Except she had something in her hand.

Was that a . . . gun?

Her heart beat harder. Her gaze shifted to the date at the bottom corner of the screen.

Last night. This video was from last night.

Her panic began to swell out of control, but Andi forced herself to hold it together.

The screen changed to another view of her. This time, Andi stopped in front of a house. Looked at it a moment. Glanced up and down the street. Then she rushed up the driveway, shoulders hunched as if trying to conceal her presence.

"Do you know whose house that is?" Gibson kept his voice clipped and professional.

Andi licked her lips. "I'm going to guess it's the senator's."

"This video puts you there at the time she was shot."

Andi swung her head back and forth. "But that wasn't me. I wasn't there last night. My whole team can back me up."

His expression remained unchanged. "Then how do you explain this video?"

Andi rubbed her throat as it began to tighten. "I have absolutely no idea."

chapter
forty-three

DUKE ARRIVED BACK at the sports complex just in time for his appointment.

This time when he walked in, a fortysomething man wearing a baseball cap, jeans, and a Seattle Seahawks jersey was waiting for him.

"Duke McAllister?" the man started.

"You must be Richard Blackmore," Duke said.

"The one and only."

The two shook hands.

"Why don't you come to my office." Richard nodded across the rink.

Duke followed him through a doorway on the other side of the building. Richard sat behind the desk, and Duke took a seat in front.

"What can I help you with? I understand from Pence that you have some questions."

"I'm following a lead." Duke explained about how all

the Lights Out Killer's victims had been to a hockey game and how he was looking for a possible connection.

"May I see their pictures? I've seen them on the news, but I wasn't really thinking about them in terms of hockey, I suppose."

"Of course." Duke pulled the pictures from his bag.

He watched Richard's expression as he flipped through each of the photos without saying a word.

The suspense was killing Duke. He couldn't read the man's expression.

The next moment, Richard set the pictures on his desk and looked up at Duke. "I do recognize a few of these faces."

Duke's breath caught. "Which ones?"

He pulled out Mark Williams's photo. "I believe Pence told you that this guy got into it with Raz."

"He did. Who else?"

He pulled out the photo of Jevonne Whitaker. "This guy wasn't as rowdy with Raz, but he made some smart comments. Raz actually found him after the game and confronted him about it." Richard shook his head. "I'm constantly on his case about getting his temper under control. He struggles with it."

"Was it a fistfight?" Duke asked.

"No, security broke it up. We know to always have security close to Raz."

"Was there someone else also?" Duke asked.

Richard pulled out a photo of Stuart. "This guy was

waiting for Raz out back. He just wanted to heckle him. Said Raz made him lose a bet with his friends, but he should have known better. It was the same old same old. Nothing really happened, but Raz got upset."

"But you don't remember the rest of the victims?"

"I can't say I do. I suppose I could look through old incident reports and talk to the players if you wanted me to."

"I may not need you to, but the police might." He was going to have to tell the authorities. He couldn't put it off any longer.

"There is one thing I think you should know," Richard said.

"What's that?"

"Raz has been on vacation in Canada for the past two weeks." He almost sounded apologetic. "So I don't think he's your guy."

Duke leaned back hard in his chair.

What? That couldn't be right. They'd come this far only to hit another dead end?

Suddenly, he felt like he was back to square one again.

And that was the last place that he wanted to be.

Gibson exited the interrogation room.

Andi was left alone—at least until Emilia came back.

Her panic grew stronger. The cold felt more biting. The darkness in the room deeper.

She couldn't stop replaying that video in her mind. The images of her in front of the senator's house were strongly incriminating.

But the truth had to be one of two things. Either someone who looked like her had made the video to confuse the police, or the video had been altered using some type of AI technology.

Those were the only options that made sense.

If the video had been altered, the person who'd done it had worked amazingly fast. He or she would have had to hack into more than one security camera system in order to change that video. All within a matter of hours after the shooting.

Which meant Andi had been set up all along. Someone had shot the senator in hopes of Andi taking the fall for it.

Who would do that?

Victor was the only person who made sense. He had both the resources and people in his pocket. In fact, it wouldn't surprise Andi if someone—or more than one person—here at the station was in his pocket.

That meant she wasn't sure who she could trust.

Last she'd heard, they were sending officers to the rental house to take statements from her friends. She knew everyone would validate her alibi. She prayed that was enough.

Andi wished there was more, something other than word-of-mouth.

But someone had gone to extremes to get her to this point . . . and she'd bet that person wouldn't back down easily.

chapter
forty-four

AS DUKE WALKED BACK into the rental house, he heard a vehicle pull up outside.

He waited in the doorway and saw Detective Rasmussen and another officer emerge from the car.

The detective stomped toward him while another officer trailed behind.

"I need to ask you and your friends some questions," Rasmussen said.

"About what?"

"About your friend and the senator."

Duke swallowed hard. "I figured the feds would have taken over."

"They did, but we're helping." The man scowled. "Now, enough talking. I have questions."

Duke hesitated one more minute before letting the men inside.

Everyone straightened when they saw the officers, pulling themselves to attention.

"I need to talk to you each one-on-one," Rasmussen muttered. "While I do that, my officer here will keep watch on the rest of you. No talking. We don't want any corroboration before you're questioned."

Duke glanced at the officer with him. Officer Rector. He remembered seeing the guy before.

"Now, who wants to go first?"

Duke raised his hand. "Why not me?"

"Very good then. Is there a room where we can talk in private?"

Duke led him down the hallway to an office.

Then he prepared himself for the questions.

The questions hadn't been as bad as Duke had thought. Then again, he had nothing to hide.

Neither did anyone else here.

He realized the police were just following protocol, but all he could think about was the time he was wasting.

Finally, Rasmussen and Officer Rector left.

Nearly as soon as the men stepped out the door, Duke's phone buzzed.

It was Helena. He'd given her the number to the burner he'd picked up.

He stepped away from the rest of the group to answer. "What do you want?"

Her aggressiveness after Andi was arrested still rubbed him the wrong way.

"In case I didn't say this earlier, I'm sorry about your friend," she started.

"We all are."

"And I'm sorry if I was pushy. I really do want to help." She let out a sigh. "I promised you I'd share anything I learned. I have a feeling I'm going to regret that promise. I want to be the first one to break this news. Can I trust you to keep this under wraps?"

News? She had news?

His spine went straight with anticipation. "All I care about right now is my friend. I don't care about ratings or advancing anyone's career. What did you learn?"

Helena hesitated another moment before finally saying, "It's about the Lights Out Killer. My source told me a hair was found on one of the victims—a hair they believe belongs to the killer."

Duke's heart pounded harder. "And . . . ?"

"They ran the DNA on it—they pushed it to the top of the queue. As you know, these things usually take months if not longer. But they got a match."

"Who was it?"

Duke held his breath as he waited for her answer.

chapter
forty-five

"I'M GOING to tell you this, but if you discover anything, you have to promise to tell me," Helena said.

"You have my word," Duke told her.

Helena hesitated another moment. "The hair belongs to a man named John Langston. He had a prior record for breaking and entering several homes in Anchorage about ten years ago."

"Did the police arrest this guy for the murders?" Duke stared out the window at the lake in the distance, his thoughts racing.

Helena frowned. "That's the thing. They can't."

"What do you mean they can't?"

"He's dead."

Duke froze. "Dead? Since when?"

"He died about six months ago. Apparently, during his time in prison, he turned his life around. When he got out he joined this cult-like religious group outside Anchorage. He kind of disappeared after that."

"Kind of?"

"His body was never found. But he's believed to have gotten lost in the wilderness, and everyone thinks he's dead."

Duke tried to hide his disappointment, but it was a struggle. His hopes had risen only to sink again. "Thank you for sharing this."

"Anything new on your end that you want to share?" Helena asked. "Remember, tit for tat."

He hesitated only a minute before telling her about the possible hockey connection. There could still be something to that theory. He'd already sent the police an anonymous tip.

"Good to know," Helena muttered. "I appreciate the information."

He ended the call and turned around to see Mariella standing there with her arms crossed. "What was that about?"

Tension stretched through Duke's chest. He probably should have mentioned his deal with Helena to Mariella and the team first. But he had to make the decision on the fly.

"That was a reporter here in Anchorage," he told Mariella. "She's been giving me some information."

Mariella tilted her head. "It sounds like you're giving her some information also."

"It's requiring a little bit of give-and-take on both of our parts. But if you want insider tips, then we need an inside contact. She has connections we don't."

Mariella's eyes narrowed as if she didn't accept that explanation. "You're also giving her information we could use on our podcast. She could report it first."

"Isn't the important thing right now that we get this guy behind bars? And that Andi is freed?" Certainly Mariella could see things from his perspective. They had to have their priorities.

"Of course, Andi being freed is important. But we also can't be giving away information we've worked hard to earn." Her gaze remained unwavering.

Duke shook his head, feeling an ache form there. "Look, I don't want to argue with you. I'm just trying to find answers, whatever the means."

"I just wish you'd asked us all first."

He swallowed hard, knowing she had a point. "You're right. I should have. But my objective is to put the bad guys behind bars, not to get ratings or to be the first one to crack something. I thought you would agree."

Based on the look on Mariella's face, she did agree—but she was still angry.

Andi curled her arms beneath her head as she leaned against the interrogation table. She wasn't sure how long she had been in here—they'd taken her phone and watch —but it felt like hours had passed.

Emilia had gone to her office to do some work there but promised to return. So she was alone again. Alone with her thoughts.

Sometimes that could be the worst place to be.

A person's mind could be their biggest asset or their biggest liability.

Finally, the door opened.

Gibson stepped inside, but Andi couldn't read his expression. Couldn't tell if he had good news or bad news. He stayed near the door, his body language stiff.

"My lawyer's not here," she murmured.

Emilia had given her an earful when Andi had told her about her prior conversation with Gibson.

"That's okay because we're letting you go," Gibson announced, no hint of emotion in his voice.

Andi flinched, certain she hadn't heard correctly. "You are?"

"We've had people examining that video, and they confirmed it was a deep fake."

Her heart beat faster. "I knew it!"

"We don't want to waste our resources investigating you when the real shooter is out there somewhere."

She stood, her thoughts suddenly racing. A touch of hope returned to her. "Have you talked to the senator? Maybe she could identify the person who did this."

"She's in a medically induced coma right now, so she's not talking to anyone."

Andi frowned. "And no one else saw anything?"

Gibson shook his head but not in response to her question—rather as a way of chiding her. "You're not a part of this investigation, Andi. I can't tell you that information."

"I get it." She raised her hand to indicate he should slow his thoughts. "But someone involved me, and now I need to figure out what's happening."

His expression remained stony. "That's a bad idea. I would stay as far away from the senator as you can, if you know what's best for you."

Andi decided to drop that subject and move on. "Are there any other charges being pressed against me?"

"Not yet. But it wouldn't surprise me if you're charged for breaking into the senator's office." He gave her a pointed look.

"I can't even fathom what evidence you might have to prove I was there."

Gibson said nothing.

That probably meant there *was* something out there. But Andi had been so careful to keep her face concealed from any cameras. Right now, however, Andi was thankful she hadn't said anything or owned up to being in the senator's office. She probably wouldn't be leaving right now if she had.

"So that's it?" She looked at Gibson. "I can just leave?"

"Yes, but you need to stay in this area."

Andi shouldn't be surprised. But she'd planned on going back to Fairbanks on Monday. Her bank account had been wiped out a month ago, and now she was living paycheck to paycheck. She had no doubt that Victor was behind what had happened, but she had no way of proving it.

She still had rent due and groceries to buy. She was making some money through the podcast but not enough to live on.

Still, she was thankful she wasn't behind bars right now.

"And Andi?" Gibson added.

"Yes?"

"You need to be careful."

There it was. A touch of the Gibson she knew. The one who was a friend not an enemy.

"I will be."

Gibson nodded to the door. "Get out of here. I have an officer lined up to give you a ride back."

Andi didn't waste any time doing just that. As soon as she stepped into the hallway, she spotted an officer there. Eisenhauer.

He'd been one of the cops looking for her after she broke into the senator's office.

He handed her the personal items they'd taken from her.

Then, without saying anything, he led her to his squad

car, opened the door for her, and she climbed inside. Andi would call Emilia in a moment and tell her what had happened.

Silence stretched the first several minutes of the ride.

Finally, Andi cleared her throat. "Any updates on the Lights Out Killer?"

She might as well try to find out some information while she had the cop's full attention.

"Like they'd tell me," Eisenhauer said, his voice emotionless and professional.

"I hope this guy is caught soon. It's terrifying to think he's out there."

"I think everyone in the area shares those sentiments. I know the police are doing everything they can to find this guy. So far, he's covering his tracks pretty well."

"For sure." Andi shivered as they continued down the road.

This guy wasn't going to give her any information.

But that was okay.

She'd take one victory at a time.

Then another thought hit her. How would she even pay for Emilia's services?

These legal bills were going to add up quickly.

She could ask . . . Alpine, she supposed. Andi frowned at the thought. The last thing she wanted to do was to take any more of his money.

She would figure that one out later.

Right now, she needed to focus on staying alive.

chapter
forty-six

EISENHAUER DROPPED Andi off at the rental house.

He waited for Andi to get inside okay before leaving.

As soon as Andi stepped through the door, everyone stopped what they were doing and stared at her.

Everyone except for Duke and Mariella, who were having some kind of stare-off.

The rest of the gang sat in the living room. But an undeniable tension stretched through the air.

Finally, Duke and Mariella broke eye contact and glanced at Andi.

Then the questions came.

"Are you okay?"

"I can't believe you're here!"

"I thought they were going to lock you up and throw away the key!"

"You look like you could use a warm meal."

"Let's give her some space and let her sit down." Duke took her arm and led her to a chair.

As she sat down, Mariella joined the gang in the living room. Simmy fixed her some tea. Once everyone was settled, Andi gave them the update.

They listened quietly.

"Does this mean you're a free woman?" Simmy asked.

Andi shook her head. "No, not necessarily. They're still keeping an eye on me. I'm still not sure how things will turn out."

"We're glad you're back with us," Mariella said.

"Very glad," Ranger added.

"I've been watching the internet for updates," Matthew said. "Nothing yet."

That was good news, she supposed.

Andi drew in a deep breath as she turned to everyone. "Anything new here?"

Duke cleared his throat. "There is one thing."

Was it Andi's imagination or did he look at Mariella when he said the words? And did Mariella scowl?

"I just heard from a reliable source that a hair was found at the scene of one of the crimes," Duke said. "The police just got the DNA results back, and the hair belongs to a man named John Langston."

Andi's heart pounded harder at the update. Maybe this guy could finally be stopped. Maybe people in the area would be safe.

"That's great news, right?" Simmy's voice rose with hope.

"Not necessarily." Duke twisted his neck as if it ached. "This guy . . . he's believed to be dead."

Andi's hopes plummeted.

"Believed to be dead?" Ranger repeated, his brow furrowing. "As in, no one has ever found a body?"

Duke nodded. "That's correct."

"Well, that certainly makes things more interesting." Ranger leaned back in his seat and shook his head.

"I'd say so." Duke blew out a long breath. "I'm not sure what all this means or how a dead man's hair might have gotten on one of the victims."

"Unless he's not dead," Simmy said.

"That's a possibility," Andi said. "Without a body, there's no proof."

"Do you know anything about this man?" Mariella's voice lilted, making it seem as if her gloomy mood may be lifting some.

"Only that he had a record of breaking and entering in Anchorage from about ten years ago. After serving time, he joined some type of cult outside Anchorage." Duke shrugged. "That's as far as I've gotten. I'm not really sure about any more details."

Mariella was already on her phone typing something in. "There's a religious cult called the Pioneers that meets outside of Eagle River. I wonder if that's the one they're talking about?"

"It could be," Duke said.

Then Mariella's eyes lit, and her back went straight. "This could be nothing. But back when I was an influencer, I did this segment once on toupees."

"What does that have to do with this?" Duke almost sounded annoyed—which wasn't normal for him.

What was going on?

Mariella gave him a sharp look. "I'm getting to that. What people don't usually think about is how toupees are made. Believe it or not, the high-quality ones aren't synthetic. They're made from actual human hair."

"Keep going." Ranger turned his finger in the air as if operating an imaginary wheel that he wanted to keep moving.

"A lot of times, companies get this hair from religious groups who, for spiritual reasons, grow their hair out for years and years, only to cut it as a part of certain rituals. Then these companies buy this hair from them, and it goes through this refining process where it's bleached and styled."

"I've never thought about it before," Ranger murmured. "So you think this hair may have come from a toupee?"

"This cult near Eagle River . . . they encourage members to let their hair grow out." Mariella still stared at her phone, spouting off facts as she came across them. "They only cut it as a religious practice on February 29— so every four years."

"So you think maybe this guy joined a cult, cut his hair there, and it was then made into a toupee that our killer is wearing?" Duke clarified.

Mariella shrugged. "It's a theory . . ."

"Do you think DNA would still be present on the hair even after it goes through the process to make it into a toupee?" Simmy leaned back and pulled a plum-colored blanket over her legs as if she were chilled.

Mariella shrugged again. "I think it's worth looking into."

Andi agreed. Maybe this was another lead.

Another viable lead.

chapter
forty-seven

I'M GETTING SLOPPY. I can't afford to get sloppy.

I raked my hand through my hair as I paced the sidewalk.

None of this was supposed to happen. How had things spiraled out of control like this?

I knew how.

It was because of Kate.

I shouldn't have ever gone out with her.

But after she'd seen that X on my chest and the anger in my eyes, I had no choice but to take care of her. I hadn't wanted it to be that way.

But I had to do what I had to do.

I'd grabbed a knife from the drawer. Before she realized what was happening, I plunged it into her jugular.

She hadn't even had time to scream.

Then I'd watched the life fade from her eyes.

For the first time, I felt regret.

She hadn't been on my list. If only she hadn't spilled that wine . . .

The moment replayed in my mind, and I rubbed my abdomen, the area where the wine had splashed. My blood heated at the memory.

I'd found a large lawn bag. Put Kate's body in it. Cleaned up the blood.

Then I had to leave for work. Later, I would dispose of her.

Which might mess up my plan to strike again tonight.

But I was on a streak. Every two days. I didn't want to mess that up.

Then again . . .

My every other day schedule was becoming too predictable. I could mix things up. Strike when it was unexpected.

The fire in my blood grew hotter.

Sure, Kate had died. I suppose she should count. I could add an X to her chest. Maybe sneak her body into her apartment.

But it was risky. I'd used a different knife.

And she wasn't one of *them*.

No, I'd decided that reporter should be next. She fit my narrative.

Kate didn't.

Kate's death would only confuse people.

I was getting more efficient and skilled now, and I decided I didn't even care if my next victim was home alone or not. I liked a good challenge.

Anyway, I'd quickly hidden Kate in my house—just in case anyone stopped by. Not that anyone ever did that. But I couldn't risk it.

My mind remained on her even while I was at work.

Hiding her in my house was the best I could do for now. I couldn't afford for one of my neighbors to see me acting out of character. I hoped none of them had seen her come to my door.

Inviting her to my house had been a mistake. A big mistake.

Later, I'd park in the garage. I would put her remains in my trunk. I'd have to be very careful to clean everything up. There couldn't be any hint that she'd been at my house.

My thoughts continued to race as I breathed in some fresh air while on my break.

A new thought hit me.

What if Kate had posted something on social media? And I needed to get rid of her car. Plus, she had friends. What if she'd told them she was coming to my place for lunch? They might come over to look for her.

Worry began to grip me.

And worry could lead to mistakes, and mistakes could lead to my downfall.

I couldn't let that happen. I rested my hands on my belt and sucked in a deep breath.

No, I *refused* to let that happen.

Things had to go off without a hitch.

It was the only way people would learn their lessons.

chapter
forty-eight

THE TEAM DECIDED to have a "situation room" meeting.

Andi knew she should probably be tracking down clues pertaining to her own personal case, but she needed to stay out of sight for now. So she stared at the murder board.

A new excitement swelled in her. With this latest development concerning the toupee, maybe they were onto something.

She added another piece of paper to the murder board: Evidence So Far. She grabbed a marker so she could add all their clues there.

"So this is what we can presume," she started. "The killer has an unusual gait. He drives a dark blue car. He uses an ulu. And he may wear a toupee."

"It's not much to go on," Duke murmured. "Tracking

down the person with those traits . . . it's nearly impossible. We still need something more."

Andi stared at the list and nodded. "I agree. Like *why* is he targeting the people he does? What's the common denominator?"

"Exactly." Duke nodded.

"I really thought we were onto something with that hockey lead," Andi said.

"So did I," Duke said. "But, at least on the surface level, I haven't found anything viable."

"So what else is there?" Matthew asked. "It would be nice if we could put someone's name under the Suspects category."

"I agree," Andi said. "But right now, we don't really have anyone."

"Get this, guys." Mariella sat up straighter, excitement lacing her voice. "There's actually a company here in Anchorage that makes toupees. Weird, right?"

"You could be onto something." Andi was feeling rather impressed with Mariella right now.

"We should definitely pay them a visit," Duke said.

"I agree, but tomorrow is Sunday." Andi took another sip of her tea, though it was lukewarm now. "There's a good chance the company will be closed."

Mariella tapped her phone screen again. "I have the name of the CEO, who lives here in Anchorage. Maybe we can pay him a visit."

Andi would have to sit out of that one. She was already in hot water. But she liked the idea.

"It can't hurt." Duke nodded slowly. "See what he says. See what kind of records or databases they keep on these people. If we could pinpoint this exact toupee and who purchased it, then we could find this killer and get him off the streets."

"Should we tell the police about our theory?" Mariella's gaze scanned each of their faces.

Andi had mixed feelings, especially considering everything that had happened today.

"What do you think?" Duke stared at her.

She blew out a long breath. "Let's think about that. It's not that I want to get the scoop before anybody else. The important thing is getting this guy locked up. In fact, maybe we should wait and see if this turns into anything first."

"Then that's what we'll do," Duke agreed.

The others nodded.

Andi hoped that decision was the right one.

Duke really wanted some one-on-one time to talk with Andi, but she'd disappeared into her room a good thirty minutes ago.

As everyone else split to do their thing, he gently

knocked on her door. She opened the door a few seconds later almost as if she'd been expecting him. "Come in."

He stepped inside and quietly closed the door behind him.

Andi walked back toward her bed. She'd changed into sweats and a T-shirt, and she'd pulled her hair back into a sloppy ponytail. Something about the look made her seem more vulnerable.

He sat on one end of the bed, and Andi perched on the other.

"What's with the tension in the house?" Andi pushed a stray hair behind her ear

Duke's gut clenched as he remembered his earlier conversation with Mariella. But he still stood behind his decision to talk to Helena. It was the right thing to do.

"Helena and I have been exchanging some information, and Mariella didn't approve of it," Duke admitted.

Andi nodded slowly as if contemplating his words—and her response. "I see. I guess you trust Helena?"

He shrugged. "I have no reason not to."

"But do you have any reason to?"

Her words were spoken like a lawyer.

He pressed his lips together, determined to give a thoughtful answer. "I looked Helena up, and she's legit. She's done some good work, especially on missing indigenous women. If we can combine our resources to find this guy, then why not do it?"

Andi bobbed her head up and down. "I see your point. But I see Mariella's point as well."

Their gazes locked.

"Justice is the most important thing," Duke stated.

"You're not going to get any arguments about that from me."

He studied her a moment, trying to read her thoughts. To figure out what was going through her mind. She was tough, but today had to have taken a toll on her.

"Are you doing okay?" he asked. "I mean, really okay? I've been worried about you."

Her lips twitched as if she was trying to figure out what to say. "Tonight definitely shook me up. I'm not going to lie. But I'm happy to be free now. I also realize I could be on borrowed time."

"Do you think Victor set you up?"

She crossed her legs beneath her and leaned back on her palms, her gaze burdened. "I think Victor sees this as a game. Some people, he'll eliminate if they get in his way. For some reason, I think he likes to toy with me. He wants to prove he's smarter."

Duke agreed with her assessment. Victor was a vile man. Duke had done his own research on the guy. A trail of trouble followed him wherever he went.

"Maybe that's because Victor knows you're the only person who can really bring him down," Duke said.

Andi's gaze didn't appear fully convinced. "Maybe. I

don't know. But if Victor is behind what's happening to me, that means he had one of his people shoot the senator and set the house next door on fire. That's extreme. I have a long list of people linked to him who are now dead. There are some powerful people on that list—commissioners and business owners and people in charge of calling the shots. But a senator? That takes it to a whole new level."

"It does. Maybe Glassine was threatening to go public with his blackmail."

"That's what I wondered as well. And how much do you want to bet that all those files are now gone?" Andi's gaze locked on his.

"But you still have copies," Duke reminded her.

"I do. And if I come forward with them then I'll be admitting I broke in. It feels like a no-win situation."

"You'll figure out the best thing to do," Duke murmured. "I know you will."

Andi swallowed hard, something in her gaze cracking. She looked away. "I hope so, Duke."

"Everything will be okay," he reassured her.

"I hope that's the truth. I'm hoping that tomorrow we'll find some answers. Otherwise . . . we might be out of time." A frown tugged at her lips as she said the words.

chapter
forty-nine

ANDI HAD HARDLY GOTTEN any sleep last night. Her thoughts were going too strong, too fast. Plus, a rainstorm had raged outside. Thunder had rumbled—a rare occurrence in this area, but the sound had reminded her of home.

She lay in bed on her back with her arms spread to her sides and staring at the ceiling.

She couldn't believe how close she had come to being locked up. If she wasn't careful, she'd be right back to where she started: with reservations to Cell 220 at the Hilton Prison Inn.

Although she felt certain Victor was behind this, she had no proof. However, if someone had doctored that security video, maybe the police would look into it. Maybe they could trace it back to the person responsible.

But it was doubtful.

After lying in bed and watching the sun come up over

the lake, she finally rose. There was no reason to stay in her room any longer. She had too much to do.

Instead, she showered and got dressed. By the time she entered the kitchen, Simmy was already making breakfast for everyone. The food smelled heavenly—especially the bacon.

Everyone else was up and called good morning as she found a seat at the table.

A moment later, a plate full of bacon, eggs, and pancakes was placed in front of her, along with a steaming cup of coffee.

"You are going to spoil me," she murmured as she took a sip.

"If anyone deserves to be a little spoiled today, it's you," Simmy said as she sashayed back into the kitchen to grab more food.

The woman was so sweet.

Andi wanted to know more about her. But she wouldn't ask. She'd wait for Simmy to share. But Andi had a feeling Simmy had come to this area fleeing from an abusive husband or boyfriend. That was what Andi picked up on through talking to her friend.

The group made casual conversation for several minutes until Duke stood. He grabbed a book from the table. A Bible.

"Normally, I'd go to church on Sunday, but I thought today I would read some Scripture, if that's okay."

Everyone murmured their confirmation.

"This morning, I felt led to this verse from Romans." He cleared his throat before starting. "And we know that in all things God works for the good of those who love him, who have been called according to his purpose."

"Interesting choice of Scripture," Simmy muttered. "It always reminds me of Esther and how we can be created for such a time as this."

Esther? Andi mused.

Beau had said Andi could be a modern-day Esther.

The Bible story had come up twice now in two days.

Coincidence?

Maybe not.

Maybe Andi was in just the right place at the right time to do what was needed. But she had to stay strong in the battle.

"I know that's a popular verse, but it's also a great reminder for all of us." Duke paused. "None of our lives are insignificant. We're all on this planet for a purpose, and whenever God shines bright, the darkness will try even harder to close in."

"Maybe you should be a preacher if this tour guide thing doesn't work out," Ranger said.

Duke chuckled. "I don't know about that."

Then Duke lifted a prayer, and they began to divide up the tasks for the day.

But Andi's thoughts remained on what he'd said. *We're all on this planet for a purpose.*

She thought she knew hers: to stop the evil that occurred wherever Victor Goodman went.

Like any good soldier, she had to be willing to risk everything for success.

Their time was running out. Everyone was leaving tomorrow—everyone but Andi.

She'd have to stay until the police released her. Which meant that after the murder club wrapped up here, she'd need to find a place to stay, which would be challenging since she didn't have any money.

Andi suppressed a sigh. She'd figure something out.

She always did.

"Um, guys . . ." Matthew stared at his phone. "There's another victim. The news headline just showed up. He's broken his pattern of striking every other day."

Duke had been assigned to go visit the owner of the toupee company.

While he did that, Simmy and Ranger would track down more friends and family of the victims, and Matthew and Mariella would get some footage of Anchorage for the video portion of their podcast.

On his way out, Duke picked up Beau at the hotel and gave him an update.

"Do you think Suzie is okay?" Beau asked.

Heaviness settled on Duke. "I talked to her earlier, and she sounded fine. She's staying with a friend for a while."

"I can't believe someone would target her." Beau shook his head.

"Only because they're targeting Andi and everyone she cares about." Disgust churned in his stomach at the thought.

"Speaking of Andi . . . how is she today?" Beau asked.

"Nothing's going to make her back down. She still has that fire in her eyes."

Beau smiled. "I bet she does. I hope she comes out of this unscathed."

"You and me both." He swallowed hard as the words left his lips.

Downtown Anchorage blurred by as they headed out of the city. At least, the day was beautiful, and the sun hung brightly in the sky.

Everywhere you turned in Alaska, the view was breathtaking.

A moment of silence passed until Beau asked. "Any updates on Celeste?"

Duke's jaw tightened as it always did when her name was mentioned. "No, not recently. Every lead I've followed has dried up. I don't even know where to look anymore."

"Keep looking. Eventually you'll find answers."

He tried to hold on to that hope, but it was beginning to fade. "I have a feeling that woman I saw who looked like

Celeste is long gone. Probably not even in Alaska anymore."

"You really think it could have been Celeste?" Beau stole a glance at him.

"I ask myself that nearly every day, and I'm still not 100 percent sure."

Before they could talk about it anymore, they pulled to a stop in front of a grand house located in the Hillside East neighborhood.

Ashcroft Gardner lived here. He had started Hair Master twenty years ago.

They were arriving unannounced. He wasn't sure if that would work to their advantage or not.

They parked and strode up the hilly driveway to the white-and-black modern-looking house with large windows.

They rang the doorbell and then waited.

A woman with blonde hair piled high on her head, an unnaturally dark tan, and a tailored purple dress answered. She looked confused by their presence.

Julie Gardner.

Duke had looked her up.

"I'm not interested in buying anything," she told them, her voice clipped.

"We don't have anything to sell." Duke kept his voice easy, not wanting to frighten her. "We're investigators, and we'd like to speak to your husband if possible."

She eyed them curiously. "What's this pertaining to?"

"His company. We think he has information that could help us stop a killer." Duke paused, trying not to overwhelm her. "I promise, it'll only take a couple of minutes of his time."

She stared at them another moment before finally shaking her head and stepping back. "I don't think this is a good idea."

She started to close the door, but Duke reached out his hand.

Julie stared at it, a trickle of fear in her gaze.

He quickly removed his hand and held it up as a peace offering. "It's about the Lights Out Killer. We believe there's a connection to your husband's company, and we're trying to find some answers."

"The Lights Out Killer?" Her hand went over her heart.

"Yes, ma'am," Duke said. "He struck again, and now it's more urgent than ever to figure out who this guy is before he kills someone else."

She stared at them another moment as if contemplating what to do. Then she let out a puff of air. "One minute."

She closed the door and a lock turned.

"We'll see if she comes back," Beau muttered.

Duke figured they had a fifty-fifty chance.

But in the meantime, he'd wait. He had to figure out some way to talk to Ashcroft, and he didn't have time to play any games.

After what seemed like five minutes had passed, the door finally opened again.

A man in his fifties answered. He had a wrinkled complexion that had seen too much sun, gleaming white teeth, and a full head of dark, age-defying hair. Based on his shorts and polo, he was about to play golf.

He was probably a good twenty years older than Julie.

"I hear you're looking for me," he started.

"That's right," Duke said. "I'm Duke, a true crime podcaster and former Army CID. This is my brother, Beau. Before we go to the police with this information, I thought it was important to verify it first. I don't want to cause any trouble if there's no need for it."

"You think this somehow ties in with my company?"

"I think it's a good possibility."

"I'm curious to hear what you have to say," Ashcroft said.

Instead of inviting them into his house, Ashcroft stepped outside and nodded to seats on a patio at the front of his house. "Let's talk out here."

Duke understood the man's caution.

He found a seat on a black metal chair.

Then he dove into his reason for coming.

chapter
fifty

ANDI HATED BEING HERE at the rental house and not doing anything.

Mostly she'd been pacing and unproductive.

And she also hated being unproductive.

But she understood why the group thought she should stay here. The more she could stay out of sight and off of the radar the better. Plus, the more she went out, the more opportunities Victor might have to frame her for something.

How was Andi going to prove he was the one responsible for killing her friend and colleague back at the law firm in Texas? For killing a long list of other people?

Based on what she'd seen so far, she couldn't.

The man was slippery. Clever. Resourceful.

She had no doubt he'd covered his tracks. Even if the police tracked down the person who'd shot Glassine, it wouldn't trace back to Victor.

Andi paused near the window in her room and let out a long breath. She needed to do something tangible. Being alone with her thoughts would make her go mad.

She'd look at those papers again, she decided. Maybe something different would stand out to her.

She spread them out on her bed and began reading through all the various files.

She stopped on one.

It was about the impact of this new oil reserve on indigenous people living in that area. According to studies, it would seriously affect their lifestyle. The caribou they depended on would be diverted from their normal migrations. Pollutants could hurt the food supply around the Arctic Ocean.

They'd fiercely opposed the project.

Until they didn't.

Two months ago, their suits had been dropped. Most of the community had changed their tune and decided the oil project would be good for them and maybe even offer jobs.

Something about this didn't ring true.

They'd been paid off, hadn't they? It was the only thing that made sense.

They'd been given money in exchange for their cooperation—and no doubt an iron-clad contract had been written up and signed.

Those people probably didn't even realize the rights they'd signed away or what this would mean for them.

Money wouldn't preserve their lifestyle—one that had existed in their communities for hundreds of years.

Her thoughts raced.

Before she could explore that anymore, she heard the front door open. Someone must be back.

She rose, anxious to see who it was and to hear what they had learned.

But as she padded down the hallway, she froze.

It wasn't a member of the murder club.

It was a man wearing a black mask and a gun in his hand.

"So you believe someone wearing one of my toupees might have murdered somebody . . . or several people?" Surprise tinged Ashcroft's voice. "That he might be the Lights Out Killer?"

"We believe that the murderer is either the person wearing the toupee or the donor," Duke said. "That's what we need your help on. Do you know if the DNA remains intact during your process?"

Ashcroft blew out a breath. "They don't have the hair follicle intact, which is where experts normally extract DNA. However, recent advancements have made it so scientists can actually get DNA from the hair itself—even hair from thousands of years ago."

"Do you keep record of who the donations come from?" Beau asked.

Ashcroft nodded. "We do. Of course I don't have that information here at my home."

"If you have a record of the donor, do you have a record of which toupee their hair was used for, and who purchased it?" Duke held his breath as he waited for the man's answer.

Ashcroft's gaze shifted before he looked back at them. "We keep records of which of our certified salons these toupees go to. These salons may keep a record of each toupee and which client has bought it."

"How can you find out that information?" Duke asked.

Ashcroft's eyes wavered back and forth a moment before he shook his head and shrugged, almost as if overwhelmed. "I'll see what I can find out for you. But it will take a while to go through all those records and call the salons. Most of them aren't even going to be open today."

"This is important," Duke reminded him.

"I want to see this guy off the streets just as much as anybody. My vice president knows the cousin of one of the victims. I know it's a distant connection, but still . . . it's unnerving."

"It definitely is," Duke agreed. "I guess in the meantime, we can assume this killer is wearing a toupee. It's something to look for."

Ashcroft touched his head, pride gleaming in his eyes. "Our toupees look very realistic and lifelike. I'm not sure if you see someone wearing one that you'll know it's even a toupee. That's always been our goal."

Duke studied the man. Other than the fact his hair looked thick and unusually dark, Duke supposed it looked natural. If the piece was worn by someone younger, whom people didn't know was bald, then maybe it wouldn't be noticeable.

But at least they had something to go on now.

"We'll keep that in mind," Duke said.

"Also, you should know that many men who are our clients are often in their early thirties, some even in their twenties," he added. "Especially the ones who are single and not ready to appear older. Our clientele would probably surprise you."

Duke extended his hand. "Thank you for your help. And if you could let us know as soon as you learn something, that would be great."

Duke reached into his pocket for a business card and frowned when he realized the only one he had left was the original pink and glittery one that Mariella had designed.

Ashcroft gave him a look as he took it, and Duke shrugged.

"Will do." Ashcroft paused as if having second thoughts. "Are you going to tell the police about this in the meantime?"

"I have a feeling that it might be beneficial."

Ashcroft nodded. "I'm inclined to agree."

Now Duke and Beau would head back to the house to find out what everyone else had learned.

chapter
fifty-one

ANDI DARTED TOWARD HER ROOM.

But as soon as she ran through the doorway, the man caught up.

He tackled her to the floor.

Her head hit the wood with a thud.

Her vision blurred, and an ache torpedoed through her head.

The man flipped her over and sat on top of her, his gun still raised.

"You think you're so smart," he growled.

Her jaw hardened with stubborn determination. "I don't know what you're talking about."

"You just don't know when to back off."

"Never. You never back off when evil men try to gain more power." At those words, she lunged at him.

Her fingers dug into his eyes until he howled with pain.

But he didn't move off her. He kept her pinned by his weight.

Andi kicked, her knees hitting the man's back.

Raged filled his eyes. "You're going to regret that!"

Metal hit her temple as the man's gun collided with her head.

More pain ripped through her. Stars flashed in front of her eyes, and her head swirled.

His other hand fisted and slammed into the side of her mouth.

Blood covered her tongue, and she let out a moan.

"Don't make me do that again," the man growled. "You need to back off. Because this is your only warning."

"And if I don't back off?"

"You don't want to know what will happen then." The man raised his fist as if he might hit her again.

Then a noise sounded in the background.

The door closed.

Was someone else here?

And if this man saw them, would he finish one of her friends off too?

Panic gripped Andi.

She couldn't let that happen.

Duke stepped into the rental house, set his keys on the kitchen counter, and paused.

Where was everyone?

He hadn't expected to beat the rest of the crew home.

Andi must be in her room. Was she sleeping? She'd had a long, hard day yesterday so some rest would be good for her.

"What now?" Beau crossed his arms and leaned against the kitchen counter.

Duke's gaze wandered down the hallway. While part of him wanted to let Andi sleep, the other part wanted to check on her.

"Give me a minute to see if Andi has figured anything out." Before Duke could second-guess himself, he strode down the hallway.

He gently rapped on Andi's door and waited to see if she answered.

A moan sounded on the other side of the door.

His heart rate ratcheted as he threw the door open.

Andi lay there, blood drizzling from her mouth, half of her face swollen, and a bruise already forming at her eye.

He fell on his knees beside her. "Andi?"

She tried to lift her head but squirmed as if it hurt. Finally, she pointed behind her.

Duke saw the open window.

Had the person who'd done this to her just run away?

"Beau!" he called.

His brother appeared.

"Stay with Andi," Duke murmured. "I need to see if I can catch whoever attacked her."

Beau raced toward her.

As he did, Duke propelled himself out the window.

chapter
fifty-two

DUKE PAUSED OUTSIDE and glanced around.

Where had that guy gone?

Just then, he spotted a figure in the distance, near another house.

Duke sprinted toward him.

From what Duke could see, the man was dressed in all black. But Duke couldn't make out any other details.

All he knew was that if he got his hands on this man after what the guy did to Andi . . .

He might lose his religion.

He pushed himself as hard as he could past one of the lake houses. Then another.

The guy kept running, surprisingly fast.

Thankfully, no one was outside. Duke didn't want any innocent bystanders to get hurt.

As he passed another house, the guy darted toward the front yard.

Just what was this guy planning?

Duke veered around the other side of the house, hoping to cut the man off at the pass.

But just as Duke reached the driveway, he paused and looked around.

The man was gone.

He couldn't have just disappeared like that. So where was he?

Duke sucked in several slower breaths as he looked for any signs of movement.

The guy wasn't going to win.

Duke wouldn't let that happen

"Can you stand?" Beau asked.

Andi cringed thinking about it. But she couldn't continue to lie here on the floor.

She lifted her hand, and Beau took it. Carefully, he helped her to her feet.

Pain ripped through her skull, and her head pounded.

She didn't think anything was broken, but she was definitely bruised.

"Let's go to the living room," Beau murmured.

He led her down the hallway and placed her in a chair in the living room. Then he ran to get her a bag of ice and a damp cloth to wipe away the blood.

All she could think about was Duke.

Had he caught this guy?

Was Duke okay? That man had a gun, and Andi had no doubt he'd use it.

Part of her was surprised the man hadn't finished her off right away.

Why threaten her instead of killing her?

Unless Duke was right. This was a game to Victor.

Beau handed her the compress, a concerned expression on his face.

"I'm not going to ask you what happened yet because I know Duke will want to know." Beau frowned, still studying her injuries. "I don't want you to have to repeat it."

"Thank you," Andi croaked out.

"Let me get you some water also." He rose and went to the kitchen.

Water ran.

Everything that just happened still seemed so surreal.

Unthinkable.

Maybe even . . . desperate.

Was Victor getting desperate? Did that mean she was getting closer? That Andi was making him nervous?

Suddenly, the front door opened.

Her entire body tensed. Was the gunman back?

How had he gotten inside in the first place? Had he picked the lock? It was the only thing that made sense.

Andi looked up. Thankfully, it was Duke this time.

He rushed toward her and knelt in front of her. "Are you okay?"

She barely heard him. "Did the guy get away?"

His expression hardened. "He had a motorcycle stashed in the woods. When I realized where he went, it was too late. He was already on the bike and gone. I need to call the police."

Andi grabbed his arm. "No, don't do that."

Duke paused and stared at her, his breath coming in shallow gulps. His emotions looked barely restrained.

Finally, he said, "You need to tell the cops what happened. And you need an ambulance so you can be checked out."

"I'll be fine. I don't want to be on the police radar anymore. If they come and ask me questions, I'm going to have to fess up and admit that I broke into the senator's office."

Duke remained quiet a moment until his shoulders slumped. "What happened?"

Andi ran through the details with him, and he listened.

When she finished, Duke took a cloth from Beau and gently dabbed her wounds.

The tenderness of his touch did something strange to Andi's heart. It made her want to reach out. To touch his face. To bury herself in his arms.

For some reason, the thought terrified her.

chapter
fifty-three

WORD WAS GETTING out about my newest victim.

I smiled as I sipped my coffee and watched the crowd in the distance.

Like a dog salivating over food, I couldn't wait to hear people's reactions. To smell their fear. To see the way they cowered like injured prey fleeing a hunter.

My craving was unquenchable.

I'd had a change of plans last night.

I'd planned on targeting Ms. Helena Gray. I had the plan all worked out. The power cut.

Then her friend had shown up, and I'd had to hide.

My gaze darkened, but I quickly corrected it. If I wasn't careful, someone might see me.

I couldn't get sloppy. I'd heard about the hair that had been found.

That wasn't supposed to happen.

No more mistakes.

Last night, I'd had to change my plans.

I didn't like changing my plans.

But I couldn't risk it.

I could have been recognized. Then my plan would be ruined.

So I'd moved on to Plan B. Things had gone swimmingly.

I'd even had time to dump Kate's body.

Finding her would probably confuse investigators. But that was okay. They were already confused. The more confusion, the better.

Tonight, things would go off with a big bang.

I'd finally send my message.

People would pay attention.

Would that be enough for me? I wasn't sure.

I'd have to play that one by ear.

I took another sip of my coffee before tossing the cup in the trash.

I got off work at six. I wouldn't have much time after that.

But I just knew my plan would work. I'd been collecting everything I needed for weeks. I'd been studying layouts. Making sure every detail was attended to.

I touched the X on my chest.

Tonight, people would pay.

chapter
fifty-four

EVERYONE RETURNED to the house ten minutes later.

Duke watched as they spotted Andi's injuries.

He saw the concern on their faces.

They all sat down, and Andi explained what had happened.

He was worried about her. He shouldn't have left her alone. But he'd honestly thought she'd be safer here at the rental house than out in the field with him.

He'd been wrong.

After Andi finished explaining , he sensed she needed a break. He turned to Ranger and Simmy.

"How about you guys?" he asked. "Did you find out anything?"

The two glanced at each other and frowned.

"Not really," Simmy murmured. "I'm sorry. I wish there was something . . ."

"I did some more research," Mariella said. "Into that cult. I might be able to head out there tomorrow to talk to some members."

Ranger's phone buzzed, and his entire body went tense.

"Is everything okay?" Duke watched Ranger, curious about his reaction. He sensed bad news.

His eyes narrowed. "No, it's not."

"What's wrong?" Simmy rushed.

He held up his phone where a picture of a school-aged girl was displayed. "This is my daughter."

"You have a daughter?" Surprise rippled through Andi's voice.

Duke was thinking the same thing. He had no idea, even though he *had* seen Ranger looking at a picture of a girl one time. He'd wondered about the story behind it.

He waited to hear what else Ranger had to say.

"Who sent you that picture?" Andi's voice sounded weaker than she would have liked.

Trembles had overtaken her. She couldn't stop them, no matter how hard she tried. In fact, the harder she tried to control them, the more intense the shaking became.

Duke had draped a blanket over her then started a fire and moved her closer to the flames.

But nothing would stop her quivers. She knew what it was: adrenaline from almost losing her life.

Even what Ranger had said wouldn't distract her.

She blinked, desperate to focus on what Ranger was telling them.

"I don't recognize the number." Fire flashed in his gaze, and he lifted his lip in a snarl.

He wasn't someone to be messed with.

And that was *exactly* what someone was doing.

First, Duke had gotten pictures of his sister.

Now Ranger had gotten a photo of his mysterious daughter.

"Do you want to tell us anything about your daughter?" Mariella asked.

His gaze darkened. His face tightened. His shoulders seemed to snap into a brooding position.

"She's older here than when I saw her last. She would be ten now." He showed them the picture again.

The girl wore a heavy coat, and the background behind her showed snow and a barren landscape.

"How did someone get that picture?" Duke asked.

"I don't know . . . especially since she drowned two years ago," Ranger finally said, his voice low and hardly discernable.

"What?" Simmy slapped her hand over her mouth. "How?"

"She was left unsupervised and probably got curious. The water . . . it's to be revered. Not something anyone should be in while alone. I told her that many times. But she was strong-willed. And her mom . . . " He didn't finish the statement.

"Where did that even happen?" Mariella seemed to mutter the question without thinking it through.

His gaze darkened even more. "Russia."

Andi's eyebrows flung up. Russia?

Exactly what was Ranger's story? Of everyone here, he was the most private.

He might have good reason for it.

He pressed his lips together, clearly not wanting to say more.

A knock at the door sliced into the silence.

This house was like Grand Central Station it seemed.

"Stay where you are," Duke grumbled before he strode toward the door.

His body language made it clear he was bracing himself for the worst.

So was Andi.

chapter
fifty-five

DUKE REACHED for the gun holstered at his waist and slowly opened the door.

Gibson stood on the other side.

Duke lowered his hand, making sure his shirt covered the gun, and then welcomed Gibson inside. "I wasn't expecting to see you here."

Duke still thought Gibson was one of the good guys. He'd only been doing his job yesterday when he questioned Andi. Yet it was still hard not to have any hard feelings about it.

"Sorry to stop by unannounced," Gibson paused just inside the house, dressed casually in jeans and a black T-shirt that showed his many tattoos.

He was someone who made Duke wonder. What exactly was his past? He had a rebel vibe to him, yet he was a cop. Those two qualities didn't always gel.

"Are you here to arrest me?" Andi stood from her

chair and lifted her chin.

"No, I'm not—" Gibson stopped mid-sentence when he saw Andi. His eyes narrowed, and he stepped closer. "What happened to you? And don't tell me 'long story.'"

Andi and Duke exchanged a look, and Duke knew Andi was contemplating how much she should say.

"Just tell me." Gibson's words sounded clipped. "I'm here as a friend."

Andi hesitated another moment, a distant look in her eyes. Then she snapped back to reality and pulled herself together. "Someone broke into the house and warned me to back off."

His hands went to his hips, and his furrowed brow made it clear he wasn't happy. "Did you call the police?"

"No, I didn't." Andi's voice sounded listless. "I don't want anything to do with the police right now. They're just going to ask me more questions I don't want to answer."

Gibson opened his mouth as if to say more but then shut it again.

Duke turned toward him. "Did you figure out who shot the senator?"

"Do you mind if I sit down?" Gibson pointed to a chair in the living room.

"Be our guest," Duke said.

As Gibson sat in an upholstered wingback, Duke grabbed a wooden chair from the dining room and pulled it into the group.

"We're still trying to figure out who shot the senator," Gibson said. "Her office was broken into and some of her files were stolen."

"I didn't steal anything." Defensiveness rose in Andi's voice.

"You didn't," Gibson said. "This just happened last night."

"I suppose you don't know who did that either?" Beau stared at Gibson, waiting for his answer.

"We don't," Gibson said. "We're trying to figure out what's on those missing files."

Duke continued to think everything through. "Did you talk to her staff?"

"We're working all the angles. For now, I was hoping you might know what was in those files that was worth shooting the senator for." Gibson stared at Andi, waiting for her to respond.

Was this a trap? That was what Andi kept thinking.

Yet she was so tired of keeping things to herself. So tired of Victor getting away with crimes.

"I may be able to find some copies of some of the files to give to you . . . anonymously, if you catch my drift," Andi said.

Gibson shifted. "I *am* an officer of the law."

"Those are my terms." Andi crossed her arms. "I don't

want to put you in a precarious position, but I also don't want to go to prison. It seems like the most important thing here is finding out who shot the senator, am I right?"

"If you give me the files, I'm sure I can work something out concerning the potential charges against you. How does that sound?" Gibson stared at her, waiting for her response.

"That sounds perfect," Andi said.

She found her phone, hit several buttons, and then sent the photos she'd taken to Gibson's email.

He scrolled them briefly before glancing back up. "So what's your theory?"

"I think Victor paid off the indigenous people living near the potential new oil reserve so they'd drop their lawsuits, thus eliminating one more obstacle to the project being completed. I think that's what he's doing—eliminating people who get in his way."

"Like Glassine?" Gibson asked.

"Like Glassine. Like me. He thinks he's untouchable."

Gibson rose to his feet. "He doesn't have anything to hold over me. And I just happen to know he's in town. Maybe I'll go pay him a visit." His gaze traveled to meet each person's in the room before stopping on Andi's. "And, no, none of you can go with me. I will, however, request an officer be stationed outside this house—especially since it's clear you guys are targets."

chapter
fifty-six

THE GROUP SAT in silence a minute after Gibson left.

They had a lot to think about.

The Lights Out Killer and his newest victim.

Victor Goodman, and the fact that Gibson was going to talk to him.

The fact that Andi had been assaulted.

The picture that Ranger had received.

Everything felt like too much. Where did the team even go from here?

Duke's phone buzzed, and he saw that it was Helena. She asked if they could meet.

His stomach tightened at the thought. He knew she was a sore subject, but he wasn't going to back down either.

He turned to address the group. "Would you guys mind if Helena came by? She has something she wants to share with us."

His gaze slid to Mariella. He was especially curious about her reaction.

"Something pertaining to the case?" Mariella's voice sounded more clipped than usual.

"Yes," Duke said. "We could be territorial here and move at the speed of a snail. Or we could work together to do what's right. What's important is stopping this guy. I think you all agree with me, am I right?"

Andi must be rubbing off on him. That was normally what she said.

Everyone in the group nodded right away, except Mariella.

Instead, she opened her mouth as if to argue only to shut it again. "You're right. That is the most important thing. I just want it to be a team decision and not something a lone ranger decides."

He understood that.

Duke texted Helena back, glad that everyone had seen things his way. He didn't want to waste time trying to persuade anyone. They really did have to have their priorities straight here. They had to keep their eyes on what was important.

He glanced at Andi again. She looked tired. Beat-up. But the fire remained in her eyes.

Then he glanced at Ranger. He looked as if he was in another world.

Simmy sat beside him, an arm placed on his shoulder as if she desperately wanted to comfort him.

Beau had stood and moved around some—probably because he couldn't sit very long because of his injuries as a POW. He hid them well, but Duke knew when his aches and pains flared.

Then there were Mariella and Matthew. They'd recently learned that the parents they'd grown up with weren't their real parents. They barely had time to comprehend that before they'd come here to work on this case.

They were each carrying burdens. Heavy, heavy burdens.

But they'd all been brought together for a reason. To find answers. Maybe to find comfort in each other. Maybe to help each other.

All that was yet to be seen.

But they had to stick together. Because they were stronger that way.

A cord of three strands cannot be broken.

Nor could a cord of six.

Helena arrived fifteen minutes later.

As Duke waited for her, he stepped outside and saw the cop there.

He sucked in a breath. It was the same one who'd been searching for Andi. Eisenhauer.

Certainly the man knew by now what had happened.

Would he recognize Duke? Charge him as an accessory?

Things could still go south quickly.

Before Duke could step back, the man saw him and nodded. "Everything okay in there?"

Duke nodded. "It is. Thanks."

"Let me know if you need me." His eyes narrowed. "Have we met before?"

Duke swallowed hard and shook his head. "I don't think so."

But the man's gaze lingered on him a moment too long.

Helena rushed up then, her eyes dancing with excitement. Duke ushered her inside and introduced everyone.

The group greeted her as she joined their circle, sitting in the chair Duke had been using.

She held a narrow pad of paper in her hands as she looked at the group. "It's nice to meet you all. Thank you for letting me come."

"You heard there was another victim?" Duke already knew the answer.

Helena's lips tightened. "I heard. They haven't released any information on him yet. It's enough to make you uneasy, isn't it? In fact, my lights went out last night."

"What?" Duke's voice rose with concern.

"I thought for sure I was a goner." Helena rubbed her throat. "I even picked up the phone, ready to call the police before this guy finished me off. But it was raining, and I even heard thunder. So I thought maybe it was the storm . . ."

"What happened?" Andi asked.

"There was a knock at the door. I didn't think the killer would knock, but who knows, right? It's not like any of the victims have survived to tell us." Her voice cracked as she said those words. "Then I heard a voice, and I realized it was my friend. Sometimes I think he showed up in the nick of time. And other times I think I was being paranoid."

"Did you check around the house to see if the electricity had been cut?" Duke asked.

Helena nodded. "The breaker had been flipped, but sometimes that just happens for no good reason."

"Video cameras?" Andi asked. "You seem like the type who would have them, am I right?"

"They went out with the electricity." Helena's gaze clouded with worry.

"We also have an update," Andi offered.

She told Helena about their toupee theory.

"That's brilliant," Helena muttered. "Good work."

Mariella's cheeks may have reddened with a blush.

"I wanted to tell you one other thing." Helena adjusted the way she sat in the chair. "The police found another body this morning, in addition to this latest victim."

"Wait . . . this guy struck twice last night?" Mariella rubbed her arms as if chilled.

"That's the strange thing," Helena said. "I don't know that it was the same guy. I mean, this body was found off the Coastal Trail near Elderberry Park. I heard someone say she was a nurse."

"Was she also stabbed?" Duke asked.

"She was. But here's the weird part. She was stabbed in the jugular. But on her chest, there's the start of a mark." Helena straightened her hand and slanted it over her heart as if to demonstrate where the mark was. "It's almost like somebody started to make an X, but then stopped."

"Do you think he got interrupted after he killed her?" Beau asked, sounding confused, "Maybe didn't have time to finish carving the X?"

"I have no idea," Helena said. "Maybe he made a mistake. Killed the wrong woman. Decided not to mark her like the others."

"Maybe, but that doesn't sound like this guy," Duke said. "He seems meticulous."

"Every killer messes up sometimes." Helena reminded him. "I was at the crime scene myself covering it, and I actually caught a glimpse of this woman when the medical examiner arrived." Her voice caught. "She was wearing this yellow sundress, and obviously blood was all over it. But on the belly area . . . there was this noticeable red mark."

"More blood?" Mariella asked.

Helena shook her head. "No, I don't think it was blood. It almost looked like . . . a wine stain."

"You think this woman spilled wine on herself?"

"It happens." She shrugged. "But that made me think . . . what if she was out on a date or something when she died? Is that thought crazy?"

"So you're saying the serial killer has a dating life?"

"Or he could be married. Who knows? I have no idea what I'm saying right now," Helena said. "But I was hoping that you guys might be able to help me figure all this out."

chapter
fifty-seven

ANDI LIKED HELENA. The woman was smart and driven. In fact, if they ever looked for another team member . . . maybe Helena would fit the bill.

They'd just have to convince Mariella of it first.

Their fearless spokesperson still seemed uneasy about Helena's presence.

Mariella clearly saw Helena as a threat.

Did Alpine have anything to do with Mariella's viewpoint? Was he pushing Mariella to be number one on the charts? Mariella came from a world where numbers were everything. A world where to be successful, you needed to be the best. Where you looked out for yourself.

But Andi didn't think like that. Not by a longshot.

"So let's spell this out." Andi suddenly felt like she was coming to life again. "This is what we think we know about the killer." She pointed to the papers on the murder board. "He drives a dark blue sedan. He has an unusual gait. He uses an ulu. He possibly wears a toupee. And he may be single and dating. Is that about right?"

"That sounds like it," Helena said. "But I still can't help but wonder if we're missing something."

Andi shifted. "I hope you don't mind me asking this, Helena. But who is this source that you're getting this information from? Like about the hair, for example. That hasn't been made public."

Her cheek twitched. "It's not important."

"I'd say it is," Mariella said. "If you want us to be upfront with you, then you need to be upfront with us."

Andi watched Helena's face, curious how she would respond.

The woman's gaze traveled back and forth with thought before she slowly nodded with decision. "Okay, fine. My source is a guy I've been on a few dates with, who just happens to be a cop in Anchorage. After he's had a little too much to drink, he really likes to open up."

Based on Helena's frown, Andi had the impression the reporter didn't really like this guy. Was she simply using him?

"Do we know this cop?" Duke asked.

"I'm not sure, but I'd prefer not to say his name," Helena said. "He really is a good guy, and I don't want to get him in trouble."

Andi could understand that. And his identity wouldn't affect this investigation.

So . . . what *were* they missing?

Helena left a few minutes later, and only the Arctic Circle Murder Club members remained.

The Arctic Circle Murder Club that was currently meeting in Anchorage. But they all still remembered their roots. Up north in the Land of the Midnight Sun felt like home. Even being in Anchorage, part of Duke missed the boreal forest, the glimpses of Denali on clear days, and the overall culture of Fairbanks.

But right now, they were working in Anchorage. They needed to put everything into this before their time was up.

"So what's next, guys?" Mariella glanced at everyone. "I feel like we're on the brink, and we're either going to sink or swim."

Duke knew that feeling well.

"I think we should continue to pursue this hockey angle," Duke said. "I know that Raz, who seems like the most likely suspect, is not supposed to be in the country. But there could be someone else we should look at. I really feel like we need to explore the idea more."

"I agree." Andi tucked her knees under her chin and wrapped one arm around her legs. The other held a compress to her temple.

He prayed she really was okay. Going through what she had . . . it could affect a person.

Duke turned toward Matthew. "Could you work your

magic and see if Raz really is in Canada right now? Confirmation would be nice."

"Absolutely." Matthew pushed his glasses higher and nodded.

"I'd like to go back and talk to Stuart's parents again." Duke's gaze locked with Andi's. "I'd like to take you with me. I don't think it's wise if you're left alone again."

"I'm going to get some looks when people see my face." She removed the ice compress from her temple and offered a weak smile.

"I'd rather weird looks than another surprise like we had earlier." Duke hadn't meant to sound grim, but his words held the truth.

"Agreed." Beau gave them both a look.

"I can talk to one of the victims' families," Mariella said.

"Maybe Beau can go with you," Duke suggested.

"Be happy to."

Duke glanced at Ranger and Simmy. "You two game for talking to another family?"

Duke wasn't sure what Ranger's mental state was after getting that photo. But he'd looked preoccupied ever since.

He used a pocketknife to carve a stick he must have grabbed outside. The motion was slow and methodical—and almost seemed like a prelude to his thoughts and what he was considering doing.

"I'm game for now," Ranger said. "But I've already

booked a flight for tomorrow morning. I'm sorry to leave early, but I need to take care of something."

Simmy's eyes widened as if that was the first she'd heard of that update.

Duke wondered about Ranger's words. The man was private and didn't like to open up.

He had secrets.

Then again, they all did. Duke wasn't one to judge.

"We should get moving." Duke stood. "We don't have any time to waste here."

Everyone nodded in agreement.

Maybe today would be the day they found answers.

chapter
fifty-eight

FIFTEEN MINUTES LATER, Duke and Andi pulled up to Josiah and Elma's. Andi had called on the way, and the couple said it was fine if they stopped by and that they'd just gotten in from church.

Sure enough, when they stepped inside, the two were still dressed in their Sunday best, and the air smelled like roast beef and gravy.

The aroma brought back memories to Andi of Sunday dinners with her family after church. Those meals had always been a priority for Andi. She'd give anything to go back and have another one with her mom cooking fried chicken.

The memories caused a sweet ache to form in her chest.

The Downings offered Duke and Andi some food, but they refused. The two of them had grabbed smoothies on the way here. Because of their big breakfast, they weren't that hungry.

Just as before, they all settled in the living room. Andi noticed the couple staring at her face and tried to put them at ease. "It's not as bad as it looks."

"I hope that wasn't because of this investigation," Josiah said.

"Just a little accident." Andi's jaw ached as she said the words, a reminder of what had happened.

This *wasn't* an accident.

That man would have done even more damage if Duke and Beau hadn't returned when they did.

She shivered again at the thought.

Josiah and Elma still stared at her, worry in their gaze.

"I'll be fine," Andi insisted.

Josiah seemed to reluctantly nod. "So . . . you have an update?"

"We're fleshing out several leads, but there's one in particular we need your help with," Duke started.

"Anything we can do." Elma rubbed a thumb across her other hand, the motion undoubtably subconscious. "This guy needs to be stopped."

"Did Stuart ever have any connection with ice hockey by chance?" Andi asked.

"As a matter of fact, yes, he did."

Andi's breath caught. Maybe the hockey lead *had* been a good one after all.

"He was the co-owner of the ice-skating rink where

the Golddiggers practiced," Elma said. "But he sold his portion of the ownership probably five years ago."

Duke and Andi exchanged a long glance.

Duke turned back to the Downings. "Was Stuart a big hockey fan?"

"He enjoyed it. Loved going to the games."

"You think hockey is connected with these murders?" Elma stared at them as if in disbelief.

"I know it sounds like a stretch," Duke said. "But we're just following a lead, and we needed to know if this could be ruled out or not."

"Do the other victims have an interest in hockey?" Josiah asked.

"We're trying to figure that out now," Andi told them.

Worry filled Elma's gaze, and she rubbed her hands even harder. "Please, keep us updated."

"We will," Andi reassured them. "Thank you so much for your help."

Their team really could be on to something.

But they needed to talk to more families before they could know for sure.

Andi climbed into the SUV and turned to Duke. "We're getting closer."

"I agree."

"What now?"

Duke cranked the engine. "I think we should talk to the family of another victim. How about Sherri Blanchard?"

"Let me see if I can find her family's information." She searched on her phone a moment before finding what she was looking for.

She rattled off the address, and they headed that way.

"So . . . what do you think about that photo Ranger got?" Andi asked after a few moments of silence.

"I don't know what to think. I don't know who sent it, but it obviously affected him deeply."

"I can only imagine. I hope he's okay." Andi rubbed her arms.

"You and me both."

They pulled up to Sherri's parents' house.

Sherri, the second victim, had been the thirty-eight-year-old housekeeper.

They met with her parents, who confirmed that Sherri had briefly worked at the rink as a custodian probably about fifteen years ago.

Another puzzle piece snapped into place, Andi realized.

After thanking Sherri's parents, Duke and Andi climbed back into the SUV and called the rest of the team.

Mariella and Beau had gone to talk to Jevonne Whitaker's wife. Jevonne was the twenty-nine-year-old DJ.

It turned out he played for a hockey team about fifteen years ago.

Andi and Duke exchanged a glance.

A better timeline was coming together in their heads.

Ranger and Simmy didn't answer their call, which might mean they were in the middle of something.

Matthew confirmed that Raz really was in Canada and hadn't been in the area in the past two weeks. They could definitely rule him out.

Duke turned to Andi. "What do you think?"

The next step seemed obvious to her. "I think we need to pay another visit to that ice hockey rink."

chapter
fifty-nine

AS THEY HEADED down the road, Andi glanced around them. At any time now, she expected to see another car following them or some kind of other threat.

Every time she closed her eyes, she remembered that masked man. She remembered the feeling of his fingers at her throat. Of the gun hitting her temple. Of his fist colliding with the side of her face.

Maybe she should have gone to the hospital, but she hadn't. And she *would* be okay.

But she couldn't deny that she was on edge.

"I really think we're getting somewhere." Duke's voice pulled her from her thoughts.

Andi glanced behind them one more time before looking back at him. "I do too. But why would someone kill various people associated with an ice hockey rink? That's what we need to figure out. It is weird. I mean, a lot of hockey players get into fights, but this seems to take it to another extreme."

"Agreed." Duke's gaze flickered to the rearview mirror. "But there has to be a reason. Do you think whatever connects these people links back to something that happened fifteen years ago?"

"It sounds possible to me."

"Maybe somebody at the rink will be able to tell us what's really going on."

He was worried too, wasn't he?

She swallowed hard before saying, "We can hope."

As they pulled into the parking lot at the rink several minutes later, Duke's phone rang. Gibson's name appeared on the screen.

Andi sucked in a breath. Did he have an update for them? Had he learned something about Victor?

Duke hit Talk, and Gibson's voice came through the speakers. "I wanted to give you guys a quick update."

Andi held her breath as she anticipated what he might say.

Duke put the phone on speaker, and they listened with rapt attention. "What did you find out?"

"I went to the apartment where Victor has been staying while he's in town," Gibson said. "Turns out I just missed him by thirty minutes."

Duke glanced at Andi and saw her countenance fall. She'd been hopeful, hadn't she?

He glanced back at the speaker, returning to the conversation with Gibson. "I'm sorry to hear that."

"I'm not going to give up," Gibson said. "I'm going to keep trying to reach him."

Duke remembered what Andi had said about the man being untouchable. Maybe he was. That was certainly how it seemed.

There had to be some way to catch this guy in the act.

"Keep us informed," Duke muttered.

"Will do."

They ended the call, and Duke stole one more glance at Andi. He was worried about her, worried about the toll all of this was taking on her.

"I'm sorry, Andi," he murmured.

"Me too." She pressed her eyes shut. "But I'm not surprised."

"I know, but I'm sure you're disappointed."

After several seconds of silence, her eyes fluttered open, and she turned toward him. "I am. But one day he's going to make a mistake. I'm going to be there when he does."

"I know you will," Duke said.

Part of him dreaded that day. Dreaded the lengths he knew Andi would go through to bring this man down.

He was going to have to take this step by step.

Finally, he nodded at the building in the distance. "Are you ready to get inside the rink?"

"I'm as ready as ever."

The two of them climbed out and made their way to the front door. Several cars sat in the parking lot, indicating the place was open. That was good news.

As soon as they walked in, the chill in the air hit them.

Duke glanced at the rink and saw several hockey players running drills. The woman behind the counter only nodded at them. But her gaze lingered on Andi just a moment too long.

That was going to be happening a lot today, thanks to her bruised face.

Just as before, Duke paused near the edge of the rink and looked out.

He spotted Coach Pence.

The man seemed like a good place to start as any. Maybe he'd remember something new this time.

chapter
sixty

ANDI WATCHED the coach a moment and already knew that talking to him probably wasn't going to be a pleasant experience.

In fact, when the man saw them, he mumbled something beneath his breath before stomping toward them.

"You again." He paused in front of them, hands on hips and a deepening scowl on his face. "What are you doing here?"

"We have a few more questions."

"Well, I don't have any answers. I don't know what you're expecting from me. I already told you Raz is out of the country."

"I still think these murders are somehow linked with this sports complex," Duke said. "We're hoping you could help us."

"I don't have time for that," Pence barked. "We're having our grand reopening tonight, and our players are going to scrimmage against a team from Fairbanks. I need to give that all my attention. It's going to be like the good old days."

"That's more important than a murderous rampage in the city?" Andi's voice sounded wispy with disbelief.

Pence rolled his eyes. "Well, of course a hockey game isn't more important than a murderous rampage, if you want to be all dramatic about it." He stared at her face and squinted. "You've been playing hockey?"

Andi frowned and touched her swollen temple. "Not exactly."

He shrugged as if it didn't really matter to him. "Look, I don't know how I can help you. Can't imagine what this place might have to do with this killer, so you're going to have to talk to Richard again. Sorry, but that guy has a lush office job and nothing better to do than gab. I'm needed out here on the ice."

Before they could say anything else to him, he strode away.

"Well, that was pleasant," Duke murmured as he and Andi headed toward Richard's office.

"He's going to win Person of the Year for sure," Andi added.

Duke almost wanted to smile, but he couldn't. He

couldn't believe Pence didn't want to cooperate, especially considering what was at stake.

They reached Richard's office. The door was closed so Duke knocked.

When no one answered, the woman behind the front desk wheeled her office chair across the floor and peeked around the corner. "Richard is out to lunch, but he'll probably be back in about twenty if you want to wait."

"Thank you," Duke called. After the woman wheeled herself back out of sight, he turned toward Andi. "It's not worth it to leave and come back."

"I agree. We might as well stay since we're here." Andi shivered and rubbed her arms.

Duke wished he had a coat or something to give her, but he didn't. This place *was* chilly.

As they waited, they paced the building. Pictures of various teams that had met and practiced here throughout the years were displayed on the walls, along with signed photos of some of the professional athletes who'd started out here.

The lineup was impressive.

"This place has been around for a while," someone said. "Back before the Golddiggers were a professional team, this was where all the little guys met and practiced."

The woman from the front desk paused beside them, her arms loaded with stacks of papers as she headed toward an office.

"You looked as if you might be interested." She shrugged. "Middle school and high school leagues have practiced here. Kids have taken lessons. Figure skaters have used the facility. It's gotten a lot of use. It was a shame when it shut down several years ago, and I for one am thrilled that it's reopened."

"The facility looks really nice," Andi said.

"Everything is state of the art—from the bathrooms all the way down to the door locks," she continued.

"The door locks?" Duke questioned.

"You know all the fancy technology they have nowadays. I don't even have to be here to unlock this place. That's pretty amazing."

"Do you remember anything out of the ordinary that happened here fifteen or so years ago?" Andi asked.

The woman thought about it a moment before shaking her head. "Not really. Well, now that you mention it . . . I do remember hearing someone talking about a custodian who got fired for setting up cameras in the girls' locker room."

"Is that right?" Andi exchanged a glance with Duke. "Do you remember this guy's name?"

"Gerald maybe? Gerald Blinken?" She shrugged. "I don't know. It's been a long time . . . I wish I could help more."

"It's okay," Duke murmured.

They'd need to wade through lots of history to find answers.

But time wasn't working in their favor.

Duke glanced back at the pictures on the walls. Were the answers in one of these photos?

It was a distinct possibility.

He found one from fifteen years ago and picked out Jevonne Whitaker's image. He studied the rest of the photos, looking for anyone else familiar.

No one stood out.

Just in case he'd missed something, Duke snapped photos of the pictures with his phone. It couldn't hurt to have a record of these.

Maybe there were answers in here somewhere.

chapter
sixty-one

RICHARD SHOULD BE BACK at any moment. In the meantime, Andi tried not to think about Victor.

But, of course, she did. She wondered where he'd gone. If he'd known Gibson was coming. What he was planning next.

She caught Duke staring at her but knew she didn't have to say a word. He clearly could read her thoughts. When his gaze traveled to the bruise around her eyes, she bristled.

Was he silently reminding her that she was safer backing off?

Andi touched the side of her face before rolling her shoulders back. "I don't regret any of it."

He raised his eyebrows. "You don't?"

"I'd do everything again if it means bringing down Victor."

He twisted his head as if surprised. "You sure are dedicated."

She raised her chin. "Someone has to step up. Why shouldn't that person be me? For such a time as this . . . both you and Beau have brought it up. I'm not calling myself a modern-day Esther. But maybe I'm here in Alaska for a purpose."

Duke only stared at her.

She cleared her throat and pointed to a picture beside them on the wall, figuring it was better if the subject dropped. "What are we missing, Duke?"

He averted his gaze to the team photo and let out a sigh. "I don't know, but we're getting closer to the answers."

"When should we bring the police into this?" Because it was only a matter of *when*, not *if*.

"Maybe after we talk to Richard—and after we hear from Simmy and Ranger. But there definitely seems to be a hockey connection, and we need to let them know."

"I agree, even though I'm not looking forward to talking to the cops again." Andi tensed just thinking about it.

"Then you don't have to," Duke said. "I will."

A footstep sounded behind them. Andi turned to see a man standing there wearing a Golddiggers' jersey and jeans.

"Richard . . ." Duke said. "Sorry to stop by unannounced like this."

The man's brow rose but not in an unfriendly way. "I can't say I'm happy to see you again because I know what this probably means. Is one of my guys in trouble?"

"I'm not really sure," Duke told him. "But we're hoping you can help us work a few things out."

Richard grabbed his keys from his pocket and unlocked his office door. "I'll do my best. Why don't you come inside?"

They stepped inside the small space.

Richard hurried to the other side of the desk and pulled out his chair. "It's a busy day. I'm sure you heard we're having our official grand reopening tonight, even though people have been practicing here for a few weeks. We're expecting a decent crowd as well as several people who used to be well-known here in bygone days."

"We appreciate your time," Andi said.

"Have a seat." He gestured to two chairs opposite his desk. "Then let's see what we can figure out."

Duke explained the possible hockey connection to Richard.

"That's disturbing, to say the least." Richard cracked his neck as if uncomfortable with the conversation. "It does sound like there could be a link. I'm just not sure how to figure out what that is."

"Were you working here back then?" Andi asked.

Richard shook his head. "I was just hired when they decided to reopen this place."

That was too bad.

"Is there anyone working here now who used to work here fifteen or so years ago?" Andi asked.

"No, when this place closed down, everyone was let go. Everyone here is a new hire."

"Since you've worked here, have there been any major incidents that might have impacted a person negatively for years afterward?" Duke asked.

Richard leaned back in his seat and let out a breath. "That's a big question. I'm trying to think that through. I'm sure you know that a lot of hockey players have a temper, so there have been plenty of fights."

Duke knew that was true, and that detail could also make this more complicated.

Richard straightened, clearly rattled by this theory. "Do you have those pictures on you again?"

Duke pulled them from his bag and handed them to Richard, who spread them over his desk.

The man studied them for a few minutes before shaking his head in exasperation. "I don't recognize any of them. But . . . I can make some calls to people who used to work here. Maybe they'll remember something. But as far as scuttlebutt I've heard through the years, I'm not much help. I can't think of anything that stands out. I wish I knew something. I truly mean that."

Disappointment bit at Duke. But he understood.

"Well . . ." Richard frowned.

Duke jerked his head back toward the man.

"I do remember something about one guy being fired," Richard said. "He was the co-owner with Stuart Downing."

"A co-owner was fired?" Andi asked.

"I mean, I guess he wasn't *fired* fired. But things got difficult until the guy quit."

"Sounds ugly," Andi said.

"Apparently, it was ugly. And it was one of the reasons this place was shut down. Lots of internal fighting. The two didn't share the same vision. This guy—Landon Peters—he made some threats afterward. I never heard what came of him."

He and Andi thanked Richard and started out the door.

Richard would need time to talk to those people. But unfortunately time was something they didn't have, not when lives were on the line.

chapter
sixty-two

DUKE AND ANDI arrived back at the rental at the same time as Simmy and Ranger.

Once they were all back inside, they sat in the living room and shared what they'd learned.

Sure enough, Chad Windsor had confirmed he played hockey about fifteen years ago. Why his wife was targeted instead of him? That was still unclear . . . unless hurting Chad's wife was a means of hurting him.

They were definitely on to something, Duke realized. Chad himself might be a suspect . . . except he was out of town when his wife's murder happened. Besides, why would he murder his own wife?

They'd confirmed that all the victims were connected to hockey in some way.

Mark Williams: former coach for a middle school team.

Sherri Blanchard: worked at rink.

Jevonne Whitaker: played hockey fifteen years ago.

Stuart Downing: co-owner of the team.

Wyatt Jenkins: avid hockey fan.

Tex Lanyard: hockey dad.

Nicole Windsor: husband played hockey fifteen years ago.

Albert Clubber . . . he was the only real wild card.

He'd been a CPS worker. How did he fit?

Andi still wasn't sure. Unless . . . unless one of his cases involved someone involved with hockey. It was the only thing that made sense.

"So what are we going to do in the meantime?" Mariella stood near the murder board, a sparkly pink baton in her hand. "How are we going to find these answers?"

"We should definitely look into Landon Peters and this Gerald Blinken guy," Andi said.

"I've already looked up Gerald Blinken." Matthew held up his computer. "He's still in the area and still working as a janitor, it appears."

"Do you have a picture?" Duke asked.

"I do." He turned his computer around.

Andi sucked in a breath. "I've seen him. He works at the car dealership with Melanie Wooden."

Duke glanced at her in surprise. "Are you sure?"

"I'm positive."

Duke turned back to Matthew. "Can you find an address or contact information?"

"I'm on it."

"In the meantime, there's only one thing that I can think of, and I'm not sure anyone is going to like it." Andi licked her lips. "But I think we should all go to this game tonight."

Duke bristled beside her.

"Do you think the killer will be stupid enough to go there?" Matthew asked.

"I don't know. But these other victims have been to the games, and they have a connection with hockey. I just feel like maybe we'll run into someone or see something. We need to get into the thick of things if we're going to figure this out."

"I hate to say this because the move could be risky," Duke said. "But I think going to the game is a good idea."

"Wait . . . what time does the game start?" Mariella asked.

"Six p.m.," Duke said. "But we should probably get there around five-thirty."

Mariella glanced at her watch. "That means we need to leave in about three hours."

"In the meantime, we need to look into Gerald," Duke said. "I also think we should call the police and let them know about our theory. It's important. They're privy to information that we're not."

Thankfully, no one argued with him.

～

Duke called Detective Rasmussen and told him their theory. He asked the man to delay the opening of the sports plex tonight.

The man laughed it off, which Duke didn't appreciate.

There was no reason not to take them seriously. Sure, the guy probably got lots of leads that didn't pan out. But they'd come up with a solid, viable theory to look into.

Duke tried to hold his frustration at bay, but the task felt impossible. He didn't like that man. Didn't like his arrogance.

Duke finished the call.

As he did, Ranger got everyone's attention. "I tracked down this Blinken guy—in a manner of speaking, at least. He's not answering his phone. I called the dealership, and they said he's on vacation. That he went fishing at some cabin he owns that's off the grid."

"So we're not going to get anywhere with that," Andi muttered.

"Unless it's a ruse," Simmy said. "Maybe he told people that so he can plan more murderous acts."

"Why don't we all take a little breather?" Andi suggested. "We'll come back and talk again in ten minutes. Okay?"

"I'm going to call Chad Windsor back in the meantime," Ranger said. "Just to put my mind at ease. Maybe he'll recognize someone in this picture."

Everyone agreed.

As everyone rose, Duke sensed Andi studying him.

"What do you say we take a quick walk out to the lake before we work some more?" Andi suggested.

"That sounds like a good idea."

They stepped outside, waved to Eisenhauer, and then strode side by side to the lake. They stood on the shore and looked at the peaceful water. Majestic mountains rose in the distance, forming quite the picture. Along the various piers and docks, boats and floatplanes were moored.

In any other circumstance, the scene would be peaceful.

Duke could say that about a lot of places in Alaska. Yet he kept encountering turbulence.

Only moments after they'd paused by the lake, Duke noticed someone walking toward them.

Dabney had emerged from the small guest house on his property where his family was staying after the fire.

He paused near them.

"How are you guys doing?" Dabney's gaze stopped on Andi. "Not good, if I had to guess."

"Just had a little run-in with a troublemaker," Andi explained with a casual shrug. "Nothing I won't heal from."

Dabney's gaze remained clouded with uncertainty. "I'm sorry to hear that."

"Any updates on the fire at your place?" Duke asked. "I hope they caught the person who did this."

Dabney shook his head. "Police assume it's someone I put in jail at one time who's now out and seeking revenge. But this person left no evidence behind—other than that matchbook—and no one saw anything. It's unnerving to say the least."

"I can imagine," Andi said. "I'm so sorry to hear that, and I hope they're able to find this person. That could have turned out so much worse."

Duke knew Andi thought there was more to the story. She thought the fire was to send her a message. And maybe it was, though other arsons could have been started with a matchbook from the same casino. Given everything that had happened, nothing would surprise him anymore.

"So I heard through the grapevine that you guys are podcasters." Dabney jammed his hands into his pockets and rocked back on his heels as he waited for their response.

"Word gets around, huh?" Duke said.

"In neighborhoods like this, yes, it does. I think that's fascinating."

"We are trying to make a difference," Andi said.

He stared out over the water, his arms crossed casually. "Duke, I meant what I said when I told you I owed you one. I don't know what case you're working on now or if there's anything I can do. But keep in touch. I could never repay you for saving my daughter."

He handed them each a business card.

That connection might actually come in handy.

Maybe not with this case. But maybe with Celeste or Victor.

Maybe.

Besides, most things didn't happen by accident. There was a reason for them.

Maybe meeting Dabney—and saving his daughter—had more than one purpose also.

chapter
sixty-three

AT THEIR INVITATION, Helena showed up thirty minutes later.

They all met again in the living room and gave her the update.

"I don't like that hockey theory." Helena frowned and rubbed her arms.

"Why not?" Andi studied the woman's face, which had grown paler. "You almost look like it's personal."

"It *is* personal to me," Helena said. "I have a connection with that ice hockey rink also. When I was a teen, my parents wanted me to go to the Olympics. The owner of the rink used to let me practice before the teams came in. I would get there at five a.m. every morning to practice figure skating before school."

Andi hadn't seen that one coming . . .

"There were noises outside my house when my power

went off last night and my video cameras went out . . ."
Helena shivered again. "What if that's really because I was
supposed to be the next victim?"

"You shouldn't be alone until this guy is caught."
Duke gave her a look. "Maybe you could tell your cop
friend. Maybe he can put a protection detail on you."

Helena nodded. "I'll do that. I'll figure out something.
It doesn't sound like I have any other choice."

Andi was inclined to agree. She glanced at Ranger.
"Were you able to get up with Chad again?"

"He said I could send him the photos, and he'd try to
remember everyone. But he was out at a job site and probably can't get to it tonight. I told him it was important,
and he said he'd do his best."

"He couldn't name anyone off the top of his head?"
Mariella asked.

"He sounded rushed," Ranger said. "And, it may have
been my imagination, but his voice changed when I
brought up the team. I don't know why."

"Maybe he's hiding something," Andi murmured.

Even as she said the words, she couldn't help but
wonder what the man might be hiding.

After Helena left to keep investigating, Duke stood and
began pacing. "We've got to figure out what this hockey
link is. Someone throw out some ideas."

"Maybe someone was cut from the team and now wants vengeance," Mariella said.

"Maybe someone was injured there and blames the rink," Simmy said.

"Maybe an employee got fired and that changed the trajectory of his life," Ranger said.

"Someone got their heart broken," Andi suggested.

Duke continued walking back and forth. "All of those could work. But why blame this group of victims? They didn't seem to know each other."

"I agree," Andi said. "Even if all these people used the rink at the same time, they didn't all fire the killer. They didn't all cut him from the team. They didn't all injure him. We're still missing something."

Silence fell between them.

"Can we see those pictures again?" Andi asked. "The ones that were hanging on the wall at the rink?"

"Of course." Duke grabbed his phone.

"I can print them for you." Mariella stood. "And maybe we can send them to some former employees to see if we can track down their names. Someone has to be able to identify these guys before Chad gets around to it tonight."

The two of them walked to the printer Mariella brought with her.

A few minutes later, she gave each of them copies.

Duke sat and studied the larger version of the photos. He stopped on one of a high school hockey team.

Twelve guys were in the photo—two of them being Jevonne Whitaker and Chad Windsor.

Could one of these other guys be the killer? Chad's wife had been murdered, and he'd been out of town. A news article verified his alibi. Otherwise, he could be a suspect.

He studied all the faces, but none of them looked familiar. It didn't help that the images weren't high quality.

"Um . . . you guys," Matthew murmured.

Duke didn't like the sound of his voice. "Yes?"

"An article just popped up online." Matthew's gaze was latched onto his phone. "It's about us."

"What?" Andi's voice rose.

"It . . . it spells out each of our identities," Matthew continued. "All of them."

Duke sucked in a breath. That was part of their agreement—only Mariella and Matthew would be known by their real names. The rest of them had reasons to use nicknames.

"It's all there." Matthew shook his head in disbelief. "Our real names, our photos, where we're from, our prior careers even."

Ranger stood, his nostrils flaring as he grunted. "Who did this?"

They all turned to Matthew, waiting to hear what he had to say.

Matthew looked up and frowned as if he didn't want to answer. Finally, he murmured, "The reporter . . . it was Helena Gray."

A pulse started at Duke's temple. No . . . this couldn't be true.

chapter
sixty-four

ANDI FELT the tension in the air.

She didn't like this turn of events any more than anyone else. She'd wanted to keep her life back in Texas a secret. She didn't want everyone in Alaska to know she'd been an attorney. That she'd been disbarred and disgraced.

"I knew we couldn't trust Helena!" Mariella jumped to her feet, outrage in her gaze.

"She wouldn't do this," Duke muttered.

"Why are you defending her?" Mariella turned to him. "Her name is on the article. How else do you explain it?"

Duke shook his head. "I don't know. But I don't think she'd do something like this."

"Do you like her or something?" Mariella snapped.

Something about her words made the air leave Andi's lungs. Did Duke like Helena? Why did that thought make her feel unbalanced?

"No, it's not like that." Duke's jaw hardened with irritation. "I just get a sense about people. And I didn't get the feeling from Helena that she'd betray us like this."

"We need to confront her." Ranger's hands went to his hips. "This isn't okay."

"I'll try to give her a call now." Duke grabbed his phone and put it on speaker.

But there was no answer.

Andi glanced around the group, her gaze stopping on Simmy. She'd been quiet, but she looked especially pale.

What was going on inside her head?

She almost seemed . . . scared.

Andi dragged her gaze away

"If Helena is responsible for this, then I'm sorry," Duke said. "I would have never brought someone into our group who wasn't trustworthy. But I really don't think she did this."

"Why would someone use her name on the article?" Mariella asked.

A new idea hit Andi, and her stomach dropped.

"Maybe because this person is targeting me by targeting you," Andi murmured.

Everyone turned to stare at her.

"What do you mean?" Duke finally asked.

"I mean, think about it," Andi continued. "Duke got pictures of his sister. Ranger got a picture of his daughter. Now this. What if someone knows the best way to make me back off from my investigation is by hurting the people I care about?"

"So you think Victor is behind this?" Duke asked. "The article? The pictures of my sister? The photo Ranger got?"

"It makes sense." Andi set her jaw, not backing down.

"I guess in some way it does," Duke murmured.

"I'm so sorry." Andi glanced at each person in the group. "I would have never pulled you into this on purpose . . ."

"It's not your fault," Duke reassured her. "We'll get to the bottom of this. But for now, we need to get to this hockey game. We don't want to be late. We can talk about this again later, okay?"

Everyone seemed to reluctantly agree.

Duke's thoughts remained on everything that had happened as he drove to the sports plex.

What a nightmare.

All of this.

The team *had* to find some answers before anyone else got hurt.

As they got in line to buy their tickets, most of the group was quiet.

Were they each reviewing the ramifications of having their identities revealed? Maybe.

Alpine had already called Mariella, and then Mariella had called Jason.

Simmy still stared off in the distance, her arms wrapped over her chest.

Ranger seemed to be silently seething.

Andi's gaze wavered back and forth as if computing everything. Flashes of guilt occasionally appeared also.

Matthew kept checking his phone looking for more articles, comments, or other updates.

Duke . . . well, he'd tried to keep his identity under wraps mostly because he'd made a lot of enemies while working for the Army CID. However, he probably had the least to lose out of everyone in the group.

The murder club was definitely being targeted. They simply needed to figure out who was behind these attacks.

Finally, they got their tickets and stepped inside the building.

Quite a crowd was already here, probably four hundred people if Duke had to guess.

He scanned the faces around him. Would there be anyone here he recognized? The killer? Future victims?

Was the killer staking out the place?

Maybe.

This was their chance to figure it out.

Duke had seen two security guards at the rink, plus three police officers on duty, probably as added security. He recognized two of the officers as Rector and Eisenhauer.

A buzz of excitement lingered in the air. No one here

knew about the theory—no one except the people the team had told. The police hadn't taken them seriously.

The officers here tonight were just for crowd control.

"Let's find our seats," Duke told the team. "Then we can divide up to watch people. Something is going down here tonight. We need to figure out what."

chapter
sixty-five

THEY COULDN'T HAVE MADE this easier for me.

Not only were people with past connections to hockey in this area invited to come here tonight, but those podcasters had shown up also.

I'd heard them talking. I knew they claimed to want to find answers. But it was only for their own sake. They wanted the glory of solving a murder mystery.

But this would be my big moment.

Not theirs.

I'd been planning this ever since I heard this place would open again.

The news had ignited something in me.

To make it even more perfect, I'd gotten my hands on something that would really help me send my message.

This wasn't like the Xs I'd been leaving. Tonight would be totally different.

I'd make a statement.

I'd let the world know what these people had done to me.

I'd make them pay.

Thankfully, I had a background in tech. Before my current job, I'd thought I wanted to work with computers. But a desk job hadn't satisfied me—even though I'd been good at it.

So I'd pivoted and gotten this new position. But I still liked to use those old skills whenever I could.

I'd use them tonight.

I'd use the skills I'd learned at my new job also.

I'd even use the skills I'd learned through hockey.

Everything would come together for my big finale.

People would finally learn their lesson.

They would know what it felt like to suffer.

chapter
sixty-six

ANDI WATCHED THE CROWD.

They filled the stands, eating popcorn and soft pretzels. Some wore jerseys and had painted their faces. Foam hockey sticks waved in the air.

An emcee gave away prizes. The mascot, a prospector, got the crowd wound up. Loud music pulsed overhead.

What kind of horrible thing had happened here to cause this killer to go on this rampage?

They needed to find someone who would answer that for them.

Andi split from the rest of the team to wander the complex. She had the picture of the old hockey team in her hands, ready to show anyone who might be able to help.

She scanned the faces around her, looking for someone familiar.

Right now, it felt like the proverbial "looking for a needle in a haystack."

Officer Rector fell into step beside her, a curious look in his eyes. "Everything okay?"

"I'm not sure. Just a hunch."

He glanced at the picture. "That's an old photo."

"I think someone in this picture might know something."

"About what?"

"The Lights Out Killer," she murmured.

His eyes widened. "Really? So you're looking to see if you can spot these people in the photo? To see if they're here tonight?"

"Something like that. We told Detective Rasmussen, but he didn't seem very interested in our theory. So we came here ourselves. Honestly, we're afraid something is going to happen."

"I'm surprised you're not lying low considering everything that happened with the senator."

Andi shrugged, deciding not to beat around the bush. "I'm not good at lying low."

He nodded slowly. "Understood. If you need any help, let me know."

"Will do."

Then Andi spotted a familiar face through the crowds.

Her heart skipped a beat.

Could he be the killer?

Duke was standing near the concession stand when he spotted someone he recognized.

Helena. She appeared just as on edge as the rest of his team.

But he felt very little compassion toward her.

He stormed toward the reporter.

Her eyes widened with surprise when she spotted him, and she paused. "Duke . . . is everything okay?"

"How could you?"

She blinked, confusion flashing through her gaze. "How could I what?"

"How could you publish that article with the real identities of my friends and me?" His jaw hardened. "We trusted you."

"I have no idea what you're talking about." Her voice sounded airy with uncertainty.

"You didn't publish this?" He found the article on his phone and then watched Helena's face carefully as she read it.

Her expression went from surprised to confused to outraged. "Duke, I promise that wasn't me. Someone used my name to set me up. I wouldn't do this."

"If that's true, then someone has been watching us. He knows we've been talking to you. He used your name to get this published."

Her face grew paler. "I . . . I don't know what to say.

But I didn't write that article, and I'm sorry someone did. I truly am. I didn't even know any of this was happening. I don't know how to prove that to you, but it's true."

Duke wanted to believe her, but he wasn't there yet. "I tried to call. You didn't answer."

"I was run off the road when I left your house." She showed him a bruise on her arm. "I'm okay, but my car is totaled."

"Run off the road? Do you think it was on purpose?"

"I don't know for sure. But the other driver kept going." Helena's eyes began to look glassy, but she blinked her tears away. "I'm just glad I'm alive. It could have been worse."

"I'm sorry that happened." Duke stared at her a moment before swallowing hard.

He believed her. He didn't see any signs of deceit in her expression.

Duke hadn't thought Helena would expose their names in the first place.

What if Andi was right? What if Victor was behind this?

That man would stoop to anything to stop Andi, wouldn't he?

That thought terrified Duke.

chapter
sixty-seven

ANDI PUSHED herself between the people milling in front of her, jostling people about, until she reached the man she'd seen. She grabbed his shoulder.

Dabney turned toward her and blinked with surprise. "Andi, right?"

"I didn't realize you'd be here." She tried to sound casual. But was her temporary neighbor connected with these murders somehow?

He shrugged. "I've always been a hockey fan. I figured I'd come out and offer my support."

"Is your family here?" Her thoughts raced as she remembered his two daughters. They'd already been through a lot with that fire. They didn't need any more trauma tonight.

He narrowed his eyes. "No, why? Is something wrong?"

Andi released a quick breath of relief before

wondering how much she should say. "I suspect something might go down here tonight."

Dabney tilted his head in confusion. "Could you be more specific? Something other than the game?"

"This might sound crazy, but I think this place is somehow linked to the Lights Out Killer. I told the detective covering the case, but he didn't listen to me. My friends and I are here trying to find answers—trying to do what the police won't."

Dabney stared at her another moment, his intense gaze appearing as if he tried to grasp what she'd said. "Are you serious?"

"Dead serious."

"Okay, then I'm going to get out of here." He stepped toward the door. "And I'm going to call in some favors at the police department to get more officers out here."

"That would be great. Please, do that. There's no time to waste."

He paused another moment. "You really think there's something to this?"

Andi nodded. "Unfortunately, I'm nearly certain."

Dabney pressed his lips together and nodded. "Okay. I'll see what I can do to help then. In the meantime . . . be safe. Please."

～

Duke settled in his seat with the rest of the gang as the game started.

"Anything?" he asked Andi, who'd just returned seconds before him.

She offered him the popcorn bag in her hands as she told him about running into Dabney. Then she asked, "You?"

He took a piece of buttery popcorn and popped it in his mouth. "I ran into Helena."

Mariella had taken a seat on the other side of Andi, and she jerked forward. "Wait . . . did you ask her about the article?"

Duke nodded. "She said she didn't write it, that someone is trying to set her up."

"And of course you believed her." Mariella rolled her eyes.

"Someone ran her off the road when she left our rental."

"That's what she said, huh?"

"I don't know what your beef is with her," Duke muttered.

"My beef is that you shared information we gathered without our permission, and then she wrote that article, and now you're defending her."

"I'm defending her because she's innocent."

"Okay, you two!" Andi sliced her hands through the air. "Stop. Fighting isn't going to get us anywhere."

Duke and Mariella exchanged a look before returning

back to the pre-game entertainment. Duke knew he and Mariella shouldn't be at each other's throats. But he didn't want to back down either. He needed to stand his ground.

Right now, he reminded himself, he had more important tasks at hand. Those were what he needed to concentrate on. That and employing all the fruit of the Spirit every time he interacted with people.

He was a work in progress.

He scanned the crowd again. Was the killer here? Staking out his next victim?

Would that victim be Helena?

Striking in a place like this would break the killer's MO. Then again, if the psychopath had killed that nurse, he was already starting to break from his pattern. Plus, he'd struck two nights in a row.

Why would he do that? Why had he veered from his usual plan?

There had to be a reason.

Duke's thoughts raced.

Something had happened, hadn't it? It only made sense. Something had caused this guy to change his pattern.

Now the killer was getting sloppy.

Maybe even desperate.

Duke's spine straightened at the thought.

He didn't know what to anticipate next, which made things even worse.

"You guys . . . they just released the ID of the newest

victim." Matthew leaned over from the end of their row and held his phone. "He's the owner of that car dealership where Melanie works. Alex Bergenske."

"What?" Duke couldn't have heard correctly.

"It makes sense," Andi said. "Think about it. Melanie said Stuart helped her get the job, that Alex was his old friend. I'm just taking a stab at this—excuse the expression —but it sounds like Alex could have been a friend of Stuart's from hockey."

Duke let out a long breath and leaned back. "You're right. Just one more confirmation that we're on the right track."

The thought filled him with both victory and defeat —a combination that made his gut churn.

chapter
sixty-eight

ANDI'S NERVES thrummed through her as the game started.

But she wasn't paying attention to anything on the rink. No, she was looking around.

The team had to make the most of their time. They had to find answers before it was too late.

Right now was their best opportunity.

To do so, she needed to keep her eyes wide open.

"You guys hockey fans?" Beau raised his voice in order to be heard over the sounds of the game and crowd around them. He sat on the other side of Duke.

"I'm a Texas girl," Andi said, unsure if she was in the mood for such casual conversation. "Ice hockey isn't a big thing there."

"Understandable."

Andi glanced at him. "You?"

"Not so much, though I always love a good game." He

paused, seeming to realize how mundane the conversation was also, and then blew out a long breath. "You really think the killer is here?"

"I think there's a good chance he's here and he's blending in." She shivered as she said the words. Especially since she knew what this man was capable of. He was a cold-blooded murderer, who made his victims suffer—all so he could send some kind of message.

Maybe he was even someone without a soul. This man was targeting innocent people, and his rampage wasn't slowing down.

She remembered the ulu. She'd done some research and had discovered they were commonly used here in Alaska. Owning one didn't necessarily narrow down their pool of suspects. But was it significant in some way? And how did it tie in with hockey?

She still had so many unanswered questions.

She glanced beside her. Duke seemed preoccupied as well, with his tight shoulders and set jaw.

Ranger still had anger brewing in his gaze.

Simmy still appeared nervous with her small jerky motions.

Matthew and Mariella were busy on their phones, probably research and recording.

This investigation had changed things, hadn't it? Especially having their identities revealed. What would that mean for this group?

Andi didn't know, and she couldn't think about it now.

The crowd cheered as the Golddiggers got the puck.

The next moment, the entire place went dark, and screams of terror erupted throughout the building.

"Is everyone okay?" Duke pulled up the flashlight on his phone and shone it onto his friends.

They were all there—but visibly shaken.

The lights had gone out . . .

Duke's blood went cold at the realization. It was no accident. The darkness had been planned.

The Lights Out Killer was here.

"We're fine," Andi said, glancing at everyone also. "We're all fine."

Around them, panic gripped people. Other cell phone lights came on, creating the effect of stars in the nighttime sky. Except there was no peace at the sight of it. Only fear and pandemonium.

The sounds of blades sliding across ice went silent as the hockey players also froze. The announcer's voice disappeared. Even the people selling popcorn and cotton candy in the stands went silent.

At any time, a backup generator should kick on. Illumination should fill the space. Make people feel a little better.

But moments passed, and nothing happened.

"Duke . . ." Andi muttered.

"I know." The killer was here. He didn't have to say it out loud.

A few seconds later, something that sounded like gunshots filled the air.

People's fear accelerated. The crowd scrambled from their seats and tried to flee.

Then a new emotion gripped the air.

What was going on?

Someone yelled, "The doors are locked. We're all trapped in here!"

More screams filled the space at the announcement.

Duke sucked in a breath.

That couldn't be right.

But what if it was?

chapter
sixty-nine

ANDI TURNED TO MATTHEW, knowing he was the best one to answer her question. "How is it possible that all the doors are locked?"

"A lot of locks at places like this are operated by computers where somebody can control them remotely." He said the words matter-of-factly.

She remembered what the woman at the front desk had told them. Matthew was right—these locks were all electronic—an upgrade. A deadly upgrade.

"So someone locked all the doors, and they're unable to be unlocked without a certain computer program . . ." Duke muttered.

Matthew nodded. "That's correct."

Panic thrummed through Andi. They were all stuck inside this place with a killer.

And what about those gunshots? What had those been about?

Had the killer totally changed his MO?

"If people can't get out, I'm guessing that means people can't get in either," Ranger murmured.

"Based on the panic in the air, I'd say that's the case." Duke's words were clipped with tension.

"So we're all trapped in here?" Mariella's voice cracked with fear.

"I can go find Richard." Duke stood. "He should know how to operate the doors."

"There *are* police here," Ranger said. "I think they'd want to step up. I'll find them and see what we can do to help. I'll tell them what we know."

"Duke." Andi's gaze locked with his. "Can you call Gibson also? Let him know what's going on since he is in town anyway? Maybe he can get through to someone with the Anchorage PD."

"I'll do that." He was already dialing.

"I'll come with you." Andi stood and turned on her phone light. "You need to see where you're going."

As she did, another terrifying thought hit her.

If the killer was responsible for turning the lights off in this place and locking them all in, not only were they all trapped . . . but what was he planning for them next?

With Andi by his side, Duke explained to Gibson what was going on. The state trooper promised to be right there —and to bring backup with him.

From the sounds of it, the police had gotten numerous calls.

As Duke and Andi left the bleacher area and headed toward the main lobby, Duke saw people throwing chairs at the windows, trying to break them and escape.

But it was no use.

This place had been upgraded to ensure that no hockey pucks would break the glass.

In other words, no one was getting out of here.

Duke reached Richard's office and, as Andi shone a light inside, he spotted the man behind his desk. His motions appeared frantic as he talked to someone on the phone.

A moment later, Richard ended the call, muttered something under his breath, and then squinted at them. "Duke? Is that you?"

"It's me." Duke shone his light on his face and then stepped farther inside. "What's going on?"

"That's what I'm trying to figure out. I called the lock company, but they're not able to unlock these doors remotely. Ironically, they say it's for safety reasons."

"It's a madhouse out there," Duke said.

Richard raked a hand through his hair. "I know. Without the system working, I can't even make any announcements to people to direct them on what to do.

All of our backup systems are down. And it's too noisy to get everybody's attention otherwise."

"Can we help you do anything?" Andi asked.

"I have no idea," Richard said. "I guess the best thing you can do right now is just to be vigilant. If you see anybody acting suspiciously, tell one of the cops on duty. I have a really bad feeling about this."

So did Duke. So did Duke.

chapter
seventy

ANDI AND DUKE wandered the crowd, looking for signs of anything suspicious.

But most of what they saw was chaos, Andi mused.

People continued to pull at the doors, desperately trying to get them open. A man rammed his shoulder against a window repeatedly until a security guard stopped him. Another group formed some kind of human ladder as they tried to reach a higher window and open it.

Did everyone suspect that this could be the work of the Lights Out Killer?

Most likely, no.

Only a few people knew about this killer's connection with hockey.

And it was probably better that way.

"You guys okay?" Officer Rector stopped them, shining his light at their faces.

Andi squinted against the glare. "We're fine. Just

trying to navigate this like everyone else. Are there any updates you can give us? What were those gunshots about?"

"No one appears to be hurt," he said. "It may have been a scare tactic."

"It worked," Duke muttered.

"Other police officers are outside but unable to get in," Rector said. "They're working on a solution—and trying to get the backup generator going. I've been trying to keep people calm, but it feels useless. There are too many people and not enough cops."

Andi reminded him about her theory. Told him she believed the killer might be here. That he might want to exact the perfect revenge tonight.

Rector went paler at her words. "You're right. This could be worse than I anticipated."

"Is there an estimated time your colleagues might have these doors opened?" Duke edged closer as a crowd ran past toward the doors.

Rector shook his head. "I know they're working as hard as they can. That's the thing with technology—it's a blessing or a curse."

"Agreed," Andi muttered. She grabbed Duke's arm as a man running past nearly knocked her over.

Just how much longer would everyone be trapped in here?

As if to answer her question, a new round of screams sounded near the check-in counter.

She, Duke, and Officer Rector pushed through the crowd toward the commotion.

When they reached the front door, they saw a man pointing at something behind the desk. "It's a bomb! According to the timer, we only have eight minutes until it explodes."

A bomb.

Duke couldn't believe his ears.

Was *this* the Lights Out Killer's grand plan?

If he wanted to instill fear in people, he'd done a great job.

"Does anybody know how to disable one of these?" Officer Rector glanced around.

Duke knew exactly the person.

Beau.

He'd worked as a bomb tech in the military.

Duke had to find him.

He dialed his brother's number. Beau answered on the first ring, but the crowds were so loud that Duke was doubtful his brother could even hear him.

"There's a bomb," Duke nearly shouted. "We need your help."

"What? You've got to be kidding me. Where are you?"

"Near the front door."

"I'll be right there," Beau said.

Duke shoved his phone back in his pocket and glanced around. The crowds had gathered around the bomb as if they wanted to see the device for themselves. But this was the worst place they could be.

Duke cupped his hands around his mouth to be heard above the noise. "You all need to get to the other side of the building, as far away from this bomb as possible. Do you understand?"

People stared at him as if dumbfounded. Then, all at once, they darted in the opposite direction. He prayed no one got trampled in the process.

He glanced back at the bomb and Officer Rector standing beside it. The officer looked pale, and sweat already dripped from his face.

Duke didn't know much about bombs but, based on what he was seeing, this one had enough explosives to take down this whole place. He wasn't sure anyone would get out of here unscathed. But the farther away people were, the safer they'd be.

However, disabling this bomb would be their best option by far.

At that moment, backup lights popped on, adding a dim glow to the sports plex.

Had the killer turned on a generator? Or had Richard figured out how to do so?

As if to answer him, a crackle filled the air over the speakers.

This killer had somehow managed to hack into the sound system, hadn't he?

"You should all be ashamed of yourselves," a man said. "All of you. Every single one."

Duke and Andi exchanged a glance. It was the killer. He had no doubt about that.

But where was he right now?

"None of you should support a place like this," the man continued. "There are people here who know why. Unless they step forward and start telling everyone what they did, then a bomb will explode, one powerful enough to take down this entire structure with all of you inside. You have six minutes to start talking. Six minutes for the guilty parties to go onto the ice and tell the world about the evil they've done."

Other people were here whom the killer wanted to exact revenge on.

Did these people even realize he was talking about them?

And where was the killer? The question took root in his mind.

If Duke had to guess, this guy was controlling the sound system remotely. Going to the sound room seemed too risky because it was the first place police would check.

Yet it sounded like this guy was inside the building. Did the killer plan on going down with everyone else in the sports plex? Did he have an escape plan?

Duke didn't know, but they needed to find him.

Beau emerged through the crowd, barely pausing in front of Duke. His gaze was set on the front of the building. Urgency marked each of his actions.

"Beau . . . the bomb." Duke nodded toward it.

Beau took off in a jog toward Officer Rector.

In the meantime, Duke and Andi needed to find the killer.

chapter
seventy-one

FEAR CRACKLED THROUGH THE AIR. Andi could feel it.

Those who'd remained calm at first were now also in a panic.

The reality of the situation had hit everyone, and anyone who had been in denial now had no choice but to face the truth.

Darkness hovered close. Danger breathed down their necks. Death might soon become a reality.

Andi wasn't sure if the lights being on helped or hurt the situation. At least in the dark people couldn't see everyone else's fear. But the emotion was like a toxin that spread without apology.

The killer was somewhere in this building, and he'd made his wishes known.

Andi's heart beat harder as she tried to remain calm.

"Let's go closer to the rink to see if anybody goes on the ice," Duke said. "If they answer the killer's demands."

He took her hand—as a practical measure—and led her through the crowd toward the bleacher area again. People still darted toward the other side of the building and huddled at the doors there.

Very few people sat in the stands. But some remained, clustered in groups. Others hugged each other. Still others tried to console those in the throes of panic.

But no one stood on the ice.

What would the killer do if no one came forward?

Even if someone did come forward, would this guy really disarm that bomb?

Andi doubted it.

She looked to the side and saw someone rushing toward them.

Helena.

"Duke, Andi." She sounded breathless as she stopped in front of them. "I think I know what this is about."

Andi sucked in a breath.

Then she waited to hear Helena's explanation.

Based on the look on her face, Helena was concerned. Duke braced himself for whatever she was about to say.

"I don't know why I didn't see this before," Helena stated with a shake of her head. "But now it makes sense."

"What did you figure out, Helena?" Andi asked with a rushed tone.

"I vaguely remember hearing something about this when I used to take lessons here. In fact, I walked in on it once when it was happening."

"When *what* was happening?" Duke tried not to be impatient. But that bomb was on a timer, and they had only minutes left.

"There was this kid who played on the high school hockey team." Helena's words came out faster. "He was a little different from the rest of the team. Not super athletic. I think his parents were wealthy and slipped the coach some money so he would make the team. Anyway, my impression is that the team captain didn't like him and wanted him gone. But the move wasn't his call. So the captain and his friends started trying to make this kid's life miserable so he'd quit instead."

"He was bullied, wasn't he?" Andi's voice tightened.

Helena nodded grimly. "At first, I think they just picked on him. But I walked in once, and he was cornered in the closet. One of the boys was taunting him with the blades of his ice skates."

Skates . . . were the blades similar to those of an ulu? Maybe not directly. But to a psychopath . . . the blades just might be close enough.

That suddenly made sense.

"What did you do?" Duke narrowed his eyes as he waited to hear what else Helena had to say.

"I tried to stop them." Helena's voice cracked. "But one of the players jerked me back, told me to mind my own business or I'd be next."

"And did you?" Duke asked.

Helena didn't seem like the type who would back off.

"They wouldn't let me get close to the closet. They held me back. So I told the coach what was happening, and he told me he'd take care of it. I trusted that he would. But he always favored his star players. I should have known better." She pressed her eyes shut and shook her head as if fighting off guilt.

"Do you remember who this boy was, Helena?" Duke asked.

She pulled her eyes open, though her expression remained grim. "I don't really remember his name. Can I see that photo again?"

Duke pulled it up on his phone, and Helena studied the faces for a moment.

Finally, she pointed at one. "I'm pretty sure it was this guy."

Duke and Andi leaned closer to get a look at the guy's face.

Something about the man looked familiar. But Duke couldn't pinpoint who the guy was or what caught his eye.

He ran through the faces of various people he'd met since they started this investigation. None of them seemed to fit. So who was he?

"Anything?" he asked Andi.

"There *is* something familiar about him." Andi frowned as she continued to study the picture.

"That's my thought too, but . . ."

They needed to find someone who could tell them this guy's name.

And they needed to do it before it was too late.

Duke glanced at his watch.

There were only four minutes left until that bomb exploded.

If they weren't careful, time would be up . . . literally.

chapter
seventy-two

ANDI SEARCHED for someone who might be able to ID the person in that photo. Coach Pence? Richard?

Someone here had to know who these guys were.

Meanwhile, Duke and Helena hurried to check on Beau.

Andi headed toward Richard's office but paused when she saw a closet in the distance.

A closet. Like the one where Helena had said she saw the bullying taking place.

And the guy behind this . . . he was making announcements from somewhere. It needed to be somewhere private.

Could it be . . . ?

Andi hesitated a moment. Then she stepped closer. Closer. Closer.

She knew there was no time to waste, yet she still hesitated.

If she opened that door, what would she find inside?

Part of her didn't want to know.

But this was not the time to be a coward.

She reached the door and grasped the cool metal handle.

She pressed her eyes closed and lifted a prayer before she tugged it open.

She fully expected to see someone inside, crouched down with some type of microphone in hand.

But instead, the space was empty.

Her shoulders sagged. So much for that theory.

Andi shook her head, chiding herself for being so scared over nothing. She was clearly overthinking things.

As she started to close the door, someone shoved her.

She tumbled into the small space, landing on her hands and knees.

She flipped over, ready to confront whoever had done this.

But before she could, the door slammed closed, a lock turned, and darkness surrounded her.

"I think I know who the killer is." Duke glanced around. "I need to find Andi."

"Who is it?" Helena asked.

"I need to find her first, run something by her."

They began searching the crowds, looking for Andi.

Duke glanced at his watch again. Only two minutes and thirty seconds left.

Sweat raced across his brow.

Andi could be in danger.

As they rounded a corner, he nearly collided with someone.

Matthew.

He appeared startled at Duke's presence and lowered his phone.

"We're trying to find Andi," Duke rushed. "Have you seen her?"

"I just passed her a few minutes ago. She was heading in that direction." He pointed toward the east side of the rink.

Duke took a step in that direction. "Was she alone?"

"She was. But I wasn't paying that much attention. However, I'm pretty sure that I saw that cop walking after her."

Duke's heart pounded harder. "That cop?"

"I don't remember his name, but he was stationed outside our rental house. He was right behind her, so I just assumed they were together."

Wasting no more time, Duke darted in the direction Matthew had seen Andi walking.

He needed to find her.

Now.

chapter
seventy-three

ANDI'S HEART RACED . . . especially when she realized someone was in the small closet with her.

The killer. He hadn't just locked her in here.

He'd slipped inside also.

In the darkness, she hadn't seen him.

Just what was he planning?

"This is where it happened," he started.

Another chill washed through her when she heard his brooding, deep voice. Yet she still couldn't see his face. Still didn't know who he was.

She swallowed hard. "I'm sorry about what happened to you."

"Turn on your flashlight," he ordered.

Andi swallowed hard as she fumbled with her phone. A moment later, she found the right button and hit it.

As she shone the light on the man, recognition filled her.

No . . .

Eisenhauer leered over her.

The cop.

The one who'd blended in so effortlessly.

The one with thick, full hair and long arms.

The guy hadn't even been on her radar.

He raised his shirt.

The light on the phone illuminated an X that had been left on his chest. The mark was now scarred over from past wounds . . . but still as chilling as ever.

"I'm so sorry," Andi told him as she pressed herself against the wall. "That's horrible. I know what they did to you."

Surprise flickered in his gaze. "No one stopped them."

"They should have," Andi said, the phone trembling in her hands. "They shouldn't have let that happen to you."

"I know!" he snarled. "But they did. Everyone turned a blind eye to it. Winning was the most important thing. They didn't dare injure Jevonne's ego."

"It was a travesty." Andi licked her lips. "But there's no need to kill all these people. They weren't the ones who put you in the closet. Who left that mark on your chest."

"But there is a need!" His voice hardened. "Everyone here represents the people who knew what was happening and did nothing to stop it. They're all the same. All of them!"

The guy's mind was made up . . . and not in a good

way. He'd convinced himself everyone was guilty and this was the right thing to do.

How would Andi change his mind?

She licked her lips and tried to loosen her shoulders, to soften her tone. "Most of the people here right now . . . they had nothing to do with this."

"Don't you see? They're still supporting this sport. They're supporting people who would do anything to win. They're supporting the evil held in this building."

Andi swallowed hard as she ran through what she could say to make this situation better.

But she knew the countdown was on.

They were probably down to less than a minute now if she had to guess.

"There are still good people in this world," she murmured. "You have to believe that. You have to believe that most of the people in this building would step in and help if they had the opportunity."

"You saw them out there! All those people were only looking out for themselves. They don't care about anyone else. All they care about is getting out and saving themselves. If they had the chance, they'd trample others to survive."

"You're focusing on the few instead of the many. I don't believe that's true of everyone."

"Then you're naive!"

"Actually, I'm not. People have hurt me too. But that doesn't mean I would hurt them back."

"They have to pay. Everyone is only looking out for themselves." He lowered his shirt, but his hand still rubbed the spot where the X was located.

"Not my friends and me. We try to help people who've been wronged. You were wronged, Eisenhauer. What they did to you should have never happened."

He shook his head. "It doesn't matter. You can't change my mind. I'm in this too deep."

Her gaze latched onto his in a desperate plea to get through to him. "You don't have to do this. It's never too late."

"You don't get it, do you? It was too late the moment the other players cornered me in this closet and carved that X into my chest." He turned and opened the door. "Now I need to get out of here before I go down with this building."

Andi lunged for the doorway.

But before she could push her way out, it slammed.

A lock twisted.

Eisenhauer had managed to trap her in here, hadn't he?

She stood and tried the door anyway. Just as she feared, it didn't budge.

She pressed her eyes shut and leaned against the cool metal.

Andi had to do something . . . or she would die in a matter of moments.

Duke reached the closet and tugged at the door.

It was locked.

He banged on it. "Andi? Are you in there?"

"Duke? I'm here."

Relief filled him. She was okay.

"It's Eisenhauer!" Andi yelled.

His throat tightened. "We know. We're looking for him. Are you okay?"

"I'm fine. But the bomb is less than a minute from exploding, Duke . . . has Beau disabled it yet?"

"He's still working on it." Duke wished he had something different to say.

Just then, a voice came through the overhead speakers. "Can I have your attention, please? Turn your eyes on the screen."

"What's happening?" Andi asked.

"I'm not sure." Duke leaned away from the closet to peer at the rink.

A slideshow had started on the overhead screens—a show displaying the people who'd been on Eisenhauer's hockey team all those years ago. Not only his team—the pictures were also of people who'd worked at the rink.

Xs were slashed across each of their faces.

At the bottom, a countdown ticked away.

Fifty-four seconds.

Eisenhauer wanted the last thing everyone remembered seeing here to be the people who had bullied him. The people that turned a blind eye.

Duke's heart pounded harder in his ears.

"Duke?" Andi called. "What's happening?"

He told her what was on the screen.

"You don't have to stay here with me," Andi said. "Go help."

"But..." He should stay with her. Help her out. She shouldn't be alone...

"We're not all going down like this," Andi said. "We're going to talk again on the other side of this. But they need your help right now."

He hesitated another minute. Contemplated the things he wanted to say.

Then Andi said, "Go!"

He snapped back into action. "Okay, but I'll be back."

He'd only taken two steps away when he ran into Ranger and Simmy.

"Get that door open!" Duke pointed to the closet. "Andi is trapped inside."

"Got it."

Then Duke darted toward Beau. He needed to see what was happening.

When he reached the area, he saw his brother still kneeling over the bomb.

Forty seconds.

"Beau..." Duke called.

"I've almost got it."

Matthew still stood there, phone in hand and sweat dripping down from his face. "I'm trying to work on those doors."

"Nothing?" Duke asked.

He shook his head. "I'm almost there too. But this guy is good. He keeps blocking me."

Duke's gaze wandered the crowd.

Where had Eisenhauer gone? Where was he hiding?

Maybe if he could find him he could convince him to shut off the bomb. To unlock the doors.

Duke wasn't sure that plan would work. But he didn't have any better ideas and time was running out.

chapter
seventy-four

"ANDI, IT'S ME," Ranger said on the other side of the door. "I'm going to get you out of there."

"That would be great. Please, hurry . . ."

Andi leaned against the door as if she might pass through via osmosis. Her heart beat at a rapid pace that made it hard to breathe.

She heard Ranger doing something on the other side of the metal. Saw the knob moving.

Finally, the door opened.

Andi nearly fell from the closet and into Ranger.

Simmy grabbed her and squeezed her shoulder. "Are you okay, Andi?"

"I'm fine," Andi murmured with a nod. "Thank you."

Then she glanced at her watch. They only had twenty seconds.

She swallowed hard.

Would this be it?

There was little she could do at this point other than wait.

She didn't want to admit defeat.

Didn't want to go down without a fight.

But . . .

Seventeen . . .

Sixteen . . .

Fifteen . . .

At just that moment, a click sounded.

Then the roar of the crowd filled the sports plex.

Feet rushed across the concrete floor.

"Matthew must have gotten the doors unlocked," Ranger said.

Andi let out a pent-up breath of air.

She prayed that was the case.

Based on the way people ran toward the exits, it was.

"You two should get out of here." Ranger glanced at Andi and Simmy.

"Simmy—you go," Andi said. "I need to stay and help clear this place."

"There's no time to clear it!" Simmy said. "There's barely time to run!"

Andi glanced at her watch again.

Simmy was right.

They had six seconds.

∼

Duke stared at his brother. The crowds ran from the ice-skating rink.

But not everyone would get out in time.

He glanced at the bomb. Saw the countdown.

He closed his eyes, knowing that all that was left to do was pray.

Which was the most powerful thing.

"I got it," Beau murmured as he bent over the bomb. "I got it!"

It took a moment for him to realize what his brother had said.

Beau rocked back on his heels, breathing heavily with relief.

Duke blinked several times as he stared at the bomb.

Sure enough, the timer had gone blank.

The device had been disabled.

Beau had done it.

Everyone was safe—if they didn't hurt themselves or others while scrambling to get out.

Duke clapped his brother on the back. "Good job."

Officer Rector did the same. "You pulled through for everyone. We all owe you."

Sweat poured off Beau's face, and he wiped it with a sleeve.

That had been intense, to say the least.

But they still weren't done.

Gibson and some officers ran through the front door and found Duke.

"He's here," Duke said. "The killer."

"Who is he?"

Duke rattled off the man's name. "Billy Eisenhauer. He's a cop."

Gibson turned back to his guys. "Let's split up and look for him before he gets away."

Duke knew it might be too late. Eisenhauer could have already slipped out with the crowd.

The only comfort that Duke found was in knowing they had this guy's name. Even if Eisenhauer had managed to escape, he wouldn't get far.

The police would track him down.

And maybe the city would be a little safer.

chapter
seventy-five

ANDI GLANCED AROUND.

But it was hard to see anything with the crowds scattering.

Where had Eisenhauer gone?

That was when she spotted someone moving in the opposite direction of everyone else. Someone with an unusual gait.

It was him.

The killer.

She pointed toward the man. "There!"

She and Ranger took off after the guy.

Ranger reached Eisenhauer before she did and tackled the guy to the floor.

In one fluid move, Ranger grabbed the man's arms and subdued him. "You're not going anywhere."

"I'm a cop," Eisenhauer muttered. "You know you

could be charged with assaulting a police officer. It's a felony! Someone help me! It's this guy! He's the killer!"

Several people stopped and stared as if they wanted to help but were uncertain.

Would Eisenhauer's ruse work?

A shadow appeared behind them, and Andi glanced up to see Gibson.

Relief swept through her so quickly her knees went weak. She caught herself on a nearby table.

"It's him," Andi explained. "Eisenhauer. It was a cop all along."

Gibson handcuffed Eisenhauer and jerked him to his feet.

"You're making a mistake," Eisenhauer shouted. "They're the ones behind this. Not me."

"We know that's not true," Gibson said. "You might as well own up to it now."

"I'm an officer of the law, just like you are!" Eisenhauer said. "I would never try to hurt anyone."

"It was terrible what happened to you," Andi said. "All those people. Your teammates left the scar on your chest using the blade on your hockey skates. The coaches and others who turned a blind eye to it. They swept it under the rug, all so those boys could succeed, so the team could get some wins. It was wrong."

The harsh look in his eyes softened. "No one cares."

"And I know you wanted justice," Andi said. "But killing all these people isn't the way to go about that."

"They needed to learn a lesson! Can't anyone see that? No one ever wanted to listen . . ."

"You said it yourself," Gibson said. "You're an officer of the law. You promised to serve and protect. That's not what you did."

"But—"

Before Eisenhauer could say anything else, Gibson motioned to Detective Rasmussen, who'd just arrived on the scene. He and his guys led Eisenhauer away.

The rest of the gang arrived, and everyone joined together in a big group hug.

They were safe.

This guy was finally behind bars.

Or at least he would be soon.

That had been close.

A little too close for comfort.

chapter
seventy-six

SEVERAL HOURS LATER, the gang headed back to the house.

They'd all been questioned by the police and cleared to leave the sports plex.

The case seemed pretty cut and dried now that the authorities knew all the details.

Eisenhauer was clearly guilty. He had a terribly tragic past.

But killing everyone he saw as a perpetrator wasn't the answer.

Still, that had been close. Too close. Everyone in that sports plex could have been killed.

If only all the Arctic Circle Murder Club's worries were over.

But they weren't.

Andi knew that better than anyone.

They still had a lot to resolve.

Almost as soon as they got back to the rental house, a knock sounded on the door.

Duke answered, and Andi saw Gibson standing on the other side.

"Can I come in?" he asked.

"Of course." Duke opened the door wider to let him inside.

Some of the gang had headed to their rooms to change their clothes or take showers. But Andi and Duke stood there with Gibson.

"Just the people I wanted to see." Gibson turned to Andi. "First of all, Andi, I wanted you to know that the charges against you have been dropped."

"All of them?" Surprise laced her voice.

"All of them. We caught the person who shot the senator."

"Who was it?" Andi rushed.

"His name is Edward Credent."

"The name isn't familiar." Andi shook her head as she tried unsuccessfully to place the name. "Did you trace him back to Victor?"

Gibson frowned. "Unfortunately, we didn't. But based on what you've told me, that's not a surprise."

"Did you give up on talking to Victor himself?" Duke asked.

"No," Gibson said. "I haven't. But he's a hard man to track down."

"I'm sure he makes it that way on purpose." Andi crossed her arms.

"Given the fact we have no direct evidence against him, I can't issue a subpoena or call him in for any other reason," Gibson said.

"Understood." Andi's voice dipped lower. "I have a feeling he's responsible for the fire next door."

Gibson's eyebrows rose. "Really?"

She nodded. "I can't prove it. But I think he was trying to send me a message."

She explained how her friend had died in a house fire and the other similarities.

She didn't bother to mention the other instances she'd been threatened. The man watching her outside the hotel. Tailing her on the road. The men who'd followed Beau to the hotel.

All Victor.

"Thank you for looking into this," Andi told him.

"Of course." Gibson's gaze locked with Andi's. "And I'm sorry if I doubted you. But I had to do my job."

"I know you did. I get it."

"I think everyone in your group should feel proud of the work you've done," Gibson continued. "This city is safer because of you all. Even if no one else recognizes it, I do."

"We appreciate that," Duke said.

Andi smiled. "Thank you."

Gibson nodded and left a few seconds later.

Duke and Andi sat beside each other on the couch. Beau—who'd gone to use the bathroom—reappeared.

Andi assumed that, now that this was over, Beau would head out. In the meantime, Duke would head back to Fairbanks.

Then Mariella and Matthew returned to the living room.

Then Ranger.

Everyone except for Simmy. What was taking her so long?

"I'll go check on her." Andi stood.

She walked to Simmy's bedroom but returned a moment later with a frown and something in her hands. "She's not in her room."

Ranger stiffened. "What do you mean she's not in her room?"

"I mean, she left this note." Andi raised the letter and then began to read. "A bad man is after me, and now that he knows where I am, it's just a matter of time before he tracks me down. I'm sorry to leave like this, but I have no other choice. I can't stay any longer. I called an Uber, and he's meeting me down the road. By the time you get this, I'll be gone. I love you all, and I'll miss you dearly. All my love, Simmy."

"Wait . . . she just left like that?" Mariella blinked in surprise. "Without talking to us first?"

"I think we've all known for a while that Simmy is running from something." Ranger's gaze darkened. "Now that her identity has been revealed, this person knows where to look for her."

"I wish she would have asked us for help." Andi rubbed her arms as a chill washed over her.

"Me too." Duke stared at the door as if he wanted to run after her.

But Simmy didn't want to be found. They had to respect that.

"I hate to say this, but I'm not sure when I'll be able to meet with you guys again either." Ranger rose to his feet. "There's something I have to take care of, something that can't wait."

"Something concerning that photo you got of your daughter?" Duke narrowed his eyes with thought.

Ranger nodded. "Originally. I need to find her—but she looks safe and well-cared for. However, I'm not sure I can say the same for Simmy. I'm worried about her. Somehow . . . I need to help them both. I don't know how yet. But I'm going to figure out a way."

Of course. Andi expected nothing less.

Her thoughts raced. There was something she knew she had to say—but she dreaded it. Still, there was no use delaying the inevitable.

"Listen, guys . . . the only reason our identities were revealed is because of me," Andi said. "As long as all of you are around me, you're at risk."

Mariella stood. "What is everybody getting at right now? Please don't tell me it's what I think it is."

"We've had a really good run at things," Duke said. "Maybe we've grown too fast. We haven't been able to keep up. Plus, we all have our own issues to deal with right now."

"So you guys are calling it quits?" Mariella stared at each of them, disbelief in her gaze.

"I'm not saying that," Andi said. "But I think we all need some resolution in our lives before we proceed."

"We have amazing video footage of what happened tonight," Mariella continued to argue. "Matthew and I are ready to put together this podcast about the Lights Out Killer. In fact, I was even hoping to get some quotes from you guys tonight. We're on fire, and we can't back out now."

"We may not have a choice." Andi frowned as the words left her lips. "Simmy had to leave. In the morning, I'm also going to leave. I can't promise what will happen after that."

"Same here," Ranger said.

"Me too. I need some resolution with Celeste. I need to put everything I have into it." Duke glanced at Andi. "So I can move on once and for all."

"But . . ." Mariella's voice trailed. "You guys can't do this. *Please*, don't do this."

The sadness in her voice was almost enough to change Andi's mind. But she knew her decision was for the best. She couldn't put the people she cared about at risk.

Nor could she stand here and stare at everyone any longer.

"Good night, everyone."

Andi stepped away. But as she did, she felt as if her heart were breaking.

The Arctic Circle Murder Club had awakened something inside her.

It had brought her friends.

It had given her hope.

But it had also awakened danger.

For those new friends.

And that threatened to shatter her newfound hope.

She needed to get some things sorted out.

Otherwise, her past might drive her mad . . . just like Billy Eisenhauer had let his prior trauma dictate all his bad decisions as well.

Andi couldn't let that happen.

~~~

Thank you for reading **Leave the Lights On**. If you enjoyed this book, please consider leaving a review.

Coming next: **The End of the Road.**

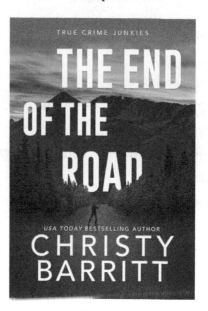

also by christy barritt:

true crime junkies series:

Just the Nicest Person

Strangers—each with their own secrets—are thrown together after the murder of a beloved true crime podcaster.

Disgraced attorney Andi Slade is seeking justice for the killer who destroyed her reputation and her career. But going undercover as an ice road trucker in Alaska to find answers is just the tip of the iceberg. A brutal snowstorm, a handsome stranger, and an unsolved cold case send Andi's plans into a tailspin.

Former CID investigator Duke McAllister refuses to give up searching for his fiancée who disappeared two years ago on the Dalton Highway. When he rescues a woman on the side of the road, he knows just how much danger she's in. Stranded together and butting heads, they discover a common interest: true crime.

When their favorite local Alaskan podcaster goes radio silent right before revealing the name of a cold case killer, they dive in to investigate only to make a terrifyingly frigid discovery. Can these strangers work together to find answers before the biting, dangerous cold claims their lives? Or even worse . . . before the killer comes looking for his own brand of justice?

He Walks Among Us

With a killer walking among them, no one is safe . .

When the newly formed Arctic Circle Murder Club meets in Fairbanks, Alaska, to investigate the mystery of the Missing Women of Dalton Highway, their plans take a gruesome turn.

Upon the group's arrival at the hotel, three women's frozen bodies are pulled from the nearby river. When a friend of one of the victims pleads for help finding out who's behind the murders, how can they say no?

The club must detour from their original plan and dive into the recesses of a killer's mind before another victim is claimed. As they seek the truth behind the murders, opposition hits them at every turn. Shocking revelations from the past along with brimming conflict threaten to end the group just as they've started.

Can this group of true crime podcasters uncover

someone's dark secrets before one of their own plunges into an icy grave?

Never Happen to You

Crime is something that happens to strangers. Until it's not.

As women continue to vanish in Alaska's Far North, the Arctic Circle Murder Club meets again to combine their skills and search for the truth. Only the evidence isn't adding up. The case of The Missing Women of Dalton Highway has gone cold, and every new possibility leaves them with frostbite.

Duke McAllister's and Andi Slade's personal investigations point them in new directions, and they're left with more questions than ever. But there's one thing they— and the rest of the true crime podcasters—know for sure: whoever is behind these disappearances will keep taking women until he's caught.

Will the team find answers and expose the truth before this madman strikes again? Or will the secrets of the infamous Dalton Highway remain as isolated as the landscape surrounding them?

Dead of Night

A woman disappears in the dead of night as a haunting crime from the past comes to life again.

When a mysterious email leads true crime podcaster Mariella Boucher to southeast Alaska on a quest for the truth about her past, she never expects to plunge headfirst into danger. But when a stranger with a troubled history saves her life, she's drawn into a five-year-old cold case that leaves her chilled to the bone.

Jason Somersby has been living in the shadow of suspicion ever since his girlfriend was murdered five years ago. When another woman disappears under similar circumstances, everyone in town looks at him with accusation—and to demand answers he doesn't have.

Mariella brings in the other members of the Arctic Circle Murder Club to help find the killer and clear Jason's name. But the more the team digs, the shakier the ground becomes. When it becomes clear one of their own is the next target, they must scramble to stop the killer before he claims another victim.

you also might enjoy: fog lake suspense

Edge of Peril

When evil descends like fog on a mountain community, no one feels safe. After hearing about a string of murders in a Smoky Mountain town, journalist Harper Jennings realizes a startling truth. She knows who may be responsible—the same person who tried to kill her three years ago. Now Harper must convince the cops to believe her before the killer strikes again. Sheriff Luke Wilder returned to his hometown, determined to keep the promise he made to his dying father. The sleepy tourist area with a tragic past hadn't seen a murder in decades—until now. Keeping the community safe seems impossible as darkness edges closer, threatening to consume everything in its path. As The Watcher grows desperate, Harper and Luke must work together in order to defeat him. But the peril around them escalates, making it clear the killer will stop at nothing to get what he wants.

Margin of Error

Some secrets have deadly consequences. Brynlee Parker thought her biggest challenge would be hiking to Dead Man's Bluff and fulfilling her dad's last wishes. She never thought she'd witness two men being viciously murdered while on a mountainous trail. Even worse, the deadly predator is now hunting her. Boone Wilder wants nothing to do with Dead Man's Bluff, not after his wife died there. But he can't seem to mind his own business when a mysterious out-of-towner burst into his camp store in a frenzied panic. Something—or someone—deadly is out there. The killer's hunger for blood seems to be growing at a brutal pace. Can Brynlee and Boone figure out who's behind these murders? Or will the hurts and secrets from their past not allow for even a margin of error?

Brink of Danger

Ansley Wilder has always lived life on the wild side, using thrills to numb the pain from her past and escape her mistakes. But a near-death experience two years ago changed everything. When another incident nearly claims her life, she turns her thrill-seeking ways into a fight for survival. Ryan Philips left Fog Lake to chase adventure far from home. Now he's returned as the new fire chief in town, but the slower paced life he seeks is nowhere to be found. Not only is a wildfire blazing out of control, but a malicious killer known as "The Woodsman" is enacting crimes that appear accidental. Plus, there seems to be a strange connection with these incidents and his best friend's little sister, Ansley Wilder. As a killer watches their every move and the forest fire threatens to destroy their scenic town, both Ryan and Ansley hover on the brink of danger. One wrong move could send them tumbling over the edge . . . permanently.

Line of Duty

Jaxon Wilder didn't plan on returning home to Fog Lake, Tennessee, following his tour of duty in Iraq. But after a gut-wrenching failure during his stint in the Army, he now faces a new challenge: his family. Abby Brennan always did her best to be the good girl and to live by the rules. When a wrong decision changes her entire life, she tries to hide from the world. However, a madman known as the Executioner is determined to find her and enact his own brand of justice. When Jaxon and Abby are thrown together in the killer's crosshairs, they're forced to depend on one another to survive. Will Jaxon's sense of duty be enough to help keep Abby safe? Or will deadly secrets lead to the penalty of death?

Legacy of Lies

The justice system failed her family—and so did her hometown. Madison Colson knows deep down that her father—a convicted serial killer—is innocent. But believing it and proving it are two entirely different things. Unable to help her father, Madison has spent most of her adult life overcompensating by helping others. When her aunt dies unexpectantly, duty calls her back to Fog Lake, Tennessee, a beautiful but painful place she'd rather forget. Terrifying events begin to unfold once she arrives, unleashing her worst nightmares. The Good Samaritan Killer—or a copycat—is back, and now Madison Colson is his target. FBI Special Agent Shane Townsend is determined to stop the deadly rampage that has sent the tightknit community into a frenzy. But he needs to earn Madison's trust first. The task feels impossible, especially considering his father is the one who put her dad in prison. With the whole town on edge and pointing fingers, tension escalates out of control. Madison and Shane must sort the facts from the lies—and fight for a legacy of truth—before The Good Samaritan Killer has the final say.

Secrets of Shame

A killer has a promise to keep . . . Attorney Isaac Colson only wants to put his tumultuous past in Fog Lake behind him and return to his life in Memphis. But when an ominous text threatens that he must come back or there will be deadly consequences, he knows he can't take any chances. Rebecca Moreno has only ever loved one man—her high school sweetheart, Isaac Colson. But when his dad went to prison for murder, Rebecca's father forbade them from seeing each other again. Years later, Isaac is back in town and old feelings are stirring. But Rebecca is harboring a secret that could change everything. When The Good Samaritan Killer strikes again, guilt pummels her. She has to tell Isaac the truth. But as events unfold, she has more to lose than ever. Isaac and Rebecca must find answers—their lives depend on it. But everyone seems to have secrets, each that forms an obstacle to finding the truth . . . and to staying alive.

Refuge of Redemption

Home is a place of refuge—unless it's a killer's playground. For years, Bear Colson has been known as the serial killer's son. But now, someone else is behind bars for the crimes his father was accused of committing. Bear wants to believe hope for a brighter future is in sight, but he has reason to suspect more than one killer was involved. Forensic photographer Piper Stephens' career crashed and burned when she trusted the wrong man. Now, after discovering an alarming secret about the infamous Good Samaritan Killer, she sets out to find both answers and redemption. But things go awry when her assistant becomes the next victim. As fear batters Fog Lake residents once again, Bear and Piper join forces to track down the truth. But the killer is determined to remain in the shadows—and he'll destroy anyone who stands in his way.

about the author

USA Today has called Christy Barritt's books "scary, funny, passionate, and quirky."

Christy writes both mystery and romantic suspense novels that are clean with underlying messages of faith. Her books have sold more than four million copies and have won the Daphne du Maurier Award for Excellence in Suspense and Mystery, have been twice nominated for the Romantic Times Reviewers' Choice Award, and have finaled for both a Carol Award and Foreword Magazine's Book of the Year.

She is married to her Prince Charming, a man who thinks she's hilarious—but only when she's not trying to be. Christy is a self-proclaimed klutz, an avid music lover who's known for spontaneously bursting into song, and a road trip aficionado.

When she's not working or spending time with her family, she enjoys singing, playing the guitar, and exploring small, unsuspecting towns where people have no idea how accident-prone she is.

Find Christy online at:
www.christybarritt.com
www.facebook.com/christybarritt
www.twitter.com/cbarritt

Sign up for Christy's newsletter to get information on all of her latest releases here: **www.christybarritt.com/ newsletter-sign-up/**

    f facebook.com/AuthorChristyBarritt
    X x.com/christybarritt
    ⃝ instagram.com/cebarritt

Made in United States
Orlando, FL
05 February 2024

43334747R00275